POLMARRAN TOWER

Also in the series

Polmarran Tower

CHARLOTTE MASSEY

A Troubadour

Edited by Lesley Saxby

MACDONALD AND JANE'S · LONDON

To Mary Caprani and to my parents

First published in Great Britain in 1975 by
Macdonald & Jane's
(Macdonald & Co. (Publishers) Ltd)
Paulton House
8 Shepherdess Walk
London N1

Copyright © Charlotte Massey 1975

ISBN 0 356 08201 6

Printed and bound in Great Britain by
Redwood Burn Limited
Trowbridge & Esher

Chapter One

Marrambridge — my first view of it was from the narrow window of the coach — appeared to be half-village, half-town. It could boast the usual tall-towered church, a hotel of sorts and a number of shops scattered along each side of its steep and narrow streets. The streets were crowded: rustic types, livestock, and the number of pannier baskets displaying an array of farm produce suggested a market day.

I leaned out of the window, but there was not much more to see because at that moment our carriage wheeled into the coachyard of The Crown, scattering the horde of peddlers and the few beggars awaiting the Exeter Mail. Two ostlers and a linkboy came to meet the coach and to assist with the baggage. From nowhere the landlord dutifully appeared and placed his bulky authority between the importunate horde and his new customers. As I was the only lady passenger, he handed me down and bowed me obsequiously into his hostelry. It too was crowded. From the taproom came the muted sound of laughter and revelry, and in the commercial room convivial groups of bagmen and merchants were comparing prices and extolling the merits of their various wares. With eyebrows raised and shoulders constantly shrugging in eloquent apology for his packed establishment, the landlord quickly conducted me to a secluded little snuggery close to his own quarters.

'A bit cramped, I'm afraid, milady, but a touch of privacy nonetheless.' Briskly he towelled a couple of stains from the surface of a tiny table and flicked dust from a seat cushion. Then, standing with arms akimbo, he enquired: 'And now, milady, somethin' in the way of refreshments perhaps? There's precious little in the way of hot vittals due to the market-day regulars and the gentlemen, but I've some nice cutlets and a fine wedge of pigeon pie if you'd care?'

'Thank you, no. I merely wish to . . . '

'If it's a room for the night, milady, I regret that I'm burstin' at the seams with customers. Gentry from hereabouts. All long since booked in and come here to wager on the wrestlin' and the prize-fightin' each market day. They have a lien on all under my roof, so to speak, and a prior call on all my best rooms. I'm sorry, milady.'

'I do not require a room, thank you. I am to meet someone here. A gentleman from Polmarran Tower.'

'The Northwoods' place, is it, milady?'

'Yes.'

'Why then, likely as not it's Mr Charles Northwood you want. He's inside, ma'am. In the taproom.' His simpering deference was now giving way to a knowing smirk. 'Mr Charles, eh? One of my best regulars. Why then, likely as not you'll be spending the night under this roof after all, if you'll pardon my making so bold. But don't worry, missy, you'll have absolute privacy.'

'You are mistaken, sir, in your conclusions. Now take me to Mr Northwood, if you please,' I demanded with the degree of hauteur which I felt the situation and his insinuation demanded.

'Eh, yes . . . yes, certainly, milady. Beg pardon if I, er . . . ' Mine host's brief essay into vulgar familiarity was quickly dissipated: "missy" was now "milady" once more, the smirk had vanished, to be replaced by a professional unctiousness as he bowed and scraped and scurried ahead of me towards the taproom.

Though there were still a few hours of daylight left the bar-parlour had already succumbed to the advance of night and was half-hidden in shadow. Both the narrow windows were open wide, to permit some of the light from a dull September evening to seep in and do battle with the heavy whorls of tobacco smoke. This had the effect of making the taproom more murky rather than illuminating it. The place was crammed with people; bluff yeoman farmers, fishermen, village artisan types, seafarers and peddlers were in the majority, but there was also the usual sprinkling of gentlemen and the ubiquitous dandies with their high collars and stupendous neckcloths. These latter appeared to be monopolizing the few women in the tavern — about seven or eight — who, from their gilt ear-rings, bracelets and faded flowers, I guessed to be Romany types.

It was to one such group, three raffish young men and two girls seated in the darkest and most obscure corner, that the landlord conducted me.

'Eh, beg pardon, Mr Northwood, sir . . . but I have here a young lady desiring a word of you, sir.'

Mr Northwood's back was to me. He had one hand on the table, clasping a brandy glass; the other was stroking the greasy lace of his companion's bodice. When he spoke he did not bother to turn round. 'Thank you, Jack, but I already have a young lady, and I'll wager a pound to a penny that my one desires much more than a few words from me.' His speech, slightly thickened with liquor, trailed off into a slurred laugh. The girl by his side giggled and nestled close to him.

'Indeed yes, sir . . .' The landlord leaned down to Mr Northwood, adding his own sycophantic chuckle to the ripple of coarse merriment now spreading round the table. 'But eh, Mr Northwood, I think this other young lady is, er . . .'

'That's quite enough, sir,' I interrupted. 'I doubt that I have anything to discuss with your Mr Northwood. Please excuse me.'

At the sound of my voice, sharp and angry, Mr Northwood released his companion and swung round. 'Hold on, my lovely, let's have a look at you.'

I was in the act of turning away, and he was in the act of rising with an unsteady, lurching effort, when our eyes met. For just a moment we paused in mutual appraisal. I don't know what he saw in my expression — a look of disdainful annoyance, I should imagine — but I beheld a face that was strikingly handsome despite the evidence of dissipation and squandered vitality. It was a saturnine handsomeness, the hair black and curly about the well-shaped head, the moustache and the eyes picking up the same coal-black colour — the sort of eyes some women call 'romantic', though they were now a trifle bloodshot and dulled from too much drinking. And his face was handsome in the way that becomes a man, with just sufficient of those minor flaws in the regularity of his features to rob them of any suggestion of prettiness; his nose was just a bit too short, his chin and jaw jutting out just enough to counter the softness of a mouth containing a tiny hint of sensuality.

Though this swift scrutiny lasted only a matter of seconds I had already left it too late to make my retreat. Even as I started to move out from the shadows his eyes were beginning to focus on me, to lose their bleariness — and then, with some peculiar glint of recognition, to dilate in surprise and shocked disbelief. He swore, his mouth no longer soft, but gaping wide with incredulity. 'Good God . . . not you!' he said hoarsley.

'I don't know what you mean, sir. We have never met before.'

8

'Yes . . . no, but . . . what the hell is going on here?' As I tried to move back, his hand closed firmly over my wrist, pulling me towards him.

'How dare you!' My own hand came into play, the open palm striking his cheek with a resounding slap. 'Let go of me!'

My blow seemed only to have sobered him. The drunken leer of a few moments ago had vanished. Anger and confusion showed on his face. The strong fingers increased their pressure on my wrist, biting cruelly into the flesh.

'Release me!' Again I swung my free hand in a wide arc. He seized it before I could deliver the second blow.

Shuffling forward, the landlord attempted a feeble intervention: 'Oh, please now, sir! Please, Mr Charles, this is most unseemly!'

'Shut your mouth, Jack, and keep off!' Charles Northwood shouldered the innkeeper aside, pulling me still closer to him as he did so, and then, clutching me to his body in some squalid travesty of an embrace, he spun me about so that my face, less than six inches from the intense fury stamped on his features, was no longer in shadow. I caught the acrid, foul smell of stale liquor from his breath. I closed my eyes and jerked my head to one side.

'Damn you, look at me, you bitch!'

Despite myself I opened my eyes to the challenging glint in his. At this range, and in the taproom's half-light, he was no longer certain. The beginnings of doubt crinkled the corners of his eyes. The fury gave way to a kind of bleary incomprehension. 'Who the hell *are* you?' he muttered.

'Take your hands off her, Charles. You're mistaken.' These words, low but hard and brittle with anger, were uttered by someone just behind me.

I turned gratefully towards the speaker. He was in the act of pushing his way through the gathering throng of onlookers, a tall, squarely-built man with hard-weather lines on his face, his long arm flashing out and the massive spread of his fingers taking a firm grip on Charles Northwood's shoulder.

'Keep out of this, Carne!'

The newcomer's arm pushed out, the elbow locked and rigid. One could almost feel the power surging down through the sinewy limb to make an enormous fist which bunched up the rich stuff of Charles Northwood's jacket, biting through to the shoulder, forcing him back a pace so that his hold on me slackened. My wrists were suddenly, mercifully, free.

'Damn you, Carne . . . you're not at Polmarran now!'

'And you're not dealing with some tavern wench, Charles.'

I was thankful for those words. Thankful for the presence of this man, Carne. Head and shoulders above the crowd he dominated the scene with quiet masterfulness. A most welcome ally too, for I was acutely conscious that all eyes were upon me. Especially his. I had the curious impression that he also seemed to recognize something in my face — as though I reminded him of someone. But if that was the case he was infinitely more successful at disguising it than Charles Northwood.

'I know damn well she's no tavern slut,' Charles Northwood was saying, jerking himself away from under the other's grip. 'Good Lord, Carne, just look at her! Is she not the very image of . . .?'

'You owe her an apology.'

Sullen-faced, and with one hand rubbing what must have been a bruised shoulder, Charles Northwood uttered some kind of angry appeal. 'Damn you, Carne, look at her, will you? Can you blame me? Look at the resemblance, for God's sake, man!'

The man called Carne *was* looking. His face revealed nothing. Only a distant echo of anger sounded through his words: 'An apology, Charles.'

'Oh, very well then.' For just an instant the handsome face teetered between petulance and contrition; then suddenly, he succeeded somehow in giving me an engaging smile. 'My humble apologies, ma'am. I own myself guilty of the most unpardonable villainy.' He made an extravagant bow, his hands spread out in supplication - or was it mockery? No, not mockery. What then? A myriad of subtle expressions were flitting through his smile - will-o'-the-wisp hints of regret, gallantry, and a kind of chastened and good-natured pleading for forgiveness. I found myself wondering if it was the sincerity of a man given to sudden and contrasting impulses, genuine and true only at the moment of utterance. I think I was ready to believe so, and to accept it for what it was worth, but the numbness in my wrists was still a very real reminder of my recent humiliation.

'Please, ma'am, if you will only signify in what way I may make amends for what was, after all, a most dreadful misunderstanding.'

'All right, Charles. That's enough ' The man named Carne then turned to me. 'He's said his piece, ma'am. Satisfied?'

'Yes, thank you.'

'Fair enough then.' With a brisk, matter-of-fact nod Carne advanced, his broad shoulders cutting off the view of Charles Northwood's rather cavalier apology. He addressed me: 'Are you Miss Katherine Ainsley?'

'Yes, I am.'

'Redmond Carne, miss, at your service.' His sun-hardened hand brushed his forehead in a sketchy salute. 'I'm Cap'n Northwood's man. He sends his compliments and says for me to fetch you to Polmarran Tower when you're ready. I've brought the carriage alongside.'

'Thank you . . .' I began.

'Here, Carne! What's this about my father sending for her?' Charles Northwood was pressing forward again.

11

I turned away, anxious to avoid another scene.

'Your lush mates are awaiting you, Charles.' With those words, and a half-contemptuous nod in the direction of the group seated at the table, Carne rebuffed him.

'Damn you, Carne, you might at least have the grace to introduce me to my father's new . . . new friend, or whatever.'

After what had so recently happened I could not be sure whether that remark was more indelicate than superfluous. At any rate it was futile. Carne was already ushering me towards the door, while Mr Northwood's female companion was in the act of successfully reclaiming a part of his attention by dint of coquettish looks and a caressing, lingering stroke of her hand along the length of his arm.

I was relieved to be quit of the taproom, and yet I was feeling a faint qualm of uncertainty now that I was alone with this man Carne. Ours was a kind of double meeting, as if we had encountered each other twice — the first time in the smoky taproom where the half-light and the circumstances made it difficult for us to engage in accurate appraisal of each other, and the second time — now — in the bright sunlight and the open, with my turning about to meet the unsmiling scrutiny of his gaze as he emerged from the door, his great shoulders almost filling it and his reddish-gold hair touching the stone lintel.

Between us there was that swift and vital awareness, that element of personal immediacy from which either deep animosity, or conversely, deep affection, can grow. Something in our respective personalities sparked it off, some subtle thing which was instantly recognizable to both of us. Unaccountably it disturbed me, frightened me a little. He seemed to tower above me, brooding and powerful, with broad shoulders tapering down to a narrow waist and lean hips. This athletic frame was somewhat surprising in a man of his years. Not that I mean to imply that he was old — far from it! I put his age at about thirty-nine or forty years, which made him my senior by just over a decade. But his face, ruggedly handsome, had the experienced look of one who had seen much of life and had clearly weathered a campaign or two; his eyes were bluey-grey, resolute, and set wide apart under heavily arched brows and a good forehead; his chin was a determined one, as was the unsmiling mouth. I noticed too that in a certain light there appeared to be just the slightest dent across the bridge of his otherwise long and well-shaped nose, as though it may have been dealt a heavy blow at some time. All in all, it was the countenance of a tough, uncompromising man who had stood four-square against all the uncertainties of an eventful life.

We continued staring at each other for a few moments, his eyes as guardedly curious as mine. I was the first to break the silence.

'Please allow me to thank you for your very timely intervention. I am indebted to you.'

When he remained silent I felt constrained to add: 'I really don't know what I would have done had you not happened along just then.'

'That was a damn-fool thing to do . . . to go flouncing into a boozing den full of market-merry lubbers!'

I was quite taken aback by his manner. 'I did *not* go flouncing in, as you put it. The fact of the matter is that, when the landlord learned that I was to be met by someone from Polmarran Tower, he took me directly to your Mr Northwood. I naturally assumed that he was Captain Northwood, the man who is to be my new employer.'

'That popinjay! Why, Mr Charles is as like to the Cap'n as a gaudy pebble is to a rock of granite.'

'I could scarcely be expected to know that. I am a stranger here.'

He took the logic of that with a curt, almost

13

begrudging nod. 'Very well, then. Now if you'll tell me where your baggage is and if you'll be good enough to follow me, we'll soon get under way.'

'One moment, please.'

'Yes, miss?'

'I wish to make some purchases before leaving Marrambridge.'

'You'll find we're well provisioned at the Tower.'

'Nonetheless there are some personal items I intend to buy here before we set off.'

'Very well, just as long as you don't take too long about it.'.

'May I ask why?'

'We've more than an hour's hard road ahead of us, that's why, miss. Also . . .' Involuntarily his eyes flitted back towards the taproom door. 'Also there is a matter of some importance to be reported to the Cap'n.'

'If it has to do with Mr Charles Northwood, and if it is on my account, then I do not wish that there should be anything more . . .'

'It's not on your account. It's business between me, the Cap'n and Mr Charles. Nothing to do with you. So there the matter is, miss, and with your permission I'll just go along and fetch your bags.'

'Were you instructed by Captain Northwood to escort me to him?'

'Aye, Miss Ainsley, I was.'

'Then I shall be infinitely obliged if you will attend on me until I am ready to depart.' With those words I turned on my heel and started towards the gate of the coachyard.

'Miss Ainsley.' His voice was little more than a whisper — the same low, deadly tone which had done so much to quell Charles Northwood earlier — yet it reached me over the din from the street.

'Yes?' I answered his look with a level stare.

'Beyond there you can see the Cap'n's equipage.'

14

With a jerk of his head he indicated a carriage and pair on the far side of the street directly opposite the gate to The Crown. 'Now I'm going into this drink parlour where at any time during the next hour I can be found refreshing myself over a tankard or two and awaiting your pleasure, so to speak. But at the end of that hour, and right on the dot of it, mark you, I'll be twitting the whip across the rumps of those nags there and I'll be heading homeward. Homeward, Miss Ainsley, with or without your company. Do I make myself clear?'

'Perfectly. An hour should be sufficient for my needs.'

'I'm glad to hear it, miss.' There was a sketchiness to his bow which made it almost a travesty of politeness. He added with a faintly taunting smile: 'By the by, keep a weather eye open for trouble on your rounds. You seem to be a dab hand at running athwart of it. Evening, Miss Ainsley.' Then he sauntered back through the tavern door.

I was very much put out by his attitude. Was I indeed a 'dab hand' at running across trouble? Certainly I had managed to run foul of both Charles Northwood and Carne in a matter of minutes. But was it all my fault? As I went from shop to shop I had plenty of time to think and it occurred to me that Redmond Carne's manner, or rather his display of bad manners, might in part be due to the fact that, while waiting for the Exeter Mail, and my arrival, he may have already spent too much time in the taproom at The Crown. If such was the case, I told myself, then I could scarcely expect any improvement in his behaviour after unwittingly presenting him with an additional hour of drinking time. Perhaps in the company of Charles Northwood!

To give him credit, though, I must say that when I joined Carne outside the inn exactly one hour later he seemed perfectly composed and displayed none of

15

the visible effects of drinking too much. He greeted me with a surprising show of pleasantness.

'Ah, Miss Ainsley, so we're ready now, are we? Everything ship-shape and sea-worthy, I trust?'

'Yes, thank you. And now, Carne, if you are ready.'

'To be sure, miss, and with pleasure.' He continued smiling, walking beside me with an easy, rolling gait and my two heavy valises swinging lightly in his huge hands. 'Oh, by the by, Miss Ainsley, and meaning no disrespect, but at the Tower I'm addressed by all and sundry as *Mister* Carne. Even the Cap'n himself always addresses me as Mister.'

'Indeed?'

'Indeed so, miss. I just thought you might like to know for at Polmarran you'll no doubt discover that my rating as the Cap'n's man of business, his first mate as you might say, will be on a level, if not higher, than your rating as governess to the young mistress.'

'Very well, *Mister* Carne, I will try to bear that in mind.'

'Well now, miss, I doubt that you'll have to do too much trying on that score as I'm likely to take the time to remind you of it should you ever prove forgetful.' The words were uttered as he was turning from me to place my bags in the carriage and, together with his grin, seemed to indicate some private joke. It angered me, but before I could think of a suitable retort he went on: 'And now, Miss Ainsley, if you'd care to travel as an outside passenger up here alongside on the box I'd be pleased to point out to you any places of interest along the route.'

'No, thank you.'

'That's as you please, miss. Only trying to be civil and friendly.'

'Are you?'

'Of course.'

'That's odd. I had begun to form the opposite impression,' I said with sarcasm.

He shrugged. 'I learned my etiquette before the mast, Miss Ainsley. No time there to pick up all the fine points of daintiness. Still, if it's as you put it, then I must offer an apology.'

Whether or not it was sincere I had no alternative but to accept it. 'Which I am pleased to accept, Mr Carne,' I said coldly, 'as I certainly do not wish to be on unfriendly terms with any one at Polmarran Tower.'

'Good. Though you may find that it won't always be an easy thing to remain on friendly terms with all at the house.'

'What do you mean?'

'No doubt you'll see the lie of the land for yourself soon enough. I reckon you to be a noticing lass, Miss Ainsley.' He looked at me speculatively.

In my uncertainty I half-turned, my hand reaching towards the carriage door.

'Stay a bit . . .' he said.

'Yes?'

'I'm genuine about the apology.' Suddenly he placed his hand on my arm, Gently. Instinctively I knew the gesture to be an impulsive one and without any untoward familiarity on his part; added to the awkward candour which I surprised in his gaze I sensed in it something of either entreaty or warning. 'And, Miss Ainsley . . .'

'Yes?'

'If it struck you that I was deliberately lacking in politeness to you, then it may well have been that, unknownst to myself, I was testing you in some way to see if you had any spirit or backbone.'

Though resting lightly on my forearm his fingers seemed suddenly to be part of this testing. Probing. I dislodged his hand by quickly withdrawing my hand from the door handle. 'And why should you feel it necessary to test me for those qualities?'

'Because I'm hoping that you'll stay much longer than the other young lady. For the young mistress's sake, I mean.'

'Miss Adelaide Northwood?'

'Yes.'

'And by the "other young lady" I take it you are referring to my predecessor?'

'That's right, miss.'

'How long did she remain at Polmarran?'

'A month or thereabouts.'

'And why did she leave?'

'I wouldn't rightly know that.' He shrugged. 'There's no accounting for the vagaries and notions of a woman's mind.'

If my patent inquisitiveness had prompted an oblique sarcasm to shape his words then I chose to ignore it. 'But surely, Mr Carne, you must have some idea?'

'That well may be, but as she gave me no reasons for leaving I'm not going to offer any which would have too much guesswork in them. Enough to say that she just gave notice of quittal to the Cap'n, cutting her moorings one bright morning as you might say, and he ordered me to fetch this carriage and drive her to catch up with the Exeter mailcoach. That's the long and the short of it.'

It was useless to struggle against the sudden flood of curiosity, but I realized that it was equally futile to pursue that line of enquiry with Carne. Still, as the hour in the tavern seemed to have loosened his tongue, and as I was determined to seize every opportunity to learn more of what I might be letting myself in for, there might be another way.

'Is Captain Northwood a military gentleman?' I asked.

'Sailor, miss. Merchantman, long since retired.'

18

'He is old then?'

'Old and tired out, I'm afraid. It's all been too much for him.'

'What has?'

He paused before answering. 'Life . . . everything . . . not half the man he was in the old days. Not by a long shot.'

'Were you at sea with him?'

'I was. Upwards of twenty-five years of it.' There was an almost imperceptible squaring of his shoulders with pride.

'And young Miss Northwood . . . what can you tell me of my pupil?'

'An angel, miss. You'll have no trouble with Miss Adelaide.'

'Good. I do so look forward to meeting her. And the rest of the family?'

'There's only Mr George at the house now. But don't worry, he won't bother you.'

'Bother me?'

'I mean like Mr Charles back there.'

'Oh, I see. Well, I must confess that's something of a relief.'

'Aye, where Charles rides the wheel of fortune from one squall to the next, Mr George keeps to his own quarters for the most part, anchored to all those old volumes and Bibles so that he's almost become as a book from so much reading.'

'And does Miss Adelaide take after him in that respect?'

'What do you mean?'

'Does she have her father's interest in books?'

'Mr George is not her father.'

'But I thought . . .' I don't know exactly what I thought, except that I was loath to believe that the half-drunken swaggerer back in the taproom was the father of my pupil-to-be. 'Surely not Mr Charles Northwood?'

'No.'

'I'm afraid I do not quite understand. In his letter to me Captain Northwood referred to Miss Adelaide Northwood as his granddaughter . . .'

'The Cap'n had another son. John, same name as his father. He was the eldest. Then came Charles, and George the youngest. John was the only one to marry. He died a few months before the young mistress was born.' The terse, quick words hinted at his desire to put an end to the subject.

'And John Northwood's widow, is she still at Polmarran?'

'No, she . . .' Redmond Carne's voice ceased abruptly. He frowned. Then as though indicating his wish to put an end to my queries he opened the carriage door.

'Thank you, but I've decided to accept your invitation to travel on the box seat with you, if I may?'

'As you wish.'

He took my arm and helped me up. Then he went round to the far side and swung himself adroitly into the driver's seat. When he was seated by my side and just about to take up the reins I ventured another question, one which I think had been uppermost in my mind all this time. 'Back there in the taproom, Mr Carne, your Mr Northwood quite obviously mistook me for someone else. It was as though I bore a close resemblance to someone of his acquaintance . . .'

'Mr Charles has a very wide circle of female acquaintances, miss. I'm not surprised that he gets faces mixed up and loses track of who's who when he's been drinking.'

'But I also had the impression that you too noticed some likeness, Mr Carne.'

He turned to give me a sharp, lingering look. I wondered if he was comparing me with some mental picture of that same woman whom Charles Northwood had mistaken me for. 'Forgive me, but even now I

have the feeling that you are put in mind of someone . . .'

'Me? No, miss. How could I? I know none of
Charles's lady friends nor do I wish to.'

'That's not quite what I meant.'

He parried that with nothing more than a laconic
smile and the words: 'And now, Miss Ainsley, I think
we're ready to cast off . . . if I can use a sea term
for the business of flicking a whip across a nag's
hindquarters.'

Both horses were already stomping, shifting about
with the nervousness brought on by a tight rein and
the expectancy of the whip's hiss.

'Please, just one more thing, Mr Carne, if you will
be so kind?'

'Yes?'

'When you remarked a little while back that I
might not always find it an easy matter to maintain
friendliness with all at Polmarran Tower, did you have
any particular person, or persons, in mind?'

'I declare, Miss Ainsley, you make very good sail
out of a few odd questions.' He smiled a little,
shaking his head from side to side. 'Why, if we remain
gossiping here much longer we'll never even make it
to Polmarran Tower tonight.' Uttered with that infuriating half-smile of his the words contained such
an unmistakable element of finality that I instantly
regretted both my question and my decision to ride
beside him. Too late now . . .

'Yup there!'

His voice and the whip's crack merged in a staccato
command, unleashing an animal's snort and the harness jingle and the wheel's scrunch across the cobbled
yard. The carriage lurched forward. Once through the
gate we began to pick up speed. Within moments
Carne had the horses moving at a brisk trot and we
were wheeling out of the village and into the open
countryside. A mile or so beyond Marrambridge we

crossed an old stone bridge spanning a turbulent rivulet. The road was narrow but passable for a small carriage such as ours, and it turned sharply after the bridge to run parallel with the stream and to climb steadily into the wild hills. We kept to this roadway for the best part of an hour, ascending all the while through beautiful but lonely and deserted slopes. The one or two farms which I spied en route stood at some considerable distance from the road, remote, lonely places, half-hidden among a cluster of windswept trees, and only approached by narrow winding lanes. On all sides rocky eminences projected starkly above the heather and the rhododendron bushes. Occasionally there was a distant glimpse of the sea.

In spite of his earlier promise to point out some places of interest along the way, my driver had really very little to say. For that matter I, too, was far from communicative. Redmond Carne's references to my predecessor's abrupt departure from Polmarran Tower, his remarks concerning the Northwood family (few and somewhat cryptic as those utterances were) and my encounter with Mr Charles Northwood, all these gave me much to ponder on for the duration of the journey.

Dusk was descending when we approached Polmarran Tower. The entrance to it was through a narrow pass, its overhanging rocks pressed close together so that there was little more than a track, a long and steep descent flanked on either side by trees and dense foliage. Once through the pass, and before making the mile-long descent, I had my first view of the tower in the distance - a dark brooding watchful thing standing high and solitary between a belt of trees on the one hand, and on the other, the jagged and forbidding aspect of high cliffs to seaward. No welcoming light shone from it. It was silhouetted against the late evening sky, indifferent alike to the sun's dying rays and the ferocity of those Atlantic

22

gales which in the past must have torn and twisted the surrounding trees out of their original shapes.

My first impression, a rather chilling one, was of something which completely dominated the dusky landscape - something timeless, immutable and jealous of all careless intrusion - a half-alive thing which had set itself up as custodian of all that had been, or was yet to be, at Polmarran. I shuddered involuntarily. Was it the sight of the tower or the echo of Carne's words - *you may find that it won't always be an easy thing to remain on friendly terms with all at the house* . . .?

Just before our horses plunged us into the narrow defile between the trees, thus cutting off my view of the tower - or the tower's morose peering down on our approach, I'm not sure which - I found myself shivering again.

'Cold?' Carne asked.

'A little. The sea breeze, I think.'

'That tower is nearly one hundred and fifty years old. The first Sir Arthur Rebstock had it built. Rebstock the Wrecker they called him.'

'Why "Wrecker"?'

'Well, you see, Miss Ainsley, we have few good harbours along this north Cornwall coast and those few well-nigh impossible to make when a gale is in full force. Many of the fisherfolk about these parts are descended from generations of wreckers, aye and a damn sight too many of them still are a dab hand at wrecking. When there's a bad storm at sea they light false flares and wave them on the cliff edge to lure unsuspecting strangers on to the rocks.'

'But . . . but why?'

'In order to loot whatever cargo might be washed up when some hapless craft has been pounded to bits on the rocks and all the crew gone to their doom.'

'How horrible!'

'Horrible indeed.'

'But what has that got to do with the tower?'

'The local needs such a landmark for his own safety, you see. He's guided to safety by the landmark of his own village church spire, or tower. It's built high on the cliffs for that very purpose.'

'So that's why Polmarran Tower was built. I see now.'

'Aye, Sir Arthur the Wrecker needed a good landmark. And so did all his descendants. They varied smuggling - mind you, I hold nothing against a bit of honest-to-goodness smuggling, miss - with wrecking of foreign ships. That's how the Rebstocks made their fortune. It was lost through gambling, and serves them right. The present Sir Arthur Rebstock had to sell the place to meet his father's debts. Probably a few of his own too, truth to tell - ah, here we are safe and sound!'

Our carriage emerged from the trees at that moment. I could now see the tower and Polmarran House at close range. Proximity did not enhance the view one whit. The house abutted, or rather grew out from the lower portion of the tower like something spawned from the pool of shadows and the time-pocked stones of the Wrecker's landmark. Though I hold myself no judge of architecture I guessed its age to be considerably less than a hundred years, and I can best describe it as a three-storied country manse, sturdy and well set-up, ivy-covered, and with coach-house, stabling and various outhouses straggling to the rear and merging with what appeared to be an extensive orchard. On the land side a jagged line of wooded hills made a semi-circle about the place. I could see too that the tower stood much closer to the edge of the cliffs than I had at first imagined. In fact, its base was actually set into the top of a precipice. Below this the crash of high water against the rocky base came to my ears.

I took in all these impressions in the half-minute

or so that it took the carriage to wheel round in the drive before the house. After Carne helped me down I had time for a better look, time to cast about for a more reassuring and felicitous first impression. There was none. As with the tower, no bright lights illuminated the facade of Polmarran House, no lantern-bearing retainer, no welcoming master or curtseying pupil awaited us on the flight of steps. The front door was closed.

I confess that nothing which had ensued in the correspondence of the previous two months - that is, since first replying to Captain Northwood's newspaper advertisement - could have prepared me for this mood of disappointment and misgiving. I could only describe the place as one about which an air of gloom and dreariness lay, and which imparted to my mind the idea of neglect and melancholy. As I stood there, looking all around me while Redmond Carne removed my valises, the wind blew cold on my face and tugged viciously at my skirt; drops of rain, or perhaps flying spume, drove hard against me. And still there was no light from any of Polmarran's windows . . .

In all, then, it was a remarkably grim-looking place, and yet there was that about it which suggested to my mind that it need not have been so, and indeed that at one time it had quite obviously been the reverse. Though the gardens to the front of the house were now but a sprawling wilderness of rank weeds and long grass there was clear evidence of an earlier care in its well-planned lay-out.

'Come, miss.' Carne touched my elbow. The gravel of the driveway scarcely made a sound beneath our footsteps. It was stifled by the matted weeds and the spread of their hardy roots. I moved closer to him as we mounted the steps.

The door knocker was of heavy wrought-iron in the shape of a lion's head. It made a dull hollow sound when Carne raised it and let it fall. As we waited, my gaze returned with instinctive curiosity and not a little apprehensiveness to the tower. It loomed above me, a mute barrier of grey, uneven stones, ivy and little tufts of moss. Its narrow windows were heavily barred. They stared back at me with unblinking severity. Just before I looked away from it, Carne said, 'Try to think of it as a landmark for sailors, Miss Ainsley.'

It seemed to me that he was inwardly amused though nothing in his earnest brown face betrayed it. He raised the knocker once more and let it fall, Presently I heard the shuffle of footsteps behind the great oaken door and then the noise of a bolt being pulled back.

Slowly the door swung open . . .

Chapter Two

Carne entered first. 'Come along, Miss Ainsley . . . this here is our housekeeper, Mrs Forrest.'

As I crossed the threshold Mrs Forrest was emerging from behind the hall door, bobbing a half-curtsey and holding a candle well out from her in order to light the way for me.

'How do you do, Mrs Forrest.' I smiled (wondering too if she noticed that in the dark) and extended my hand. The housekeeper - I would put her age at about fifty years - was a short, plump, grey-haired woman, the whitish strands twisted neatly back from a face that was shrewd and quick-witted, though not unkindly.

'You're most welcome, Miss Ainsley. I hope you had a pleasant . . .' The words dried up as the candle's glow was brought to bear on my face. There it was again! That same open-mouthed recognition of something in my face, that likeness, reminder, resemblance, call it what you will. 'I hope you had a pleasant journey, miss,' she managed to finish. Her eyes darted with a kind of troubled questioning to Carne's. Mine got there first, just in time to catch the slight forward nod of his head and the eyes narrowed in affirmation and caution.

'We had some delay,' Carne said. 'Mr Charles is back. I ran into him at The Crown.'

'And . . .?' Mrs Forrest was looking at me.

'Same as ever, Mrs Forrest. And so far gone with

grog that he mistook Miss Ainsley for one of his fine lady friends from London town.'

'Well, no cause for us to stand here in a draught chattering about him,' the housekeeper said with the slightest hint of relief in her tone. 'I'm sure this young lady is tired from her travelling and would like to refresh herself. If you'd care to follow me, Miss Ainsley.'

Carne closed the door behind us. I felt suddenly cut off from the outside world. The echo of my footsteps on the stone floor rang through the high-ceilinged hall with a lonely distinctness - Carne's and Mrs Forrest's seemed hardly to make a sound, and this fact in some way seemed to add to my feeling of separateness, of not being 'one of them'.

From what little I could see of it in the shadows, the interior was in keeping with the outside appearance of Polmarran House. It was bleak and dark, its scant furnishings sheltered from the wavering candlelight by the all-pervading gloom. The windows flanking the main door were secured with shutters on the inside. No paintings hung upon the massive stone walls, no curtains or decoration of any sort to relieve their gaunt paleness. I looked up. There was no chandelier that I could see, only the huge blackened oak beams shedding ghost-like shadows on the ceiling as the dimly burning candle led us down the hall.

We were a silent trio who mounted the staircase. It branched off in opposite directions at the first landing. Mrs Forrest chose the left one and I followed her along a short gallery before ascending a second flight of steps. My room was at the end of a corridor. Redmond Carne took my bags in, informed me that Captain Northwood would be happy to receive me in his study within the hour, Mrs Forrest to conduct me there when I was refreshed, and in the meanwhile she would be pleased to attend on me for anything which I might require. I thanked him, and without more ado he departed, presumably to report my arrival and to impart to Captain Northwood his own impressions and observations concerning the character of the new governess. Perhaps, too, my new employer would have to be forewarned of my resemblance to . . . who?

I had for my quarters a small parlour and bedroom on the second floor; both were neatly and tastefully furnished, with windows looking out on the east side of the house towards the wooded hills. Thankfully there was no view of the tower. Mrs Forrest had prepared a good tray and there was a blazing log fire in the grate which struck warm and gleaming echoes on the polished furniture - an escritoire, wash-stand cabinet, clothes press, a small circular table with a flowered-filled vase as centrepiece, bookcase, and a number of tall slat-back chairs. The fire, together with a well-nigh extravagant use of wax candle illumination, bathed everything in a glow of light, and was a most welcome contrast to the shapeless mass of shadows with which I was greeted in the front hall such a short time before. I began to feel much better. There was security in the bright illumination.

In addition to the many indications of capable domestic management, Mrs Forrest showed a genuine desire to make me comfortable in every regard, carefully checking to see that each item was to my satisfaction. Crisp white linen, soaps, rose water, towels . . . more hot water, miss? Above all, she possessed that quality of polite and matter-of-fact talkativeness which made me glad of her company.

'You'll meet the young mistress at breakfast. She's abed now and sleeping, exhausted from the excitement of your coming.'

'I am so anxious to meet her. I do hope she will like me, Mrs Forrest, as I think it of the utmost importance that teacher and pupil . . .'

'She'll like you as you'll like her. A sweet lass

with taking ways as you'll soon discover, Miss Ainsley. Though, mind you, like the rest of 'em she can be a bit strange in her ways betimes. Comes of being without proper ladylike supervision most of her life I expect. I mean, I do my best in my own simple way whenever called upon but I don't have the book-learning and the ways of gentlefolk. Never had children of my own neither, so I don't have the trick of dealing with Miss Adelaide's strange little ways.'

'In what way is her manner strange?'

'Well now, I'm not sure as how I'd put it.' Pausing, Mrs Forrest put her head to one side in momentary concentration. 'I suppose really she's as bright and cheerful as any seven-year-old, but there's times when I find her creeping about the place, playing her own little secret games in odd corners and out-of-the-way places. And she's much given to whispering and talking to herself.'

'But surely that is only to be expected in one so young? Especially as she has no companions of her own age here.'

'And that's as I always says to Mr Forrest, but I'm not a native of these parts no more are you, Miss Ainsley, nor am I a superstitious woman. And my husband says that all Cornwall people are a queer mixture of pagan and believer and that it's easy enough to be be pixylated when you're actually born here.

'I'm very pleased to hear that we are neither of us superstitious. As to being pixylated, well . . .' I could not help dismissing the suggestion of sprites and magical powers with an indulgent smile.

'Still, there's the matter of Mr George and his illnesses . . .'

'What sort of illness?'

She shrugged her ample shoulders - not knowing, not caring too much, despite her odd reference to it. Apparently Mr George Northwood's illnesses were an accepted part of the household routine.

'Does he have the doctor frequently?'

'Doctor, miss? No, it's never anything serious like that. It's more in the nature of . . . well, I'm not sure really how I'd put it. I suppose you might just say that he has his moods, so to speak. Keeps to his room for days on end and with the door locked for the most part. Locked, mark you. Mr Carne always attends him at such times. Meals and clean linen and what not. My husband always says that young Mr George just likes to pamper himself and that there's really nothing sickish the matter with him in the least save what he imagines in the mind.'

'Hypochondria, I expect.'

'No, miss, I don't think that it's anything medical-like. More like in the mind. My husband says that's what comes of reading all those old volumes.'

'I see.'

We continued in this vein for a few minutes. I began to wonder if there was any particular significance in the fact that neither of us made any reference to either Charles Northwood or the young mistress's parents. I began to wonder too if I should attempt to repair that omission . . .

'And what of Mr Charles Northwood?'

After just a moment of hesitation the housekeeper said, 'I'm not rightly sure I should be telling you all this. Mr Forrest always says that talking to me is like telling all to the ship's parrot. But howsoever I'll not deny that I like this family here. Every one of 'em. And I don't believe all I hear said about them, nor should you. So better you hear some things from me than from some of those church-going ladies in Marrambridge. Or the Rebstocks, even. You could hear it worse from them. Now you ask me about Mr Charles . . . well, Miss Ainsley, all I can say is that he has a way of life as tousled and unruly as that black curly hair of his. But no matter what they says, he's not the worst. His mischief-making is out in the

31

open for all to see. So says Mr Forrest. My husband thinks the sun shines out of Mr. Charles, he does, all on account of such things as being able to ride near to fifty miles in two hours, or drink no end of indifferent booze, or have the girls ogling and chasing him, or being a good hand at cards or dice. Anyone who's in favour of a good fling is all right by my Jem, alas.' The last was uttered with just a slight sniff of disapproval.

'I take it that your husband has some position here?'

'Aye, I suppose you might say that he has, though what exactly the nature of that position is, the pair of us are often at a loss to know, miss. If this were a proper regulated household - the sort of place I was accustomed to before coming here, (not that I'm criticizing in any way, mind you) - but if this were a proper regulated household so to speak, then my good man would most likely be set-up for a life with the position of butler. A butler, no less. That is of course if he had the correct training and the manners to go with it. My Jem, I'm sorry to admit, is a bit lop-sided in the matter of etiquette. As it is, he gets his position here by virtue of having been a first-rate boatswain on the Captain's old ship and, if you'll pardon my being the one to say so, by Mr Forrest having the wit to marry quite a bit above his station. So there you have it pure and simple.'

I felt certain that I was going to like Mrs Forrest with her good-humoured candour and chattiness. That feeling encouraged me to ask: 'What of Mrs John Northwood, my pupil's mother? Is she here?'

Mrs Forrest was suddenly all bustling efficiency again, continuing as though I had not spoken. She put another log on the fire and said, 'Now, that'll be blazing away nicely when you come back from meeting the Captain. I'll bring you down whenever you're ready . . . oh my, what a pretty gown in this light! It becomes you, Miss Ainsley, and with your hair done up like that.'

'Thank you. I must try for a pleasing effect on my first meeting with Captain Northwood. I confess to being just a teeny bit nervous.'

'Little need for that, miss. My husband always says as how the Captain always barks more than he bites.'

'You still haven't told me anything of Miss Adelaide's mother . . .' Although I had not failed to notice the housekeeper's earlier words: *Comes of being without proper ladylike supervision most of her life,* I continued quite casually: 'I expect Mrs Northwood will be present to meet her daughter's new governess?'

Mrs Forrest looked at me speculatively, and then, investing her question with a curiously troubled expression, she enquired: 'What has Mr Carne told you?'

'Nothing. I just wondered if . . .'

'Nothing, eh?' She silenced me with a brisk shake of her head. 'So-ho, the least said the easiest mended.'

'I beg your pardon?'

'Forgive me, Miss Ainsley. Just a manner of speech. My Jem is always saying such-like phrases - you know the sort of thing: "What's done is done", "little use talking about what there's no use talking about", "least said the easiest mended". My husband is a great man for such-like.'

There was a tacit rebuke in her casual words. I felt colour rushing to my cheeks, embarrassment tinged with the beginnings of frustration. 'I merely asked if Miss Adelaide's mother . . .'

'Now you look here, Miss Ainsley,' - it was not said in a sharp or unfriendly manner - 'Jem Forrest and me are only servants and has to do as told and are not supposed to know certain things. You'll find, miss, that we knows our duty.'

'I'm sorry. I quite understand.'

'And now, Miss Ainsley, meaning no lack of compliment to your comeliness, but I doubt if the Captain will pay much notice to your finery if I delay you into unpunctuality. Whenever you're ready, if you please.'

On descending to the ground floor again I found that it was now less shadowy than before. A two-pronged candle-holder had been set up on a small table near the foot of the stairs. Its feeble glow showed me that the brick-paved hall seemed to be the principal ground-floor apartment, that it extended from the front of the house to the back, passing on either side of the central staircase, and that it communicated with other rooms on both sides. It was to the door of one of these rooms that Mrs Forrest directed me. Just before she tapped on the thick wooden panel she laid her hand on my arm. She leaned closer, and in a tone compounded of hurried advice, warning, friendliness, whispered: 'Now, miss, from time to time here you'll happen on situations that are unexpected. From the start you'll be best advised to show no feeling of surprise or curiosity. Do you follow me?'

'No, Mrs Forrest, I'm afraid I don't.'

'Just you mind well what I said.' She rapped on the door, disengaged herself from my side and stepped back.

Redmond Carne opened the door. He stood squarely in the entrance, momentarily barring my way as he paused to subject me to a swift scrutiny. Unpunctual or not, he at least seemed to take considerable notice of my appearance, yet much to my annoyance his stance compelled me to brush against him as I entered the dimly-lit room. It was impossible to determine his precise facial expression but in the quiet flicker of the room's solitary candle I had just sufficient light to glimpse his bold, half-smile, yet not enough to make out with any great degree of clarity the shadowy form of Captain Northwood standing by a window at the far end of the room.

In the very first moment of entry, and even in the dim light, I was instantly struck by the bizarre décor of Captain Northwood's study. As near as I could tell, it had been remodelled to look like a ship's stateroom or master's cabin. The walls were panelled in some dark wood and made to resemble bulkheads; the ceiling was very low and fashioned from the same substance, and from one of its broad rafters hung an unlit hurricane lamp; a slant-topped chart table stood against one wall and on it there was a huge waist-high globe. The solitary window at which Captain Northwood stood with his back to me was low and wide; it was uncurtained and the crowded lattice-work framed small thick panes of glass, the whole thing set into the panelled walls at an angle, with the uppermost part tilted outwards to give the impression of a vessel's stern window. At any moment I expected the floor, or deck, to rock slowly from side to side with a heaving swell!

'Cap'n, this is Miss Ainsley.' Redmond Carne spoke from behind me as he closed the door.

The other man advanced to meet me, moving slowly into the pool of light made by Carne as he applied the lighted candle to four companions set in a brass candelabrum which he placed on the top of a large table in the centre of the room. Captain Northwood I perceived to be a tall, spare figure, clad in a black coat and a white neckcloth, both of which were of a style long since out of fashion. His shoulders were stooped, though his height of over six feet and the general build of the man suggested to my mind that in his younger days he had been strong and powerful. But what immediately held my attention was the face of my new employer - a face having the paleness of marble, gaunt and lined, with a great hooked nose and a square chin which gave the impression of severity and sternness. I guessed his age to be somewhere between sixty-five and seventy years. But, above all, the main characteristic was one which

35

immediately suggested a cold aloofness. It was this quality which I was most aware of as he approached me - for with the added illumination from the extra candles I saw clearly a face on which the flesh had sunk inwards, throwing into prominence the high cheek-bones, the strong hooked nose and two coldly piercing eyes.

'Captain Northwood, sir . . .' I began.

'Mister Carne informs me that you expressed considerable curiosity concerning the dismissal of your predecessor. Is that so?' he bluntly enquired. He appeared not to see my outstretched hand as he pointed towards a chair for me while he remained standing and peering down at me. So even the gesture of a handshake was being withheld! What else had Carne told him? Had he been warned in advance of my apparent resemblance to someone who was clearly known to Mr Charles Northwood, Redmond Carne and Mrs Forrest? Certainly he evinced no surprise; there was no tell-tale glint of recognition in his slow and careful study of me.

'Well, Miss Ainsley?' In the silence of the room his words sounded harsh.

'I beg your pardon?'

'I asked you a question, young lady.'

'Oh yes, so you did.'

'Well then?'

'About my predecessor? Yes, I was curious.'

'I see.' He shot a quick glance at Carne. 'Very well, Miss Ainsley. I propose to make some concession to your feminine curiosity. The reason for the other young woman's dismissal can briefly be attributed to the fact that she presumed to extend her duties into matters of family privacy. In short, your predecessor proved unsuitable because of her unseemly meddling in affairs which did not concern her.'

This by no means satisfied my curiosity but it was quite obviously the wrong time for any further dis-

36

play of inquisitiveness on my part. I confined myself to replying with a terse nod and the words, 'I quite understand.'

'Do you, Miss Ainsley?' The implacable hostility of the Captain's gaze held an unmistakable challenge. 'I question whether in fact you do "quite understand", as you put it.'

'Forgive me, sir, but you will have to be more explicit.'

Turning to the chart table, the surface of which was littered with numerous papers and maps, Captain Northwood selected a single sheet of paper. The candlelight showed it to be a handwritten page.

'Amongst the letters of recommendation which you sent to me when applying for this position there is one here, Miss Ainsley . . .' He tapped the sheet with a skeletal forefinger, raised it to the light and for a moment or two peered at it as though searching for some particular passage. '. . . One here from a previous employer in which, while he bears witness to your excellent qualifications as a tutor, he nonetheless thought fit to describe you as . . . as . . .' Once again he peered at the paper, seemed unable to locate the particular passage, and then passed the letter over to Redmond Carne. 'You read it, please, Mr Carne.'

The Captain was now able to focus all his attention on me. Despite a growing irritation I was determined to show no lack of composure under his cold gaze. The notepaper rustled in Carne's huge hand. 'Er, with your permission?'

'Certainly.' I nodded.

'Well then, let's see . . . ah yes, here it is. It says here: "However, it must be added to the foregoing that the said Miss Katherine Ainsley is of a self-assured and independent spirit of mind not usually to be encountered in young ladies of her station; it is an independence of character which has on more than one occasion during the period in which she was a member of my household led her into dispute with me, and to intrude her opinions on family matters, the latter arising from our different views on what best constituted the welfare and upbringing of my children" . . . Do you want me to read on?'

'Please do,' I said, still maintaining a level stare in the direction of Captain Northwood. It had the effect of drawing the following question from him: 'Do you not wish to explain the contents of that letter?'

'I see no reason to. It's self-explanatory,' I replied calmly, perhaps a trifle smugly. It was now my turn to deny both men the satisfaction of whatever curiosity they may have been experiencing.

'But . . . but, Miss Ainsley, I fail to see why you should include this one letter amongst what are otherwise excellent references. Its omission would not have mattered, whereas its inclusion could give cause for some misgivings on the part of a prospective employer.'

'And has it caused some misgivings in this instance?'

'We shall let that pass for the moment . . .'

'No, sir, we shall not let that pass for the moment!' There was defiance in my assertion. 'If you had misgivings about my suitability you should not have sent for me. Your last letter to me . . . I have it here, sir, should you wish to be reminded of what you said . . .'

'I know full well what I wrote.'

'Then you will know that your letter expressed satisfaction on all heads. It is only now, when you meet me face to face, that you appear to have reservations. I think I am entitled to know why. Your own son, Mr Charles Northwood, when I encountered him quite by accident this very evening at The Crown Inn at Marrambridge under circumstances of which Mr Carne has undoubtedly informed you . . . your own son quite obviously mistook me for someone else, someone I apparently resemble to an extraordinary degree, for I have the impression that both Mr Carne and your housekeeper, Mrs Forrest, were also put in mind of someone else by my appearance. Perhaps you, too, have . . .'

'Nonsense! I do not know what you are alluding to.'

'Forgive me, sir, but I think you do. And I think that this is the reason why you suddenly find me unsuitable. The fact of my coincidental resemblance to someone of your son's acquaintance is a matter of no import to me, nor does it concern me except insofar as it now appears to render me unsatisfactory for the position of governess here. In which case, I feel entitled to make some protest, having gone to some inconvenience in quitting my last post and undertaking such a long journey.'

'I did not say you were unsuitable. It's just that . . .'

Carne interrupted him. 'If I may be allowed to put in my oar, Cap'n, Miss Ainsley has been signed on fair and square and is in the right of it by all accounts. With all due respect, Cap'n, you can't give the word to go about just because Mr Charles made a bit of a nuisance of himself at The Crown.' He turned to me. 'That's our only concern, miss. Yes, I'm bound to say that you must bear an uncommon likeness to someone he must've known, or still knows. But Mr Charles does not reside here any more, so there's no need to go worrying about him pestering you. You may lay to that, Miss Ainsley. I have Cap'n Northwood's say-so on such matters.' His eyes shifted back to Captain Northwood.

The older man nodded his head: 'That is so, Miss Ainsley. If you will allow me to apologize on my son's behalf?'

'There is no need.'

'And if we could have some comment about this letter?' His eyes went back to the paper in Carne's hand.

'Very well,' I said, relenting. As my temper subsided I found myself responding to an old man's desire to have his mind cleared of some lurking doubts. 'That letter was included with the others simply because it recommended me as a competent tutor and because it described me as possessing "self-assurance and an independent character". If that description is true - and I am vain enough to hope it is - then I see nothing to be ashamed of in that letter.'

'No? What about this business of conflict with your last employer, of intruding your opinions on family matters?'

'It stemmed from our opposing points of view on the subject of disciplining children.'

'In what way precisely?'

'Simply that I made strenuous objections to the severe physical punishment which my late employer frequently visited upon his two youngest children. Often for the most trivial of misdemeanours. It was so cruel!'

'You do not approve of physical punishment?'

'No. Thankfully, I have never had recourse to it, and certainly where children are concerned I have never been convinced of its necessity or desirability.'

Captain Northwood was silent for too long. His eyes peered out from their deep sockets, watching me. Disturbing me with their icy hue. It was impossible to tell what thoughts lay behind them, but I felt certain that my last remark could not have held any great appeal for a grim-faced old sea captain. Even a private governess cannot but hear dreadful accounts of floggings and keel-hauling. What was my employer-to-be thinking? Opposed to physical punishment, eh? Bah! What next - mutiny? No, from the expression on his face I suddenly felt that he was not going to be my employer after all, that I had just arranged for my own dismissal. Well, I thought fiercely, he asked for my comments! Now let him make of them what he will.

When he finally broke the silence his words held no clue to his thoughts. 'It is a somewhat unusual attitude for a teacher, I should imagine. I confess that I hadn't expected such.'

'Well, I'm glad to hear it anyway,' Carne put in. 'She's a gentle little thing, is Miss Adelaide. And if you can give her an education without too much strictness, Miss Ainsley, then I for one think it's all to the good. Aye, Cap'n?'

Was Captain Northwood's prolonged silence a rebuke? Dissatisfaction?

'If you gentlemen would like me to outline my teaching methods, or if you wish to put any questions to me concerning the course of studies which I propose to . . .'

'No, that won't be necessary. I'm perfectly content to leave all that sort of thing to you.' To judge from the peremptory gesture with which Captain Northwood cut short my words, his professed contentment seemed to border on either indifference or impatience. 'My only concern is that you do not disturb the child with all this delving into past events . . . into private family matters I mean.'

'I am afraid I do not quite understand what you mean, Captain Northwood.'

As though in response to the troubled and hurried glance directed towards him Carne immediately broke in: 'You see, Miss Ainsley, the Cap'n's granddaughter was orphaned at a very early age. Sad doings for one so young, you will agree, but above all Miss Adelaide is not to be bothered or upset with the mention of such things. That's what the Cap'n means.'

'Precisely.' The older man nodded. 'Miss Adelaide is not to be pampered or encouraged in her occasional melancholy. Nor should you as her governess give any credence to her childish notions and fancies. Indeed, I would expect that, in addition to schooling and whatever other accomplishments are necessary to a young lady's correct upbringing, you will also make time to devise innocent games and recreations . . . suitable amusements, that sort of thing . . .' The words trailed off into nothingness and the vague gesturing grew into a helpless outspreading of his hands.

'We menfolk are not much use at that kind of thing.' Carne's hesitant and half-wincing grin mirrored the other man's helplessness. 'So we're counting on you, miss.'

'Oh, I should be delighted to!'

I meant it. My natural sympathy with all children had suddenly, and almost inexplicably, grown into a protective compassion for this parentless child I had not yet seen. In that instant I had a picture of what her life must be like in this grim barracks of a house under the baleful shadow of Polmarran Tower - a sensitive and gentle child, lonely, left to her own devices by a group of adults who were too immersed in their own affairs. And what an odd assortment of adults! A stern, uncompromising old sea dog; the mercurial Mr Carne, at first rude and sullen, then pleasant and talkative, now full of an amiability tinged with a kind of watchfulness; and Charles Northwood - when at home would he be the same pleasure-seeking, quick-tempered tippler? Mr George Northwood, as yet unknown to me. From Mrs Forrest's remarks it was an easy thing to imagine a solemn, studious young man, perhaps weak both in body and determination, keeping out of everyone's way and taking refuge from the dominance of these two tough seamen before me by cloistering himself in a room full of books. What an odd household!

'So, it's all settled then?' Carne jerked me out of my musing by slapping his knee with the air of a man who had just witnessed a market-place bargain settled to his own satisfaction.

Captain Northwood was not nearly so demonstrative. He confined himself to a curt nod. That left it up to me to force a smile. Carne alone seemed happy with the way everything had gone. After that, our meeting petered out inside about ten minutes. During that time practically all matters touching on the child's schooling were initiated by me, but to my disappointment they failed to evoke any great interest on Captain Northwood's part. When it was time for me to take my leave, Redmond Carne escorted me to the door, but not before he had effected some subtle reminder to the older man - a look, a gesture, a nod, I don't know which - but I am certain that by some oblique signal he prompted Captain Northwood to add: 'Oh yes . . . just one more thing, Miss Ainsley. The west wing of the house and particularly the tower . . . you would be well advised never to go there.'

'Why not?'

The silence was like a breach - and once again Redmond Carne was stepping in to defend it with his half-smile. 'You see, miss, part of the old tower is little more than a ruin. All loose masonry and rotting timbers in some places. Really quite dangerous unless you know the lay of it. For reasons of safety we . . . the Cap'n, that is . . . can't allow anyone to go wandering about over there. I'm sure you understand.'

'Thank you. I will be careful.'

'Take care that you never go there . . . under any circumstances!' The Captain's sharp command was much more appropriate to a ship's deck than to the precincts of a country house.

I felt Carne's hand plucking at my sleeve, checking me. He must have guessed that I was on the point of making an equally sharp retort. He leaned closer to me, and in a voice scarcely above a whisper muttered,

'Please now, Miss Ainsley . . . he means it only for your own safety.'

'Thank you, gentlemen. Good night.' In the act of bobbing a curtsey I swiftly dislodged Carne's hand from my arm, and turning sharply on my heel, I departed with all the dignity I could muster. The door closed behind me. I stood for a moment in the hall, only vaguely aware of the low murmers drifting through the door from the Captain's room. Or was it a cabin?

I was alone in the hall. Mrs Forrest was not on hand to light me back to my room. The only illumination was from that one sputtering candle on the table near the foot of the stairs. It glinted slyly on the polished wood of the lower balustrade. The blackness stood firmly and impenetrably at the top of the stairs: there was a stealthy creeping in of doubt to fill all the dark recesses of the hall. I walked over and took up the candle. The movement roused a new batch of shadows from their slumbers and sent them crawling noiselessly across the stones of the hallway. I mounted the stairs and hurried on up. At the landing I turned to the left.

I had only gone a few paces along the gallery when I heard a faint sound from somewhere behind - a gliding footstep, a door or a floorboard creaking, or perhaps a loose shutter tap-tapping in the night wind. Whatever had caused the faint noise also had the power to make me stop abruptly and swing round. I looked across the landing at the other gallery, the one leading back towards the west, or tower, side of the house - had I seen something moving just there for the fraction of a second?

In a slow, wide arc my gaze swept round, trying to prise every detail from the shadows. They were banked up against the walls, purple-black and deep, and together with a certain combination of some indistinct furniture - a tall linen cupboard, or grand-father clock, or a half-open door - they gave an exact representation of a figure standing motionless, and watching, against the wall. I stood looking and wondering if it really was some person. The dark shape made no movement, no sound. From down-stairs the muffled voices of Carne and my employer drifted upwards and then ceased. Everything was still and silent. No, not quite silent! From the opposite gallery my hearing caught at the unmistakable sound of someone breathing!

Someone was there, watching me! I looked fixedly at the dark shape, faceless and ominous, my hair tingling oddly at the roots. My thoughts passed through a few moments of indecision and emerged on the other side with something akin to determi-nation. If somebody was watching me covertly then I wanted to know why.

'Hallo . . . is there someone there?' The candle trembled in my hand. For one terrible moment I waited for the sudden movement, the gesture, the words of response.

'Who is there? Who are you?' I forced myself to take a small pace forward.

There was an answering footstep from beyond, or was it the echo of my own timorous step?

'Hallo . . . is there someone there?' I called again.

The floorboards whimpered under hurrying, re-treating footsteps. The combination of shadow and indistinct furniture became blurred with a wavering movement, a darker huddled tone detaching itself and flitting away, moving in time to the stealthy tread. A few moments later I heard a door opening softly, then closing.

Someone had been watching me. Who? Why?

I turned and with quick, nervous steps hurried to my own room, holding the candle well out in front so that my long and crooked shadow could re-connoitre each foot of the way. A moment later some-thing - some impulse which it did not occur to me to analyse at the time - urged me to lock my door after me and to secure myself against all possible intrusion.

Intrusion, but why?

An inner voice provided one possible answer before I had time to stifle it: *I would have to secure myself against all intrusion because of my striking resem-blance to another woman, a woman of whom I knew absolutely nothing but the fact that Charles North-wood could refer to her in drunken anger as a bitch!*

Chapter Three

I slept late and did not rise until past 7 o'clock next morning.

As usual after a day of travel and incident I had expected that, as soon as my weary limbs touched the crisp, freshly-laundered sheets and warmed them, I would find myself floating off into a deep sleep. Instead, I had felt cold and uncomfortable in the great four-poster bed. I had tossed from side to side, my mind pondering the significance of the evening's events. Though far less acute and imponderable in the bright morning light, the same thoughts still remained with me. Had there really been someone lurking in the darkness of the opposite gallery last night, or had some peculiar arrangement of shadows and my own strained senses conjured up the whole thing? Perhaps. I couldn't be sure. Anyway, I told myself, even had someone been there, there was probably a perfectly ordinary explanation - a timorous servant, maybe, or someone in night attire suddenly surprised by my swift ascent of the stairs. It might even have been my new pupil, an over-tired, nervous, half-frightened child unable to resist taking a peep at the ogress of a new governess. Poor little thing, how I must have startled her with my sharp 'Who's there?'

Yes, so many things to think about. And to reproach myself with. I seemed to have bungled my first encounter with everyone here. Charles Northwood, Redmond Carne, The Captain. Possibly even

Mrs Forrest now that I recalled her *'Forrest and me are only servants - you'll find that we knows our duty.'* And last night's interview with my new employer! Whether or not I pleased, offended or merely disappointed Captain Northwood, it was perhaps still too early to say, yet somehow I suspected a combination of the last two - offence and disappointment. It would be idle to pretend that there was not an element of mutuality about the whole thing. One thing was certain. Never before had I been interviewed for a position in such a cold and probing manner, nor had I departed from one with the feeling that more questions had been raised by what had transpired than had been answered. But for Redmond Carne's presence, I felt sure Captain Northwood would have dismissed me there and then.

And what of this man, Redmond Carne? He possessed a certain rough charm when it suited him, and he was undeniably handsome in something of the same rough way. His fairish hair was thick and carelessly arranged, almost to the point of untidiness: his eyes were quick and lively, glinting and narrowing all the time with intelligence and humour. He looked confident and secure. And vigilant? I could not be sure, but from the very moment of our meeting I had detected something in his look which seemed to offer to me personally either a warning or a threat.

The breakfast gong cut through my thoughts and they receded with the fading echo. I made my way downstairs. The shutters had been opened and daylight streamed into the hall, but it looked no more cheerful than the night before.

My arrival at the door to the dining-room was greeted by Captain Northwood, Carne, and Miss Adelaide. I was immediately taken with her. She was small and delicate of stature, even for a seven-year-old. Honey-coloured hair haloed her angelic face, the blue eyes were full of innocence and simplicity. The

Captain introduced me with a stiff formality which would have daunted even the bravest of children.

'Adelaide! Step forward, girl. This is your new governess, Miss Ainsley. She is to supervise your lessons and you must attend to them diligently at all times.'

The poor child! She looked so forlornly shy and diffident, her face reddening with embarrassment as I reached out and took her hand. I continued to hold it, smiling, and longed desperately for something cheery to say.

'Good morning, Miss Northwood. I so looked forward to our meeting . . .' but it sounded so futile, such a cold echo of the Captain's stern politeness.

Thank heavens for Redmond Carne!

'By the powers, Cap'n! I declare if I ever saw two fine shipmates as chummy as our two young ladies here - bless me, but that's a handsome hand-clasp between them!'

He winked boldly at me, laid his hand on the child's shoulder and gently nudged her forward. She drew a dainty bouquet of flowers from behind her back and presented it to me.

'Oh how sweet! They are beautiful. Thank you so much, Miss Northwood.'

'Redmond told me I should . . .' She plucked nervously at her pinafore.

My eyes came up to meet Carne's, blinked just a little before his steady smile, and then returned to the child. 'Thank you. It was most thoughtful . . . a delightful welcome.'

'Are we to stand here all morning? Breakfast is waiting.' Captain Northwood glared impartially at all of us and then ushered us into the dining-room. There was no sign of his son, George Northwood.

The dining-room at Polmarran was a most impressive place - grotesquely so! Just inside the door I halted involuntarily as my curious gaze fell upon

49

something between a museum and an arsenal. Sundry mementoes of a lifetime's voyaging in foreign parts festooned the walls and jostled for pride of place with various odds-and-ends of English weaponry. I beheld a weird array of fierce-looking spears, knives and shields, Indian arrows and machetes, Arctic harpoons, voodoo masks, cutlasses and ship's pennants: slightly more familiar (though no less fearsome) were the pikes and halberds of yeoman England, the crossed flintlock muskets, the horse-pistols, sabres, daggers and blunderbusses, the armour breast-plates, helmets and shields.

The whole effect was one of bizarre and hideous incongruity in a spacious hall which had originally been designed as the main room of an English manor. It was vividly illuminated by the light pouring in from two projecting bay windows. The sunlight sparkled on the metal of gun barrels and blades, on the varnish of great oak pillars which supported a beamed ceiling of the same wood, on the candelabra, the plate, the silver and the cut-glass decanters. The panels on the lower half of the walls were of the same black oak, and the floor, its polished boards partly covered by a scattering of fine rugs and large animal furs, appeared to be made of the same material. Decorating the rough-hewn stone of the chimney-breast were the horns of a stag, grown black with age and the smoke issuing from a big, open fireplace graced by hefty brand-irons. It might have been a bright, sturdy, hospitable room but for the collection of war-like knick-knacks hanging on the walls.

I was still standing just inside the door, looking all around me in wide-eyed surprise and perhaps shuddering a little when Captain Northwood muttered, 'Come along, Miss Ainsley.'

Carne hung back a pace to lean towards me and whisper with sly humour: 'We're well set-up to repel boarders, eh?' Then he stepped up to the massive mahogany breakfast table and held out a chair for me, one of a dozen or so throne-like affairs with great stiff backs which were placed on either side of the table. He sat opposite me, Captain Northwood at the head, and his granddaughter close by him and at my side of the table.

To add to my sense of unreality in that museum-like room we were served at table by the oddest of menservants - a bald, squat fellow of about sixty years, with an old scar on his cheek. From the decidedly 'lop-sided' nature of both his etiquette and his attire I could only deduce that this was Mrs Forrest's husband. He wore a livery of sorts - a faded, bluish coat with brass buttons down the front, which, for all I know, may have been the remnant of some obscure nautical uniform. He skipped all round the table with great alacrity, directing no end of inquisitive glances at me, half-smiling now and then in a manner that was somewhere between familiarity and diffidence. When not actually serving at the table he hung about the room casually rubbing the glasses and polishing the decanters, too casual by half, with his constant eyeing of us, and unabashed listening in - until Captain Northwood eventually dismissed him with a curt, 'That will be all, Forrest.'

Apart from that, my employer remained silent throughout the rest of the meal. Indeed, that first breakfast was to more or less set the pattern for all future meal-times at Polmarran. I soon discovered that conversations at table were rarely conducted by Captain Northwood, but were instead watched over and influenced by his cold aloofness. Whenever he did condescend to join in, it was generally to comment upon the happenings of the day: he would ask questions of us all, invariably of a kind that could, or should, only be answered in the bleakest affirmative or negative. Yes sir, no sir. I can recall only two or three occasions when this taciturn old man at the head of the table actually waxed quite voluble (from just a little too much wine, perhaps?) and on those rare occasions, by way of contrast to his usual mood, he would hold forth on those subjects which he had much to heart - sea-lore and navigation, foreign ports, shipping, lighthouse construction and a host of related topics - and always intoned in a style that gave to what he had to say the air of state-room lectures or instructions from the bridge rather than leisurely table-talk.

At that first breakfast, Carne was quite talkative and breezy and he helped me enormously with the child, for I was beginning to form the impression that she was of a more thoughtful and introspective nature than clever or amusing. Her interested gaze alternated between my face and the milk-moat surrounding the little castle of porridge in the centre of her bowl. Pixylated? Unbidden, the housekeeper's words came back to me. Nonsense! Naturally Miss Adelaide, like all children, had her own secret thoughts - trivially sweet, childish things; hopes and gossamer-like daydreams that were all the more precious to her because they were intimately her very own.

After breakfast, the better to become acquainted with her (and not to put her off with too great a readiness to commence lessons) I suggested that she be allowed to plan our first day together as she wished. Rewarding me with the sweetest of smiles she immediately invited me to take a walk with her. Wonderful, I thought. I could not have planned it better.

The warm sunlight kept us out of doors for more than two hours. The air, with the tang of the sea in it, had a biting freshness. Adelaide first took me in the direction of the sea.

'It's perfectly safe, Miss Ainsley. There is a little

pathway leading down to the cove. Look, over there. Come, I'll show you.'

'Please be careful. Let me take your hand.'

The pathway was railed on one side, hugging the cliff side on the other, and appeared to have been gouged and twisted from the rock face. It led down to Polmarran Cove. On either side the cliffs rose dark and steep. The channel into the cove entered at an angle so that any vessel out at sea would discern nothing more than a dark crease in the unbroken line of cliff-face extending along the coast.

'Redmond says that it is a perfectly safe anchorage,' Adelaide explained. 'Polmarran Cove was used for the smuggling trade long long ago.'

'Yes, Mr Carne told me. Rebstock the Wrecker picked an ideal haven for himself.'

'He built the tower as well, hundreds and hundreds and hundreds of years ago.' Adelaide pointed a finger.

I looked up. The tower cast its long shadow across the facade of Polmarran House. Even in the bright sunlight it seemed to point out some dark, obscure message.

'Only Grandpapa and Redmond are permitted to go up there. Do you see the very top window?'

'Yes . . .?' It was little more than a narrow slit and it was set deeply, almost buried, in the massive walls.

'Well, Grandpapa often sits up there with his big spy-glass. He can see for miles around. He let me look through it once, but not from up there. Only from the ship window in his study.'

I wondered if Captain Northwood was up there now. Watching us?

'Adelaide?'

'Yes, Miss Ainsley?'

'Would you mind terribly if we did not go right down to the cove just now? That breeze is quite cool.

Perhaps the far side of the house would be more sheltered.'

'Very well, Miss Ainsley. I could show you the orchard, and there is a little pathway through the woods.'

'Yes, I would like to see that.'

She took my hand and led me back again through the long tousled grass of what had been the lawn. Ugly patches of weeds streaked the once-proud flower-beds all round us. The sea winds had bowed and shaped the nearest trees, giving them a decided slant to landward. Like me they seemed to be drawing away from the cliff-edge and the tower as though in distrust.

'Are you afraid of my grandpapa?'

Adelaide's question took me by surprise. 'No . . . no, of course not. Should I be?'

'I suppose not. After all, Miss Ainsley, you are a grown-up.' A filigree of leaves from a low-hanging bough hid her face from me.

'Well, even grown-ups can be afraid of each other sometimes.'

'But you are not afraid of him?'

'I see no reason to be.' This was hardly a time for exactitudes. I drew closer to the child, parting the leaves and chasing the dappled shadows from her face. 'Why did you ask me that question, Adelaide? Are you afraid of him?'

'Sometimes . . .'

'But why? I feel sure you have no real cause to be.'

Adelaide reached up to pick one of the leaves, half-turning from me as she did so. 'Do you like Redmond?'

'Mr Carne? Why . . . why yes, I suppose so. But I have only been here for less than one day.'

'Have you met my Uncle Charles yet?'

'Briefly. In Marrambridge yesterday.'

'In Marrambridge! Oh, then he is back again!' She

clapped her hands in joyful anticipation. 'Perhaps he will come here to visit us! Uncle Charles is so funny. Can you twizzle your eyebrows?'

'I'm not sure, but I'll try. Like this?'

Anxiously, wide-eyed, she watched my performance and then with enormous sympathy gave her verdict. 'Well, perhaps you haven't really had too much practice, Miss Ainsley. My Uncle Charles has very funny eyebrows. He is a champion at twizzling them. I'll ask him to do it for you if he comes . . . and Miss Ainsley?'

'Yes?'

'If my Uncle Charles comes back, will you fall in love with him?'

I laughed. 'What an odd question!'

'I'm not too young to ask such questions, am I?'

'Too young, h'm . . . let me see now.' I pretended to look grave, pursing my lips and cocking my head to one side. 'H'm! Seven years of age, isn't it?'

'Nearly seven and a half,' Adelaide quickly corrected me.

'Seven and a *half!* Dear me, you are quite a grown-up young lady indeed.'

'Then I can ask you such questions.'

'Well now, I didn't exactly say that . . .'

'Will you?'

'Will I say that you can?'

'No. Will you fall in love with my Uncle Charles, that's what I mean. Well, will you?' She plucked at my sleeve, teasing, anxious, pleading. 'Will you, Miss Ainsley?'

'I don't really think so . . .'

'But you might?'

'I doubt it.'

'I think my last governess was in love with him. She went walking in the woods with him one day when he was here. That was before Grandpapa sent her away. I didn't mind her going. I didn't like her.'

55

'Why not?'

'I don't know.' Adelaid shrugged her shoulders. 'I just didn't like her, that's all.'

'And why was she sent away?'

'I don't know.' Again she shrugged disinterestedly, her gaze suddenly wandering off through the trees. 'But I really don't think you should be asking me all these questions, Miss Ainsley. If Grandpapa knew he would be most annoyed.'

For an instant I was at a loss for words. In some simple, innocent way this little girl had turned the tables on me and was now gently scolding me for indulging in a gossipy conversation which she had played no small part in starting. Should I let it pass? No, it might be as well to get things straight from the beginning.

'I certainly didn't mean to pry, Adelaide. And remember . . . you asked me the first question in this curious little conversation, didn't you?'

'That's because I like you so much, Miss Ainsley.' She smiled with such winning sweetness. Again I felt completely out-manoeuvred. 'I do not want Grandpapa to send you away. If you fall in love with my Uncle Charles maybe we could keep it a secret . . . yes?'

'Don't worry on that score, my dear.'

'It's only because I like you, you see. Do you like me?'

'Of course! I'm sure we're going to be great friends.'

'Oh yes . . . I do so need a real friend! A friend of my own.'

I put my arm around her shoulders. Her hand crept into mine. Poor child! Adults here impinged so little on her world, and yet meant so much to her.

'Miss Ainsley?'

'Yes, dear?'

'If we are to be real friends, may I call you Katherine? Please may I?'

56

'Yes, of course. I would like that very much.' I curled my hand about hers reassuringly.

'Thank you . . . Katherine.'

I was pleased with the way our very first morning was progressing. Too pleased to waste time in trying to guess at the reasons behind her questions. It was enough for me that I had succeeded in establishing a rapport with my young pupil. Katherine and Adelaide. We were friends already, hand-in-hand, chatting amiably about everything, and nothing, remarking casually on the many things which fell within the compass of our observation as Adelaide conducted me through the orchard and the surrounding woods. The sun was high over the trees, carrying the cool essence of the leaves down and spreading it all around us. How pleasant and easy it all was, this gradual forging of a bond of companionship and trust during the course of our morning stroll.

It was past noon when we returned to the house. As we emerged from the trees Adelaide suddenly disengaged her hand from mine and cried happily, 'Oh look . . . here's Uncle Georgie!'

She broke from my side and hurried on, my eyes following her as she ran, and then flicking beyond her to settle with interest on the figure of a young man coming down a row of steps at the back of the house. So this was Mr George Northwood . . .

The Captain's youngest son was of medium height, slight build, and about twenty-five or twenty-six years of age. The stark, unrelieved darkness of his attire and the blackish curls served to accentuate the pallor of his face. I was immediately conscious of the resemblance to Captain Northwood: the same deep-set eyes, the same pallid and tense features; but whereas the years had busied themselves by greying the hair and etching deep lines and a commanding aloofness on the father's face, the son's had a delicate beauty, almost classic in outline. It was impossible for me to imagine Captain Northwood ever looking like this in his youth, for despite the initial and superficial resemblance, the essential characteristic of the older face was that of uncompromising sternness and of a man possessing immense reserves of mental vigour and purposefulness. The younger man's face? I wasn't sure, but something in the delicate, shy smile hinted at effeteness and a want of determination. I know that in the moment of first seeing him a ridiculous picture sprang unbidden into my mind; I found myself visualizing him on a ship's deck, a frightened, bewildered, sea-sick passenger. Totally unlike his father. Or his brother Charles for that matter - for I could not possibly imagine George Northwood swaggering like a dragoon amidst the tavern wenches!

A ripple of childish laughter dispelled my thoughts. Her hand firmly encircling his slender wrist, Adelaide led the young man to me.

'Uncle Georgie, this is my new governess. Her name is Miss Ainsley. But I am allowed to call her Katherine because we are to be friends.'

'We are already friends, Adelaide. How do you do, Mr Northwood.'

'P-pleased to m-meet you, Miss Ainsley.'

I noticed the stammer and wondered if it had been brought on by the sudden confrontation with a stranger, or if it was of a more permanent nature.

'I owe you an apology, M-Miss Ainsley. I should have b-been introduced to you at b-breakfast this morning, b-but I was unwell and could not leave m-my room, you see . . .' The rush of words echoed the torture of an earlier rehearsal; his lip trembled. 'I t-trust you will f-forgive me . . .'

'Oh, but there is really no need to apologize.' I assured him with a smile. 'And are you quite recovered from your illness?'

'I think s-so. At any rate Redmond has allowed me out today. I am to go w-walking with him. He thinks the air will be g-good for me.'

He was facing me, but our eyes never quite met. His had a nervous habit of flitting about and blinking hesitantly, like the visual counterpart of his stammer. I watched him closely, intrigued by the oddness of his remark. *Carne had allowed him out.* Was he some kind of prisoner?

'Please, Uncle Georgie, may I tell my friend Katherine our little secret concerning your walks with Redmond?' Adelaide tugged at his arm. 'Please.'

'Secret?'

'About the gun.'

'Oh that.'

'You see, Katherine . . .' Adelaide now took my hand. I was flattered, not so much by her eagerness but by the fact that at least one person at Polmarran seemed ready to let me in on a secret. Any sort of a secret! 'You see, Redmond always takes his big gun with him when he goes walking with Uncle Georgie . . .'

'Actually the g-gun belonged to my late brother, J-John. He w-was . . .' A shadow crossed George Northwood's face. His lip trembled again. 'He w-was killed accidentally while cleaning it . . . a long time ago . . . John's g-gun . . . b-but we don't talk about that any more . . .' He murmured the words, half-talking to himself, his eyes sad with memories. For just a little while he seemed unaware of our presence, then Adelaide recaptured his attention by pulling at his arm and imploring: 'Oh please, Uncle Georgie! May I tell Katherine? Please let *me* tell the secret.'

'Oh yes . . . s-sorry.'

'Well then, Redmond always carries this dreadfully huge gun with him when he goes walking with Uncle Georgie . . .'

59

'R-Redmond is an excellent shot, M-Miss Ainsley.'

'But he knows that Uncle Georgie does not like him to kill any game . . .

'I am opposed to the k-killing of any of the Almighty's c-creatures.' He stammered an explanation. It was accompanied by a tremulous smile that was at once naive and solemn. 'The commandment expressly s-states "thou shalt not k-kill". We m-must always keep the Almighty's commandments.'

'Oh never mind all that, Uncle Georgie!' Pouting, Adelaide dismissed his solemnity with an airy wave. She flashed a mischievious smile at me. 'So even though Redmond is a first-rate shot . . . and he fires on everything he comes upon while out walking with Uncle Georgie . . . he always misses his target!' The last words rose to a peal of laughter.

I wondered if I too should laugh. I compromised with a polite smile, for I was by no means certain of the point of the story until a secret nudge from Adelaide directed my attention once more to the young man before me. With a timid grin Mr George Northwood involved me in their secret.

'You see, Miss Ainsley, as Redmond persists in aiming his g-gun at the various creatures I p-pray silently for their protection. Unknown to p-poor Redmond the Almighty invariably answers my p-prayers and is m-most merciful to the birds.'

For a fleeting moment I suspected some kind of a joke. But no - his expression was so full of earnest naivete, so certain that both Adelaide and I fully sympathized with and shared his secret - that if there was any suggestion of a joke or prank then Redmond Carne was the unwitting victim. A harmless stratagem, and entirely without malice, for it obviously had the Lord's endorsement and co-operation.

'I understand . . .' Mine was a muttered inadequacy, for there was something in George Northwood's simplicity and goodness which instantly touched me.

Adelaide had danced around behind him and had her hand over her mouth, trying to suppress a titter. With a swift, severe look of reprimand I helped her smother it. The young man seemed not to notice. Silence followed, deep and embarrassing for all but young Mr Northwood. He continued to irradiate a kind of fervour and purity which I had not reckoned on finding at Polmarran.

'The Almighty w-will always hearken to our prayers, is that not so? We have but to ask. If only poor Redmond knew how f-futile it is for him to go s-shooting . . .'

His flitting, wandering gaze had now settled on something amongst the trees. With the focusing his eyes gradually lost their inner glow. His lips tightened. 'Ah, there's Redmond n-now.'

Carne, a large fowling piece in the crook of his arm, stepped out from the underbrush and waved to us. 'Ready, George?'

'Yes.' He turned and bowed to me. 'P-please excuse me, Miss Ainsley. I look forward to s-seeing you tonight at s-supper . . .' He took a pace or two, and then as though it was an afterthought, he said to me: 'Forgive me, Miss Ainsley, but h-have we met before some time?'

'Hardly. This is my first visit to these parts.'

'I'm so sorry . . . it's j-just that you remind me of someone. For the life of me I c-can't think who.' He shook his head in a slow, bemused way, then smiling with embarrassment and apology he mumbled: 'Sorry . . . my memory, you see . . . sometimes . . . m-maybe it will come to me. You are very pretty too . . .' His face reddened suddenly. 'P-please forgive me!'

He turned abruptly and hurried over to Carne. Carne fell into step beside him. I was struck by the contrast in their appearances: the slight frame and nervous gait of George Northwood; the bold, easy stride of Redmond Carne, head and shoulders above his pale companion, powerful, formidable, armed. Was he in fact some kind of gaoler?

When they had disappeared amongst the trees Adelaide released her suppressed laughter. 'Oh, isn't it funny! You see Redmond knows all the time about Uncle Georgie's silent prayers for the birds . . . I told him and that's why he deliberately misses. Poor Uncle Georgie!'

'Is it really so funny, Adelaide? I think your Uncle George is a very sweet and gentle person.'

'Oh yes, but he is such a ninny, don't you think?' A faint mockery lit her childish features; it had an almost adult quality. When she looked up and met my gaze it disappeared and was immediately replaced by a smile of the most angelic sweetness.

'Yes, Katherine, Uncle George is so gentle and sweet really, isn't he? Will you fall in love with him, do you think?'

'Seven and a half. I think that's what you said, didn't you?'

'Yes!' she cried eagerly.

'Dear me, what a pity. That's actually an eight-year-old question.'

'Will you tell me then?'

'Yes, if I know the answer myself. Come along now.'

As I took her hand and we entered the house I found myself wondering vaguely if I really understood our little Miss Adelaide.

Chapter Four

The room full of books on the ground floor which enjoyed the somewhat pretentious appellation of 'the library' showed many of those features of neglect and infrequent usage which were so much a part of Polmarran. It was to the end of the hallway, close to the kitchen quarters, and in addition to its prodigious number of books it contained so much of Jem Forrest's odds-and-ends that it was plain to see that the ex-boatswain had gradually taken over the place as a store-room, or - to judge from its collection of rusting scythes - as an ideal 'hide-away' from at least one form of landlubber's work. Many of the books had been removed from their shelves to make room for pots of boot blacking and varnish, parcels of spare buttons, pieces of string, rope, leather, pen-knives, boot-trees, horse-brushes, and the like. A jumble of fishing rods and landing-nets, saddles and harness, headstalls and spurs, littered the floor. And as for the collections of empty wine and spirit bottles! Their accidental discovery, more than Jem Forrest's truculent muttering when he was ordered by Captain Northwood to clear out the entire room, convinced me that the housekeeper's husband was a secret tippler.

It was during my second morning under Captain Northwood's roof that he suggested 'the library' as a suitable place for my pupil and I to conduct our studies. He invited us to make full use of it. Also, he pointed out, among its numerous volumes I might discover many which would undoubtedly augment that modest store of text books which I had brought with me. I thanked him, though the invitation was couched in such terms that I was left in no doubt that 'the library' would also be a most suitable place to consign two tiresome females and get them out from under his feet.

Jem Forrest was none too pleased with the new arrangement. Stripped down to his shirt and breeches, begrudging and surly, he spent the morning shifting out all his 'necessaries', mumbling all the time about 'newcomers with their high-and-mighty notions and a-wastin' of everybody's time with all this book-l'arnin' nonsense'.

Eventually Adelaide and I had the room, and about seven hundred books, all to ourselves. Our first task was to return them to their shelves in some sort of order.

'Well now, where shall we begin? Any ideas?'

'There are so many of them, Katherine. Just look!'

'Then let's make a game of it.'

'A game . . . how?'

'Let me see now . . . ah yes! Now I have it. Do you see that tall, well set-up dictionary over there . . . ?'

'This one?'

'Yes. Now, Adelaide, that shall be the Duke of Wellington. So soldierly and important, don't you think? Now behind him we shall group all books of reference, lexicons, and the like. They shall be his staff officers, his intelligence, and his aides. All books of poetry and those of a serious literary nature shall be . . . let me see now . . . yes! We will make them the ministers of government and the ambassadors and diplomats. We will put them over here.'

'Officers and ministers on the second shelf?'

'Exactly.'

'And what of this big atlas?'

'I think atlases and map-cases and books of geography should be travellers and explorers perhaps . . .'

'Sailors?'

'Splendid idea! That set of blue ones can be a squadron of the Royal Navy.'

'And the big atlas shall be Admiral Lord Nelson . . . see, Katherine, how the binding is torn here, like one of his battle wounds. Poor Lord Nelson . . . shall I put him here?'

'The very place for him.'

'And this hymn book?'

'Hymn book . . . a chaplain?'

'Oh yes. . . just look at his nice black coat!'

'And what about novels and romances?'

'I know! We will make them dashing cavalry men!'

'Marvellous.'

Thus we spent a most pleasant two hours, marshalling our motley regiments of books and then 'billeting' them in their respective quarters. When we had filled most of the shelves we were left with only about a score of 'irregulars', a miscellaneous collection of volumes that were not easily recruited or pressed into service with their fellows. Adelaide passed one such book over to me with the words: 'A book in some foreign language, Katherine. French, I think. The Emperor Napoleon, perhaps?'

'Then we shall have to find a suitable St Helena for him . . .' I said, as I took the book from her and skimmed idly through the pages. To my surprise I discovered a French translation of Boccaccio's *Decameron,* a rather cheap edition, profusely and far too explicitly illustrated, and bearing on its fly-leaf the signature *Eliza Northwood* and the date *1823.*

Curious, I enquired: 'Tell me, please, Adelaide, who is Eliza Northwood?'

With a kind of absent-minded, yet almost brutal simplicity, the child replied: 'Eliza was wicked.'

'What did you say?'

65

'I said that Eliza was wicked. She was a very wicked lady.'

'But who was she?'

'I don't know.'

'What? But . . . but you have just said she was wicked?'

'She was.'

'Adelaide, please . . . is that a just and charitable thing to say about someone you do not know?'

'He said she was wicked.'

'Who?'

'The man.'

'What man?'

'The man who came into my room that night. I don't know who he was. It was such a long time ago and I don't remember it all very well . . . but I do remember that it was raining very heavily and the wind was smashing the shutters so loudly. I think that's what woke me. Oh, Katherine, I was so frightened!'

'What was it that frightened you?'

'The storm, I think.'

'And this man . . . tell me about him.'

'He was in my room, and he kept saying that Eliza was wicked . . . that she was a very wicked woman and that she must be punished.'

'And you do not know who this man was?'

'No.'

'What did he look like?'

'It was too dark and shadowy. And the shutters were crashing so loudly.'

I risked a dangerous question: 'Adelaide, might it have been your Uncle Charles?'

'Uncle Charles? Of course not! Besides, he is seldom here.'

'The voice . . . did you not recognize the man's voice even?' I persisted recklessly.

'No, the wind was so loud . . . and the rain and the

shutters banging . . . and that awful man was screaming and shouting . . . I was so frightened!'

A swift surge of concern pushed my wild curiosity aside. 'This man . . . he didn't harm you in any way?'

'No, I hid under the bedclothes most of the time. When I stopped crying he was gone and Mrs Forrest was there . . . She was always nice to me.'

'You poor child!' Suddenly I took her in my arms, at once trying to reach back into time and to comfort her on that night of fear, and at the same time deeply ashamed of myself for the curiosity which had taxed her with enquiries and had made her re-live it all again. 'I'm sorry, Adelaide. I shouldn't have . . . please forgive me.'

Her response surprised me. Instead of the smile of forgiveness which I hoped for, Adelaide's face held a withdrawn and petulant expression.

'Please! Please, Miss Ainsley . . . you must not keep asking me all these questions.' It was uttered in a sharp cry. Her eyes swept past me and appeared to focus on something - or someone - behind me.

'A charming picture indeed.'

Turning quickly, the child still in my embrace, I saw Redmond Carne standing in the open doorway. He was leaning against the jamb, his head inclined at a jaunty angle and a broad smile upon his face.

'By the powers! If more children could see you like this, with arms about each other, they'd have little fear of schooling.' He came towards us, slowly, his eyes shrewd and watchful behind all the teasing light. 'When I was a lad, Miss Ainsley, I always held to the notion that teachers were tyrants who were for ever frightening children with endless questions . . . questions about nouns and verbs and such like, I mean.' He finished with an odd smile.

Had he overheard?

When he was beside us he placed his hand gently

67

on the child's shoulder. I wondered if he was in some way disputing my hold on her. As she was still partly in my arms this action of his brought him very close to me. He said: 'You two young ladies are becoming right good friends, eh?'

It was hard to know if he approved. Likewise it was difficult to know which emotion contributed most to my growing confusion - the suspicion that he had been listening at the door, that he might not approve of my friendship with Captain Northwood's granddaughter, or the fact that he was making no attempt to hide a kind of bold and frank interest in my person. Adelaide regained her composure much quicker than I. She withdrew a little from my arms, smiled up at Carne, and brought up her small hand to rest on his.

'We have just completed the task of sorting out all these books,' I mumbled, seeking an escape from his scrutiny by turning from him and placing the last few books on one of the shelves.

'Here now, Miss Ainsley, you must let me help you with some of those heavy books. Far too hefty work for a slim young lass like yourself.'

'Thank you, Mr Carne, but there's only a few remaining. I can manage them. Perhaps you have other things to attend to . . .'

'Not at the moment.'

There was nothing I could say, or do. Redmond Carne remained with us for the best part of the next hour. Nothing in his manner indicated that he had overheard our conversation, but I felt that I should take the precaution of assuming that he had, that he would be opposed to my questioning the child on some past happening here - and that like a loyal member of the crew he would duly report to the skipper! That thought sobered me. All the guesswork raised by the accidental discovery of Eliza Northwood's book had quickly to take second place to some

68

hasty plan of defence. For by now I was certain that, at my next meeting with my employer, I could either expect some form of harsh reprimand from him or, what was equally to be feared and averted if possible, that implacable coldness with which he had first greeted me.

Which?

There was certainly one way to find out. All I had to do was take the initiative by producing the book, as I think I might be entitled to do as a tutor, with some tactful comment to the effect that it was accidently discovered by my pupil in the library and I took it from her on the grounds that it was unsuitable for inclusion on the bookshelf. That sounded reasonable enough.

But that very evening - the barrier of a huge, polished supper table stretching between us, and the candlelight giving an unearthly pallor to Captain Northwood's impassive features - it seemed a much more difficult plan to put into action than I had anticipated. Still, I had to try, if only to forestall anything Redmond Carne might say. And with the book already removed from my reticule and placed on the table I knew it was too late to draw back.

'Oh, by the way, we found this book in the library this afternoon. I take the liberty of drawing it to your attention, Captain Northwood, as I'm sure you will share my view that it is not the sort of thing for a young girl to . . . well, you know what I mean . . .' I pushed the book across the table, and quite by accident it fell open at the page containing the signature.

Captain Northwood reached out and took it up, his eyes immediately settling on the handwriting. His expression altered very slightly; only the eyelids flickered for a moment before narrowing to a guarded look. Then they came up slowly, meeting mine across the table in silent conflict. I felt that with his gaze alone he had effectively set up a shield of caution between us. For what reason? Did he think that I was deliberately alluding to the signature? I wanted to say, *'Look at the illustrations, and not the signature!'* But how does one suddenly blurt out an invitation to examine a collection of inartistic prints which border on the obscene?

When he spoke his voice was calm and controlled. 'A cheap edition of some French book . . . so?'

'No, not just that, sir. If you would care to look at . . . at the . . .' I felt my cheeks flushing with embarrassment.

'The signature, is that it?' he snapped. 'Any particular reason why you should feel obliged to bring that name to my attention?'

'No, of course not. Though naturally I wondered about the name on the fly-leaf as well . . .'

'What about it?'

'Just, well . . . who is Eliza Northwood?'

Neither he nor Carne chose to answer the blunt question. I felt bewildered as I watched Captain Northwood passing the book across to Carne, never once taking his eyes from me. I sat in silence, at first attempting to return my employer's stare and then looking down at my clasped hands and trying to pick up the courage to repeat my question: *'Who is Eliza Northwood?'* After all, it was a perfectly ordinary question, and one to which a perfectly ordinary answer might reasonably be expected. Yet somehow I just couldn't bring myself to ask it.

I looked over at Redmond Carne. His head was lowered over the open book, his eyes apparently focused on the autographed fly-leaf. I could not make out his expression, but his hands were restless: the nervous fingering and tapping of the cover and the thumb-nail riffling the olivine edges - all hinted at suppressed excitement. Without looking up from the book he said, 'You never told me of this find when I was in the library with you and the young mistress this afternoon.'

He looked first at me, a mere glance - intended perhaps as some kind of rebuke - and then switched his gaze to Captain Northwood. I wondered if Carne's words were intended, too, as an explanation, an apology to his Captain for a lapse in vigilance. I sat staring ahead of me, half-scared to break the silence and at the same time experiencing a growing determination not to be bullied by words or brushed aside for daring to ask a question.

The echo of that question still lingered.

'Who is Eliza Northwood?' In the stillness of the rooms my words sounded harsh.

'I think, Miss Ainsley, that I informed you of the reason for your predecessor's dismissal, did I not?' Captain Northwood demanded coldly, like a judge examining a prisoner in the dock.

'You did, but . . .' My words dried up while I fell to wondering what he would say if I suddenly blurted out, '*Your granddaughter told me that Eliza was a very wicked woman!*' But I had the feeling that the less said now the less chance of provoking my employer's wrath towards the child. Towards myself, as well. I finished feebly, 'I just wondered, that's all . . .'

Carne, his fingers ceasing their nervous handling of the book, made a brave try at being casual. 'Just an old book, that's all . . . still, I'm sure Captain Northwood appreciates your bringing it to his notice. I am bound to say that it would be an unseemly thing for the young mistress to come across by accident. As like as not, Jem Forrest had it stowed away in there with a few bottles of grog . . .' He returned the book to Captain Northwood, dismissing the thing with a careless wave of his hand. 'And speaking of Jem Forrest's odds-and-ends, Cap'n, reminds me of another item which was unearthed amongst all his junk today . . .'

Thereupon he launched into a spirited account of how some gardening implement, which had been mislaid the previous year, came to light again only today. Even more than the pretence of absorbing interest in the matter of lost and then found horticultural implements, I recognized the quiet desperation of two men who were afraid of a silence which might be turned against them by another question from me. Twice I had bluntly asked about Eliza Northwood. There was no telling what I might ask next, as far as they were concerned, so it became necessary for Redmond Carne to fill every threatening pause with an unbroken run of words. Had I given his words even half of my attention I might have learned a great deal about the number of farming and gardening implements which were frequently mislaid at Polmarran, only to turn up again in the most unlikely places, thanks to Jem Forrest's haphazard storing arrangements - but my mind was on other things. I had to consider whether or not I was placing too much importance on Adelaide's story: had the night of the storm lent vision and sound to some nightmarish imaginings on her part?

I might have begun to believe so if I had not looked up at that moment. Though a half-smile still lingered on Redmond Carne's lips it reached nowhere near his eyes; they were guarded and watchful. The Captain's, when not actually peering morosely at the book still clenched in his hand, were focused on me - decidedly wary and hostile. In that instant I instinctively knew that the child had helped me to stumble on some mystery concerning the identity of Eliza Northwood. I felt convinced of it when I looked up and surprised the traffic in odd, meaningful looks passing backwards and forwards between my table companions.

I shuddered. All around me the hideous memorabilia of the Captain's voyaging hung in silent, life-

72

like vigilance - the grotesque, heathenish masks quietly grinning, the firelight glinting slyly on the spears and knives - all mocking my inability to comprehend. *Who was Eliza Northwood?* My pupil's mother? Or the woman with whom I shared a remarkable similarity in looks, whom Charles Northwood described as 'a little bitch', 'a tigress'? For that matter, I had to ask myself, whether she was one and the same person - Adelaide's mother - and my double - and the same person who some mysterious and over-wrought man on a stormy night in the past denounced as 'wicked' and who would have to be punished? And was all this part of that punishment - that her name should never again be mentioned at Polmarran?

'Are we boring you with all this talk?' Carne cut in on my thoughts. His slight, infuriating smile held just a trace of mockery.

'Why, not in the least!' I retaliated airily. 'I simply adore stories about lost scythes and hay-forks and all that sort of thing. But as you gentlemen no doubt wish to smoke while engaged in such engrossing topics, and as I am rather tired, I am sure you will excuse me.'

The only sound was the scraping of chairs as they both stood up. In the chilling silence which followed I left the table.

Without looking back I knew that Carne was making for the door also. I lengthened my stride; I felt that I could do without his little tricks of politeness just then. I got to the door before him and was just reaching out for the handle when the door opened suddenly from the other side.

Jem Forrest stood there, bowing stiffly from the waist in what I should imagine was his very best imitation of a butler; and then, as he straightened up again, he loudly announced: 'Beg parding, Cap'n sir . . . but we have company a-calling . . .' In a low aside he muttered to Carne: 'More of the high-and-mighty, mate . . .' I was treated to a kind of cunningly malicious grin and the words: 'So sure of themselves and of what's right and wrong that they're holding all hands under suspicion . . .'

'Hold your tongue, Jem!' Carne snapped. Frowning, he said to me: 'I think you'd best stay a while, Miss Ainsley.'

Before I could reply Forrest was already ushering the visitors into the dining-room - Charles Northwood first, cloaked and booted, his gauntleted hand encompassing our entire group in one wave of greeting.

'Good evening, Father . . . Carne . . . ah! Miss Ainsley, isn't it?' He removed his gloves and hat, shoved them at Forrest, bowed, then snatched my hand and pressed it to his lips extravagantly. I pulled away, recalling all too vividly my first meeting with him. 'Please, Miss Ainsley . . . I was drunk then. Be assured that I am perfectly sober now. Sober and contrite.'

He was neither. With a slight unsteadiness he introduced his companions to me. 'Miss Ainsley, permit me to present Sir Arthur Rebstock and his charming sister, Miss Margaret Rebstock.'

The passage of introduction, greetings and civilities occupied us for more than five or six minutes. I had time to study the Rebstocks.

They were very much alike, the same dark hair and pale skin, the eyes deep grey and flecked with blue. Each had a good face with a strong, shapely, patrician arch to the nose, a feature which was becoming in Sir Arthur, a trifle less so in his sister. Sir Arthur was almost as tall as Redmond Carne though not nearly so broad in the chest and shoulders, and his waist was beginning to thicken with the approach of middle-age. He moved with a lounging and careless grace, and like Charles Northwood there was something of the dandy about him. When he doffed his cloak it was to display a dark blue sporting cutaway, trousers, waistcoat and satin neck-cloth of the same colour, though a much paler hue, the latter adorned with a silver breast-pin and the former set off by glossy tipped riding boots.

In sharp contrast Miss Rebstock wore black, like someone in mourning, the sombre clothes unrelieved by either lace, locket, bracelet or jewellery of any kind. Her dark tresses were braided severely and dressed close to each side of her head. Her face was coldly beautiful, almost haughty, and with that something about the eyes and mouth which hinted at latent passions held permanently in check.

Her brother's face combined frailty and strength to an unusual degree, full of scurrying, half-held expressions that seemed to contradict each other. In short, I had the feeling that early in life Sir Arthur Rebstock had learned to quell whatever spontaneity had been in his nature and to out-think himself from impulses by favouring an habitual restraint in all things rather than gamble with the uncertainties of life.

During those few minutes of polite chit-chat Sir Arthur and Miss Margaret Rebstock had, by the same token, ample opportunity to study me. It was obvious that they had been apprised by someone (probably Charles Northwood) of what to expect. In their case there was a deliberate absence of that to which I had almost grown accustomed - that initial look of incredulity, that stunned unexpectedness at my co-incidental resemblance to someone known to all of them, but as yet unknown to me. While they were careful to evince no surprise, nor to subject me to too close or curious a scrutiny in the moment of first laying eyes upon me, it was abundantly clear to me that they were inwardly taken aback. By graduated looks and gestures, by the odd word or inclination of the head in my direction now and again, they appeared to communicate by means of some private, family code. I could imagine each nod and gesture having its own particular meaning . . .

Well, what do you think?

Yes. A remarkable resemblance.

I agree.

So?

For the present let us act as though unaware of anything.

Very well. We shall wait and see.

Charles Northwood seemed also to be divining their thoughts. Mine too? He held us all with mocking eyes. 'Well, Arthur, what do you think of Polmarran's new governess, eh?'

'Most charming . . . and quite beautiful. I envy your niece the hours she must have in Miss Ainsley's delightful company.'

How heavy-lidded, somnolent and provocative Sir Arthur's dark grey eyes were! I felt colour rising in my cheeks, embarrassment (with just a tinge of vanity perhaps) dispelling my wariness.

'And you, Meg m'dear, what do you think of Adelaide's new tutor?' The teasing light in Charles Northwood's eyes flashed from face to face.

Margaret Rebstock offered a smile of extraordinary brevity, but said nothing.

'Come now, Meg, does not our charming Miss Ainsley put you in mind of someone? I confess that the first time I set eyes on her, tipsy and all though I was, I was immediately struck by . . .'

'Sir Arthur . . . Miss Margaret . . . as always you are most welcome here,' Captain Northwood cut in hastily, investing the interruption with a note of cordiality. 'Please to be seated with us. Forrest, attend to the needs of our guests!' Then turning to his son, his voice changing, hardening subtly, the Captain asked: 'Well, Charles, and what brings you to your father's house this time? Not filial respect, I'll

76

warrant. Is it that a full purse is much less common these days than long credit with your tailor and tradesmen?'

Charles met this rebuff with a careless laugh. 'In the old days they used to kill fatted calves for prodigal sons.'

'Only for sons who repented their prodigalities.'

'Repentance is only for sinners, Father.' He managed to look amusingly surprised at such an imputation.

'And what else but sinning is gambling and wagering?'

'If there was anything inherently evil in gambling or tippling, the Commandments would surely have numbered twelve instead of ten.'

'Insolent and irreverent as ever. Bah!'

The Rebstocks seemed not to be discomfited by any of this. I could not say the same for myself. Twice I tried to withdraw, opening my mouth to beg leave to be excused, only to have my request anticipated and waved aside by Charles Northwood. 'Please, Miss Ainsley, Sir Arthur and his sister have ridden over especially to meet you. Is that not so, Arthur? It is indeed! As for myself . . . I am here to make amends for my rudeness at our first meeting. To quit us now would be most ungracious, don't you think? So please, Miss Ainsley . . . and, with my father's permission, Forrest shall fetch up a couple of good bottles from the cellar for us, and the Lord only knows how many for himself. We shall have us a merry evening.'

By no stretch of the imagination could the ensuing hour or two be termed a merry evening. Charles Northwood alone (and possibly Sir Arthur Rebstock, though to a much lesser extent) exhibited anything approximating merriment. Captain Northwood sat stiffly at the head of the table, barely sipping his wine, polite enough to the Rebstocks but scarcely bothering to include me in a conversation revolving mainly about local and farming topics. I wondered if my question about Eliza Northwood still rankled with him. Carne, too, for that matter. He spoke only when addressed directly and drank no more than the Captain. The dishes placed before the Rebstocks were only nibbled and politely picked over, while Charles Northwood's plates were taken away again untasted. Not so with the wine. He had Forrest make more than one trip down to the cellar. The Rebstocks, sister and brother, matched him glass for glass. When not talking up and down the table, by turn gay and taunting, Charles Northwood was strutting about the room, a wine-glass in one hand, a cigar in the other, pausing every now and then before the mirror to give a slight upward brush to his moustache, or passing comments on the Captain's wall souvenirs.

'And tell me, Arthur . . . you too, Meg . . . what do you honestly think of this place now that my father has turned it into a museum? Look, over here . . . a witch-doctor's mask. My word, but it's a frightful bloody thing, isn't it? And here, did you ever see a more savage-looking weapon? What do you think of it all, Meg m'dear? Horrified? Not what you remember from your childhood days here, is it?'

'Stop it, Charles!' Margaret Rebstock's voice was sharp.

'Please, Margaret . . . Charles is only in one of his teasing moods.' Sir Arthur turned solicitously towards his sister. Then leaning across the table to me he explained: 'You see, Miss Ainsley, this used to be our home. Polmarran House and the Tower of course is perhaps the least valuable part of the former Rebstock estate. The farmlands, the pasturages, the timber - that's where our father's real wealth lay. That is, I should add, before our late father began to fly his numerous kites.'

'Kites?'

'Promissory notes, Miss Ainsley. Notes of hand and

IOUs. Flying high and wide all over the country and each one bearing the signature of our dear departed Papa. And the shylocks and the creditors began to haul them down, one at a time at first, then snatching at them in handfuls. A piece of farmland here, a few acres of pasturage there, an avenue of fine trees to the timber merchants one day, another tenant farm the next . . . '

'Please, Arthur. Must you?' His sister looked down with embittered eyes at the wine-glass twirling in her fingers.

Charles Northwood looked at her in a challenging manner. 'Why not? Everyone knows that your father crashed through money like he took a bog hedge at the hunt.'

'That's enough, Charles!' Captain Northwood rapped his knuckles on the table. 'You are hardly in a position to lecture anyone on matters of thrift or prudence.'

'Or how to turn a once-bright home into a museum, a gloomy receptacle for worthless odds-and-ends and a . . . a storehouse for sad memories . . .'

Beneath the careless taunt I suspected that there was a lot of hurt and disappointment. I began to realize that there might be just a little more to Charles Northwood than that of my first impression of a tavern carouser. Had he been driven to that mode of life by an austere, unloving father?

'Charles, I command you to keep a civil and respectful tongue while under my roof.'

'I can always be induced to leave, Father. A trifling sum would see me quickly on my way.'

Silence followed, deep and embarrassing for everyone but Sir Arthur Rebstock. Was he secretly pleased to see the present master of Polmarran and his son at each other's throats? I wondered.

He turned back to me and continued with a kind of unmoved pleasantness. 'Fortunately for my sister and I, our good host here rescued us from disaster. Is that not so, Margaret?'

'Yes. I suppose so . . .'

'You suppose! Come now, Margaret, had not Captain Northwood paid us handsomely for this house, what would have become of us? Yes, Miss Ainsley, Captain Northwood did not stoop meanly to profit from our difficulties. Why, if I remember aright, you paid us nearly twice what this place was worth. Is that not so, Captain Northwood?'

'I paid what it was worth to me. I have never regretted the transaction, Sir Arthur.'

''Pon my honour, sir . . . most kind of you. Allow me to toast your health!' Sir Arthur stood up and raised his glass towards Captain Northwood. When he sat down again he looked over to me and smiled. 'We still have some property of course, Miss Ainsley. Not much, I admit, but it suffices to permit me to live as a gentleman should.'

'Which is?' Charles was grinning again, his teeth white and sparkling with mockery, his eyes teasing.

'A real gentleman, Charles, is one who . . . while he may have no visible means of livelihood or of gaining it, and who may have long credit with the tradespeople . . . is, above all, one who can move about in good society. In short, Charles m'lad, one is a real gentleman when one has social consideration.'

'Which you have, Arthur?'

'Which he most certainly has,' Margaret Rebstock said with aggressive pride.

'Which I most certainly have, Charles, despite a certain reversal of fortunes over the past ten years. As I said, Miss Ainsley, we still have some property. By thrift and industry and practical management of our affairs Margaret has succeeded in enlarging it somewhat. And then, too, the Rebstock name still stands for something in these parts though, alas, we are never likely to recover Polmarran Tower . . .'

The last was uttered with a peculiar blend of ennui, regret, and perhaps just a trace of bitterness, no doubt brought on by the steady drinking.

'It is no longer worth recovering,' Charles Northwood said, his eyes moving from his father to Carne.

'Oh, where there is life there is hope.' Sir Arthur smiled. 'And we cling to life.'

'Wretchedly enough,' Margaret Rebstock added without smiling.

I felt out of it, and was glad to be uninvolved. My curiosity had dimmed. I wasn't sure I wanted to know any more about this house and the Rebstocks' attitude to it. I had my own problems concerning Polmarran House and its evil-looking tower. Besides, the Rebstocks and the Northwoods, and their intertwined history, seemed to be a closed corporation. And all this steady drinking seemed to be bringing out some of the worst aspects of it.

I looked down at my still-full wine-glass, trying to find the right words to release me from their presence. Carne, because of his brooding silence throughout all this, seemed just then to be a kind of ally. I looked over at him.

'Maybe Miss Ainsley would like to retire? It's getting late.'

'Maybe Miss Ainsley is getting bored,' Charles said, coming round behind my chair. 'Or maybe she feels unaccustomed to our ways and her new surroundings. Has she been shown the west wing of the house yet?' He laughed in an odd kind of way, giving with his forefinger a little flick to his silk cravat.

'There is no need for her to see it.' Captain Northwood glared at his son. 'The west wing is deserted.'

'True, but it was not always so, was it? It once was the most beautiful part of the house. Was it not, Meg?'

'Yes.'

'Please, Father, have I your permission to show Miss Ainsley the ballroom, or would even that simple request inconvenience any of your affairs?'

'Of course not.' Captain Northwood looked both angry and uncomfortable at the same time. Then with a wave of his hand he added: 'Go ahead. The house is yours.'

'Is it? Since when?' Charles affected a tone of mock surprise. 'Did you hear that, Arthur? Apparently I have been written back into the will. I am deeply touched! Overwhelmed!' With the sardonic gleam still in his dark eyes he turned to Redmond Carne. 'Well, Redmond, my old salt, it seems that you have not entirely replaced myself and poor brother George after all.'

Bristling with anger Carne half-rose in his chair. The Captain flashed a swift, disapproving look at both men. 'Sit down, Mr Carne. As for you, Charles, I forbid you to address anyone here in this manner. Your guests are present, and on your behalf I shall offer an apology. Now take Miss Ainsley and Miss Rebstock to the west wing if you wish. Come, Mr Carne, we have some matters to discuss . . .'

'If I may have a word with Mr Charles first?'

Miss Rebstock took my arm. 'Please, Miss Ainsley, I would be very happy to show you the ballroom, to let you see what remains of all our former splendour.'

'Thank you, but if you don't mind, Miss Rebstock. It is rather late . . .'

'Oh, but I do mind!' Her expression was imperious. 'Am I to be left here amongst these gentlemen with their smoking and their squabbles?' She took my arm, and leaning closer, whispered quickly: 'Besides, there is something I want you to see. Come.'

Intrigued, indeed quite overpowered, I allowed her to lead me from the dining-room.

The men remained silent as we withdrew. When we were at the door I threw back a quick look over my

82

shoulder. Charles Northwood was half-sitting, half-leaning, against the side of the table. From one corner of his sensual lips a long cigar projected. He deliberately exhaled a thick column of tobacco smoke in the direction of Redmond Carne's head. Carne, unblinkingly, looked across the table at him. The resentment and animosity was plain for all to see.

Chapter Five

'This is actually the main hall, but we always called it the ballroom. Sixty couples - seventy or eighty, in fact - could dance here all at once. With the orchestra over there . . .'

Margaret Rebstock used the candlestick to point across the room. The flame leaned away from the draught sweeping in through the open double-doors just behind us. A tiny brilliance flared up and dimly revealed the outlines of a balustraded dais at the far end of the hall. I heard the plop of hot candle grease on the veneered parquetry.

'. . . And we always referred to that as the musicians' gallery. Oh yes, Miss Ainsley, nearly eighty couples . . . and all with perfect ease and any amount of space, as you can see. Quadrilles, waltzes, the minuet, everything! And there was sufficient room for servants . . . In my father's time we had as many as fifteen servants, Miss Ainsley. Fifteen! . . . And in here, notwithstanding so many couples dancing, there was more than enough room for servants to go about with trays of refreshments, and we had side-tables along the walls over there, and sofas, and the most exquisite draperies, and potted flowers . . . Oh, it was such a splendid place then! Almost every week Father's guests down for the shooting, and the Hunt, and his parliamentary associates. Did you know that my father was the Member for this constituency?'

'No.'

'He was.' Her haughty, yet sorrowful and defeated eyes moved slowly about the vast room. She was so absorbed in memory that she did not notice my yawn. 'So full of brightness and gaiety and laughter in those days. Do you see those chandeliers, Miss Ainsley? Yes, up there. The two in the centre. Imported from Italy. Beautiful craftmanship and with sconces for literally hundreds of candles!'

But the chandeliers were bagged now, the deserted room mute with rolled carpets and dust coverings on the furniture. Through chinks in the window shutters a few long needles of moonlight pricked the gloom with a pale and slender light. Here and there on the panelled walls the gold-leaf decorations had long since peeled away; only a few tarnished vine-clusters graced the cornices of the pillars which had the appearance of propping up the shadowy ceiling.

Margaret Rebstock seemed unaware of my presence. She continued to look about her with sad-eyed nostalgia. How difficult it must have been for her to connect this bleak, deserted place with the memories of swirling silk and lavender and gay music! For a few minutes I stood beside her, silent, not knowing what to say. Polmarran's past meant nothing to me; for her the gay merriment of the Rebstock days were gone for ever. I stifled another yawn.

'You said that you wanted to show me something.'

With a sigh Margaret Rebstock returned to the present. 'Yes. Over here.'

I followed her. Over the carved fireplace one solitary portrait looked helplessly down on the darkened room, a head-and-shoulders study of a young officer, his dress jacket richly laced with gold, the pelisse trimmed with sable. As she raised the candle higher I was able to see the face clearly and to make out the Northwood features - the handsomeness of Charles, the gentle, youthful eyes of George, the high cheek-bones and the aquiline nose of Captain Northwood.

'John Northwood.' she said. 'He and I were to be married . . .' It was a flat, simple statement that said everything. And nothing.

'I'm sorry.'

'Sorry? And why should you be sorry?'

'Well, I mean . . . well, I heard about his death . . . the accident . . .'

'Accident!' Margaret Rebstock gave a short, bitter laugh. 'It was no accident, Miss Ainsley. A man like John! A man so used to guns all his life . . . do you think for one moment that such a man would attempt to clean out a fowling-piece which was already primed and loaded? No, Miss Ainsley, she killed him! As surely as if she had pulled the trigger herself. Suicide. And she drove him to it!'

'She?'

'Eliza!'

The name was uttered with such vehemence, with such a hiss of pent-up hate and jealousy, that I actually stepped back from my companion in alarm. Her face was suffused with passion, the eyes narrowed with pain and rancour and glinting cruelly in the candlelight. Only then did I notice in some odd and detached way that she was considerably taller than me, older too by nearly a decade, and that for a woman she had an uncommonly large-limbed sturdiness. Why I should suddenly take note of such details just then I do not know, unless it was that, in those surroundings, in that vast, shadowy hall full of her bitter memories, and because of her earlier drinking and present mood, I half-expected her to lash out with her hand and strike me. It was an absurd thought, I know, but there was something in the manner of her peering into my face that sent a tremor of fear through me.

She continued eyeing me for some considerable

time, the hate-filled recollections fading slowly from her scrutiny - but only to be replaced by something equally menacing in her tone as she remarked: 'You are like her, Miss Ainsley. Indeed, you could very well be her sister, so definite is the resemblance.'

I wondered if she actually suspected that possibility! Hastily, and with a great show of airiness, I smiled. 'I have no sisters, Miss Rebstock. I am an only child.'

'Strange, I distinctly remember that she said the very same thing when we first met.' In some indefinable way her words seemed to invalidate mine, to cancel out the irrelevance of a second coincidence and to replace it with a new sense of mystery. 'Apart from that one remark I never knew Eliza to mention anything else about her family background. She kept it a close secret. Even from poor John. But then a constant air of secrecy and allurement was always so much a part of Eliza's fatal charm, wasn't it?'

Margaret Rebstock had placed the candlestick on the mantelpiece, much closer to me than to her, so that her face was now partly masked by wavering shadows: in this half-light it was very difficult to know whether the question was intended for me or was merely a part of her soliloquy. Opting for the latter I remained silent. She resumed, a faint echo of her earlier, bitter little laugh rippling beneath the words: 'Yes, always so mysterious and secretive . . . and such a liar too! Oh, you have no idea, Miss Ainsley! Lies, lies, lies. So that one could never really be sure if Eliza was an only child or anything else which she claimed to be in those days. What's the matter, Miss Ainsley? Does all this disturb you?'

'No, but . . .'

'But what? Haven't they remarked on your extraordinary likeness to Polmarran's former mistress?'

'They?'

'Captain Northwood and that ruffian Carne.'

'They've said nothing to me.'

'Nothing about Eliza?'

'Never.'

'I see. So this is the very first time you heard the name Eliza Marisch?'

'Marisch? I thought Northwood . . .?'

'Marisch was her maiden name. Naturally she became a Northwood on her marriage to John.' Her eyes, no longer rancorous but dark with pain and loneliness, flitted upwards to the portrait of the young officer.

'Eliza Northwood . . . Yes, I came across that name for the first time today. Quite by accident really.' I went on to explain about my discovery of the signature on the fly-leaf of the *Decameron*.

'How like her . . . to keep such a book and to advertise her ownership of it by a brazen autograph! Typical of Eliza. Lascivious and wanton. I doubt, Miss Ainsley, if even its most lurid illustrations could rival some of her unspeakable escapades.'

'Oh, really now, Miss Rebstock, please.'

'You never knew her. Eliza was wicked!'

Margaret Rebstock's use of those words bore no resemblance to Adelaide's childishly matter-of-fact utterance in the library earlier that same day. *'Eliza was wicked!'* The phrase reverberated with a kind of sinister hollowness through the empty ballroom.

She turned away from me suddenly, her eyes sweeping up towards the portrait. 'She was wicked and cruel. He could *never* have loved her, not really . . . He loved me. Me! If she had not driven him to taking his own dear, sweet life he would have come back to me in time. I know he would!'

For just an instant she appeared to be on the verge of some hysterical outburst. Her hands lay before her on the mantelshelf, trembling now, then clenching and unclenching. Grief and pain were shadows wavering across her features as she fought to control herself.

88

'Please, Miss Rebstock, try not to distress yourself so.' I laid my hand on her arm gently. 'Come. Perhaps we should leave now. Your brother must be wondering what keeps us.'

'My brother?' She turned to look at me, a quick movement of her arm deliberately dislodging my hand. Her eyes remained on mine for a long time, her expression dark and inscrutable. When she eventually spoke her voice was strangely calm, cold even - as though spurning all sympathy. 'Yes, perhaps Arthur is wondering about us . . .' Then, as though unable, or unwilling, to let go of her obsessive theme she returned once more to the subject of Eliza Northwood.

'Did you know that Arthur and she were betrothed? No, how could you? Yes, they were. Like John he too was completely infatuated with her. Like all the men, in fact, who came into contact with her. That season, when she came to Marrambridge first, nobody knew anything about her, or her background, but I suppose that only heightened her intriguing qualities - men can be so foolish and ridiculous over that sort of woman, can't they? Arthur certainly was. In next to no time they were engaged to be married. Oh, she made no secret of her ambition to be mistress of Polmarran. And then, when she learned that Arthur was compelled to dispose of this place and most of our lands, Eliza Marisch just as quickly broke off their engagement. She was so cruel to Arthur! So heartless!'

In spite of my uneasiness with her I had grown curious. 'And was it then that she set her cap at John Northwood?' I asked.

'No, not exactly. John was away with his regiment at the time. Eliza very quickly transferred her affections - if shameless fortune-hunting can be dignified by such a term! - quickly transferred them from my brother Arthur to the new owner and master of Polmarran.'

I turned incredulously. 'Surely you do not mean Captain Northwood?'

'I do.'

'But . . . but he is so old! Old and forbidding in his manner.'

'He was not always so. Eight or nine years ago he was quite different. Besides, wealthy widowers, no matter how old or forbidding, are not infrequently the prey of unscrupulous young beauties, are they?'

'True, but . . .'

'But in this case, Miss Ainsley, while Captain Northwood may have been flattered by her charming attentions, may even have amused himself with her for all I know, he was shrewd enough to see through her and her wiles. The same with Charles. He was a match for her. Wayward and wilful, Eliza and Charles had a great deal in common and could see through each other. Poor John . . . he was not so experienced.' She paused, momentarily, to cast another fond look at the portrait. 'Yes, poor John! What chance had he against her? When she learned that he was the eldest son and heir she quit Marrambridge suddenly. She went off and sought him out, contriving an invitation to one of the regimental balls. How she must have beguiled him. Trapped him! Oh, you have no idea, Miss Ainsley, how easily she could twist the menfolk about her little finger. The first any of us knew about it was when John Northwood arrived at Polmarran with Eliza as his new bride. They had been secretly married. Married . . . and John had not even written one word about it to me!' Her voice rose on the last words, tremulously, fighting back the sob of bitterness and reproach.

How she must have loathed Eliza in those days! Eliza . . . the usurper of her place in John Northwood's affections, the woman who had so carelessly jilted her brother, Sir Arthur, destroying both their prospects with her capricious and wayward nature.

90

And what else had she destroyed here? Captain Northwood and Redmond Carne could not even bring themselves to speak of her; and Charles Northwood - who, mistaking me for Eliza, had flared into swift anger at our first meeting - in what way had she affected his life? Or George Northwood, for that matter? And my pupil? Adelaide only knew of Eliza as a name hurled in anger amidst the fury of a storm, something wrenched from an unknown man's fearful rantings, a nightmarish echo from the past. What an awful tribute to Eliza's mysterious superiority over all their lives! That name seemed to haunt Polmarran like a guilty conscience . . .

Why had the word *haunt* sprung into my mind? Was Eliza Northwood dead? The question which had been nagging me almost from the moment of my arrival here now found utterance in the darkened ballroom: 'My pupil . . . she is Eliza's child?'

'Yes.'

'And where is Eliza now?'

There was no reply.

I recalled Redmond Carne's words at the time of my interview with Captain Northwood: *"The Cap'n's granddaughter was orphaned at a very early age."*

'Is she dead?'

Still no reply - only a veiled, meaningless glance.

'When did she die?'

'Miss Ainsley, if I could be certain that Eliza Northwood was dead I would be happy. Dead and damned!'

Her steady voice, little more than a whisper, in no way lessened the venomous hatred in Margaret Rebstock's tone.

I recoiled from her - from a face that was pale and tense with remembered hate, from words still echoing malevolently through Polmarran's main hall.

'How can you say such a thing, Miss Rebstock!'

Pin-pricks of anger glinted in the grey-flecked eyes.

Her hand, cold and sharp, gripped my wrist. 'You . . . in these shadows . . . you *could* be Eliza.'

'That's absurd!' My laugh rang out. It was tinged with just a trace of alarm, like a child whistling in the dark.

At that moment we were interrupted by the sound of approaching footsteps. Her hand fell away from my wrist.

Charles Northwood and Sir Arthur were talking of boxing, or cock-fighting, as they came through the open doors; the latter dropped his voice to a becoming whisper as he entered the ballroom, as if such a conversation was hardly fit for the ears of ladies. Just then I was ready to welcome any topic of conversation. Ready to seize the earliest opportunity to withdraw.

'Ah, ladies, forgive us . . . men's talk. No, please don't go, Miss Ainsley.' Charles Northwood's white teeth were clamped firmly about a cigar stump. The tip was barely an inch from his lips, its glow illuminating the smile. 'Well, Miss Ainsley, and what do you think of our handsome ballroom, eh?'

'It's . . . well, it's certainly an impressive room. When in use it must have been very beautiful.'

'Yes, very beautiful,' Sir Arthur agreed with a nod, his eyes wandering about with a vague, nostalgic look. 'I wish you could have seen it in those days.'

'I told her what it was like,' his sister added.

'And has Meg been showing you my late brother's portrait?'

'Yes,' I replied.

'Good for you, Meg. I declare that if you had your way you'd turn it into a shrine, with regular pilgrimages and all that sort of thing.'

'Come, Arthur, let's go.' Margaret Rebstock took her brother's arm. 'This place depresses me.'

'But I thought you loved it here, Meg?' Charles Northwood, in the act of stepping over to leave his candelabra on a small table just inside the door, succeeded in cutting off the Rebstocks' exit. Mine, too, for I had already started inching towards the door. I had no wish to be left alone with him in the deserted ballroom.

'I hate Polmarran now.'

'Hate? Hate, Meg?' Charles Northwood turned round, his expression one of challenging, mock surprise.

In a tired and listless sort of way Sir Arthur Rebstock brushed his hand across his forehead. 'All right, Charles, I think that's enough.'

Charles Northwood shrugged, his teasing look still directed at Margaret Rebstock. 'Oh well, for some people hate has a more intense and enduring satisfaction than love.' Then as though anticipating a caustic rejoinder from Sir Arthur, he switched his gaze to me and hastily added: 'Naturally I'm alluding to my sister-in-law, Eliza Northwood. Has Meg told you about Eliza? Come, don't be shy with us, Miss Ainslcy. What did Meg tell you?'

I glanced at Margaret Rebstock. She said nothing.

Charles Northwood continued: 'Eliza . . . now there was a great hater! An even greater lover, 'pon my word. What do you say, Arthur, aye? Did she not have a great capacity for loving? Yes indeed, Miss Ainsley, you would have found our Eliza a most impressive woman. As pretty as Old Nick she was, and resembling him in all the qualities of pride, wilfulness and mischief. In short, our Eliza was the most interesting of women.'

'She was wicked!'

'But interesting, Meg. Damned interesting.'

'She was unchaste. Without virtue.'

'Come now, let us not confuse chastity with virtue. Would you agree with me, Miss Ainsley, that not all who are chaste are necessarily virtuous?' Despite the question his eyes were on Miss Rebstock.

93

'I'm sure I wouldn't know. Now if you'll excuse me, please . . .'

'But why?' He was quite obviously enjoying himself.

'Because it's late and I'm tired. Also, I have little or no interest in your word games.'

'Word games! 'Pon my soul, did you hear that, Arthur? Word games, I merely wished to make a point, to wit, that many a fine lady sees only virtue in chastity, no matter if that same chastity is much to her liking. So, Miss Ainsley, if one likes being chaste and prim, then where's the virtue in that?' Charles Northwood spread out his hands in a gesture of amused regret, as if he were sorry to be the one to speak such an obvious truth. 'No, one can hardly call that sort of thing a real virtue. To my mind, charity is a real virtue. And by charity I mean the act of loving and giving. Now, in that respect, Eliza was virtuous. Loving and giving. Am I correct, Meg?'

She looked decidedly ill at ease.

'Well, Meg?'

Sir Arthur broke in: 'This is too much, Charles! Miss Ainsley was right. Damned word games. I'll have none of it. Come, Margaret.' Turning to me he bowed gracefully. 'Our apologies for detaining you, Miss Ainsley. A very great pleasure meeting you. You must visit us soon. Oh, by the by, shall we have the pleasure of meeting you at church on Sunday?'

'Yes indeed. I shall look forward then to . . .'

'Ho-ho!' Charles laughed. 'Institutionalized virtue now, is it?'

'Good night, Charles.' Sir Arthur was curt.

'Wait, I'll have Forrest get your horses.'

'No need.' Margaret Rebstock was equally curt. 'We still remember where the stables are.'

Before I knew it the Rebstocks were through the door and out into the corridor. I started after them.

Too late! Charles Northwood moved with a litheness that checked my escape, his arm stretched out. 'Please, Miss Ainsley. Just one moment.' He was no longer smiling.

'Mr Northwood, if you dare to . . .'

'Please. I promise I will not offend you in any way. Oh, I know what you're thinking . . . that evening in The Crown at Marrambridge, and my behaviour to the Rebstocks just now . . . but, please, just hear me out!' The taunting gleam was gone from his dark eyes. He lowered his arm, the palm of his hand outward, like some kind of peace gesture. 'Yes, I know I appeared half-drunk and deliberately rude and sarcastic tonight. And I know what you must think of me for that, but, please believe me, I had my reasons. I want you to trust me, Miss Ainsley . . .' He took a half-step forward, instinctively affecting a tone of intimacy by dropping his voice to a confidential murmur - no doubt this was one of his conquering ways with women. Well, there was a surprise in store for him - I was neither ready to be conquered by him nor to trust him.

'If you have something to say, Mr Northwood, then I must ask you to come to the point and, with respect, to be as brief as possible. I am anxious to go to my room.'

'Very well. I'll be brief.' Like someone not knowing how to begin he stood before me for a few seconds, nervously tapping the closed fist of one hand into the open palm of the other. 'Miss Ainsley, how long have you been earning your living as a resident tutor?'

'Five or six years. Why do you ask?'

'And with how many different families in that time?'

'Three. But what has that got to do with . . .?'

'And during those years of tutoring, of mingling with all types in different households, you have quite obviously developed a certain poise and self-assurance and, more important perhaps, a degree of perception and awareness which you might not have otherwise acquired . . .'

'Tell me, what's the purpose of all this?'

'Would you say, Miss Ainsley, that every family has a - how will I put it? - has a skeleton in the cupboard, so to speak. A dark secret that nobody wishes to discuss?'

'And if so, then what of it? It's hardly an affair to concern a resident tutor or governess, is it?'

'Supposing that in some way it affected her pupil?'

'Pupil . . . what do you mean?'

'Or, it directly concerned the governess herself?' The governess - me?

I looked up and said sharply, 'What are you driving at?'

'Don't you know? You must have some idea.'

'Not the remotest.'

'All right, Miss Ainsley - tell me, why have they brought you here?'

'They? I take it you are referring to Captain Northwood and Mr Carne?'

'Precisely. Why did they select you for the position here?'

'Why not?' I shrugged. 'Presumably because of my qualifications . . .'

'Or your appearance? I suggest to you, Miss Ainsley, that you were deliberately recruited because of your appearance, your particular brand of beauty. In short, because of your striking resemblance to Eliza.'

'But that's ridiculous! I never met your father, or Mr Carne for that matter, before coming to Polmarran. I simply replied to an advertisement in a newspaper. I never set eyes on anyone from this house prior to this week . . .'

'Hah, but Carne might have seen you before. He might have travelled to wherever it was you were staying, looked you over without your knowing it, and then reported back here to his skipper . . . Yes! I'll lay a guinea to a bent penny that something like that occurred.'

'But . . . but that's absurd. Why would he? For what reason?'

'Can't you see, Miss Ainsley? They're up to something. I don't know what. But they have some new scheme afoot. I'll swear to it. The coincidence of your appearance, your uncanny resemblance to Eliza . . . why, it's just too much to take.'

'You are mistaken.'

But was I? What he had just said made some kind of sense. Redmond Carne could have journeyed to Exeter, seen me at close quarters without my being aware of it, noted the resemblance, and then . . . And then what? And why select me for the position solely because of my likeness to somebody else? I thought I had gained this position on merit, but it was just possible that I was an innocent dupe. Brought here for no other purpose than to be a pawn in someone else's schemes.

'Yes, Miss Ainsley, I think I know what you're thinking. And I think you're right. Someone here wants to use you.'

'For what reasons?'

'I'm not sure. But together we could get to the bottom of all this . . .' His voice had fallen to a whisper. He reached out with both hands and took my wrists, not harshly, but with sudden and unexpected gentleness. Even so, the touch of his fingers on my flesh brought back a vivid recollection of my first meeting with him. I looked down at his hands and said coldly: 'If you don't mind, Mr Northwood.'

He let go. 'I'm sorry. I know how you must feel about me, but I want you to trust me, Katherine . . . I may call you Katherine?'

'No, you may not.' Instantly I regretted my words; I don't know for what reason, but I could think of nothing else to say as I stepped round him and moved towards the door.

He made no attempt to halt me. I noticed as I swept past him that his face had hardened at my words and that the cynical, half-mocking glint had returned to his eyes.

'Good night, Miss Ainsley. Perhaps I have misjudged you after all. It could well be that you are not so much an unsuspecting dupe caught up in their schemes as a willing accomplice. If so, you may warn them of my suspicions as to their motives.'

'I haven't the faintest notion what you're talking about. I am nobody's accomplice. I know of no schemes. I am merely your niece's tutor. Nothing more, nothing less.'

As I turned on my heel he was already selecting another of his cigars from his coat pocket; the hand that held it waved me off with a gay flourish. Was this his habitual response to every repulse, a devil-may-care nonchalance? Was his dissolute mode of living a near-permanent reaction to some earlier, deeper rejection and disappointment? From whom - his father? Eliza? And those odd suspicions of his, inexplicable yet disturbing, had they any real foundation? Certainly he had tried to warn me in some obscure way, had even offered his trust and co-operation to get to the root of any mystery which might possibly attach to the circumstances of my selection as governess. Thinking about it all as I climbed the darkened stairway, I wondered if I had wronged him on some scores. On every score.

Then, too, there was the matter of his display of bad manners, his goading of Carne, and Captain Northwood, and his nastiness towards the Rebstocks just a little while ago in the ballroom. He had implied that it was a pretence. That he had his own reasons for deliberately acting thus. What were they? Something to do with Margaret Rebstock?

And what sort of person was she? I knew that I would not easily forget that woman's look of hate, and her words, whenever she referred to Eliza Northwood. I had already (and quite easily) come to the conclusion that she was a woman whose life lay entirely in the past. In the ruins of disappointed love, tragedy, family traditions, and pride in the local eminence of the Rebstock name. All vital memories to her. And Charles Northwood had said that hate could be a more vital force than love. I was ready to believe that of Margaret Rebstock.

I was still pondering the significance of all that I had seen and heard when I reached the first landing. So engrossed was I in thought that I almost failed to catch the faint noises coming from the area of deep shadow over on the west gallery - the same noises as before - floorboards whimpering under the pressure of a stealthy tread. I spun round. No one. Nothing. Only the same deep, purple-black night tones. They shimmered with my imaginings: the shape of a tall man standing, watching me; then that of a small crouched figure pressed against the wall, hiding from my questing gaze. And yet there was no movement. No further sound.

'Is there someone there? Hallo . . .'

There was no reply, but quite distinctly I heard the rustling sound of some garment, the whisper of silk or satin against the wall as somebody moved away from the sound of my voice.

'Adelaide, are you out of your bed?'

There was a flicker of movement through the pile of shadows and the echo of a retreating step.

If only I had the courage to follow! I turned instead and hurried away in the opposite direction.

For the second time since my coming to Polmarran I locked and bolted the bedroom door. But I did not sleep too well. The name Eliza Northwood sounded repetitively through my fitful slumber.

In the bright morning sunlight it still echoed - a macabre clarion call to my growing curiosity. Margaret Rebstock had implied that my pupil's mother was still alive, whereas Carne had described Adelaide as an orphan. Which was correct? And why had it been so important for Captain Northwood and Carne to hide all knowledge of her from me after I had produced the book at supper last night? Because she was wicked? Or because I resembled her? It came to my mind with a stab of surprise that, in spite of myself, I was being drawn into the affairs of Polmarran House in a way which had never been my intention.

Perhaps Charles Northwood was right in everything he had said to me in the deserted ballroom. If so, then I certainly owed him something in the way of an apology.

But when I went down to breakfast, Mrs Forrest informed me that he had already ridden away.

Chapter Six

On the following Sunday I attended Divine Service at the parish church in Marrambridge. Redmond Carne drove me there; somewhat reluctantly I should think, for I was the only person from Polmarran House to attend. Adelaide was not permitted to accompany me.

At breakfast on the day before, when I had raised the subject of church-going and enquired the times of service, Captain Northwood had informed me that 'as a family we are no longer much impressed by the spirit of religion or of the outward show of it.'

I pointed out that I considered it very necessary to a child's proper upbringing and that Adelaide at least should not be denied contact with the local ministry. He agreed, reluctantly, and said: 'Well, perhaps at some future date she may go with you if you think it so important, but for the present I do not wish her to attend.'

Having already formed an impression of George Northwood's simple and devout nature I was disappointed, too, when I sought some support from that quarter. He seemed afraid to go against his father's wishes and could only murmur something about 'preferring the solitude of my own room for private prayer.' Not for the first time I had to rely on Redmond Carne's presence and intervention. 'Fair enough, Miss Ainsley. If you're dead-set on going to church then I'll be pleased to hitch up the team in the morning and take you. But now you look here, miss, don't expect me to go in to perch on a hard bench and listen to some long-hauled sermon.' With this I had to be content.

Once we were clear of Polmarran and its precincts it was by no means an unpleasant ride to church. I say 'once we were clear' because, as we were preparing to leave, I noticed Captain Northwood mounting the central staircase with a big brass telescope under his arm. I felt certain that he was climbing to his tower. I looked back a couple of times as our carriage took us up through the trees and I could not help thinking that he was already positioned at that top window, spy-glass pressed to his eye, watching us depart. To me that window was like a gimlet eye, full of malice, deeply embedded in a stern face of rough-hewn stones. It seemed to belong to a dim and distant past which was as old as the Cornish cliffs upon which Polmarran Tower stood, something dark and secretive peering down on all who came and went. I breathed a sigh of relief when we passed through the rocky bastions standing close by the entrance to Polmarran.

Yes, a pleasant enough ride from there on - until we were about two miles or so from our destination. The sun brightened everything around us. The reddish earth had the glow of rude health, and wild thyme and bog myrtle and pimpernel made a vivid tapestry beneath the scattered elms. Then, when we were approaching Marrambridge and could see the top of the church steeple in the distance, Redmond Carne turned to me, and pointing to the steeple with the coach whip, said: 'You made your point with the Cap'n. Once you hold to it that church business is necessary to turning out a refined young lady, he won't stand in the way of the young mistress or yourself for long. Just give him time to get used to the idea, and if he proves a bit slow in coming about then I'll step up and speak for you.'

'Thank you.'

'No thanks needed, Miss Ainsley. I never had the chance of church-going in my young days, but I hold that it's good practice for children. Just give the Cap'n his own time and he'll come about.'

'You seem to know Captain Northwood's mind pretty well.'

'I ought to. Sailed with him for the best part of my life. From cabin boy right up to first mate on his last ship before we buried the anchor.'

'Buried the anchor?'

'Figure o' speech, Miss Ainsley. It means retiring from the sea for good and coming ashore to be a landlubber.'

'So you gave up the sea at the same time as Captain Northwood. Why?'

'Because he asked me to.'

'You are very loyal to him, aren't you?'

'Aye, I suppose so.' He gave a self-deprecatory shrug as though he had never really taken time off to consider the matter before.

'He must have been kind to you at sea.'

Carne smiled. 'The master of a sailing vessel has little or no time for dispensing kindnesses among fo'castle hands, Miss Ainsley.'

'But you rose to be his first officer?'

'The Cap'n never had favourites aboard ship, if that's what you mean. I did my duty and learned the ropes as a lad, and I earned promotion by hard work and good seamanship.' There was a manly pride in the sudden jut of his chin and the shake of his head. 'Kindness had no part in it. Just as it has little or no part in the Cap'n's nature.'

'Then why is it you have remained loyal to him all these years?'

'I have to pay my score with the Cap'n.'

'Score?'

'Aye, miss. He saved my life once by risking his own when I was only a raw lad. Not many ship

103

masters I know of would do that for a cabin brat. And also because . . .' Carne's voice suddenly fell, became low and vibrant with emotion, surprising me with its earnestness. 'Because Cap'n Northwood was the first and only person to treat me fairly as a lad, and with strict justice and respect for the dignity of a full-grown man. Harsh betimes, I do admit, but always just. Always fair and square.'

He turned and looked at me. Something in my expression must have encouraged him to continue. 'You see, Miss Ainsley, I never knew my folk. Orphaned and kicked about from every Billy and Jack who didn't want me until I upped and ran off to sea when I was about ten years old. And I think I could have been forgiven as a boy had I believed my name to be a certain foul obscenity, for such was the term generally used by all and sundry in ordering me about. Ordering, bullying and beating for the most part. But the Cap'n gave me a name the first time he found me at Kingston, Jamaica, and took me aboard. A name borrowed from a coxswain who had come down with the Yellow Jack and just been fed to the fishes and so therefore had no longer any need for it. Gave me a name and the respect due to it, and he's stuck to that all these years. So you'll no doubt see now why I know my duty to that man.'

I had a sudden impulse to reach out and take his hand, to communicate to him something of the compassion and gratitude which welled up inside me. Yes, gratitude - for so much had just been explained to me by Redmond Carne's words. I felt certain it would help me to understand something of the relationship between both these men, help and encourage me to be less distrustful of attitudes and motives which I had so far failed to grasp. But the impulse passed almost as swiftly as it had occurred. Instead I murmured, 'Thank you, Mr Carne. I am glad you told me.'

I think my voice betrayed me a little with its unexpected softness. I looked away from him, out over the steeply angled fields and the stone walls of a nearby farm, but without really seeing anything. Carne too had become silent. Inexplicably I found myself wanting to trust him, to have my mind disburdened of those suspicions planted there by Charles Northwood's words a few nights before.

'Mr Carne, why do both you and Captain Northwood consider it so necessary to discourage all reference to my pupil's mother, or the fact that I apparently resemble her to some marked degree?'

The question took him by surprise. He turned to me quickly, frowning with sudden confusion and annoyance. 'Where did you come by those notions?'

'Miss Rebstock remarked on my resemblance to Adelaide's mother.'

'Miss Rebstock had much more to drink than is decent for a lady.'

'Perhaps, but I doubt if it affected her eyesight. Besides, while she may have been the first to mention the matter she is not alone in noting the fact of my likeness to Eliza Northwood.'

'Only in the matter of looks . . . you may thank the Lord when you're in church that you resemble her in no other respect!'

'What do you mean?'

Quite obviously he regretted that unguarded outburst. 'I'll be obliged to you if you put an end to these questions.'

'Why all the mystery? Surely if . . .'

'It's you who is making the mystery, Miss Ainsley. Not me.'

'On the contrary, Mr Carne, why only the other night when I produced that book bearing her signature . . .'

'Look, Miss Ainsley' - he shook his head with a kind of quiet helplessness - 'I don't want to give offence, but in these matters you might say that I'm engaged on what seamen called sealed orders. I'm to do as the Cap'n bids me.'

'And did he bid you to help him select someone as governess who bore a close resemblance to the child's mother?'

'What do you mean by that?'

His scowling expression told me nothing. I decided to come right out with it. 'The other night when I was in the ballroom with Mr Charles he offered as his opinion the view that . . .'

'Mr Charles, be damned! Where that popinjay is concerned I've had to stand-off for too long for the Cap'n's sake.'

'That's your affair. What concerns me is what he said . . .'

'I can imagine the sort of things he'd say when he'd have you alone in that old dance room! And you . . . woman-like, hanging and simpering on his every word!'

His outburst took me by surprise. There was nothing of vanity in my wondering if his sudden anger was tinged with some kind of jealousy. I felt only alarm. And just a little anger of my own.

'Mr Carne, if you think for one moment that I . . .'

'Enough of this talk! Already I'm damn-well near enough to breaking my word to the Cap'n.'

He stood up quickly and with quite unnecessary force cracked the whip across the horses, urging them from a steady canter into as near a thing to a gallop as the narrow and uneven roadway would permit. After that, even if I had wanted to continue the conversation, it would have been impossible, due to the bumping and buffeting about which I received as Carne lashed the horses towards Marrambridge.

'If you cannot treat the animals with actual gentleness, Mr Carne, then at least try them with less severity. I assure you I am not in that much of a hurry to get to the church.' These were the only words to pass between us for the remainder of the journey.

We arrived well in time for the service. When he brought the steaming beasts to a halt outside the wall of the little church I breathed a sigh of relief - as much for the poor horses as myself.

'Do you think you will be long with this business?' With a gruff voice and a careless toss of the head Carne indicated the church.

'You do not have to wait.'

'And if I don't, how do you propose to get back to Polmarran?'

'The Lord provided me with a pair of feet,' I replied with savage insouciance.

'Don't be ridiculous. I'll wait.'

'As you please, Mr Carne.' I stepped down and walked quickly up the path and through the church portal.

I found a pew at the back of the little stone church. Not until I was seated did I become conscious of the curious looks of those parishioners who were already inside. Presumably they guessed who I was, and once again I was made aware of that condition which is frequently the lot of the resident tutor - the hybrid position of being at once neither connected, nor unconnected, with the family at Polmarran. To the Northwoods and Redmond Carne I was an out-sider; to the villagers, one of the Northwood house-hold. A strange feeling, and much more disconcerting than flattering. Especially when one or two people began nudging their neighbours, slyly indicating the newcomer with a nod, and began whispering. I could see that I was to be given a wide berth; no one wished to sit close to me. I wondered how many of them had known Eliza Northwood by sight, and whether or not they were confusing me with that singular young lady. I stared straight ahead of me, and saw the

Rebstocks, right up at the very front, with a family pew all to themselves.

The minister - a Reverend Mr William Cooper - entered the pulpit and preached an excellent sermon from Proverbs X:5; it contained apt allusions to harvest operations, showing how man should improve his spiritual harvest time, and enforcing on the young people the importance of utilizing the harvest time of youth with diligence. What a great pity Miss Adelaide and Mr George Northwood were not present, I thought.

After the service I was met in the porch of the church by the Rebstocks, who introduced me to the minister and his wife, both of whom warmly welcomed me to the parish. In spite of their reduced circumstances the Rebstock name apparently still stood for something in these parts; among the group of parishioners still lingering about the church door there were many indications of that deference invariably accorded to representatives of a neighbourhood's most eminent family. Sir Arthur, to judge from the bevy of young ladies and matrons who so quickly whisked him away, must have been accounted one of the most eligible bachelors in the area. Margaret Rebstock likewise had her coterie - all female, though, and similar to her in demeanour and dark attire. They stood in a small group just outside the door, exchanging prim compliments and, I imagine, the weekly garnerings of tittle-tattle.

This left me alone with the Reverend William Cooper and his wife. As a couple they shared a natural amiability and courtesy which added to their contrasting personalities; in their mid-forties (and childless, I gleaned early in our talk) she was short, exceedingly plump, forthright and merry; he was tall, lean and shy. With her lively eyes and gay chatter she appeared almost frivolous compared with her husband, whose character, while the essence of polite good humour, possessed some of those mannerisms peculiar to the pulpit.

After only five minutes of the most pleasant and easy talk Mrs Cooper linked her arm through mine in the most natural fashion and smiled. 'Now then, Miss Ainsley, you must come and have tea with us. Please! I'll brook no excuses. We must get to know each other.'

'Yes, miss, you must,' the Reverend Cooper added. 'As you can see, my wife is determined to have you and to make the most of a new face. I must warn you that she is a most persuasive woman where new parishioners are concerned.'

'Thank you, William.' Mrs Cooper swung her smile from her husband's face to mine, winking at me. 'Usually he warns people that I am a dreadful gossip, but this morning he is in excellent humour because his sermon was so well received. Did you like it, Miss Ainsley?'

'Yes indeed. It was most edifying.'

'Oh, you are too kind.'

'There, William, what did I tell you? It was an excellent sermon. He worries so, Miss Ainsley. Stays up half the night writing and re-writing. Missing his sleep to perfect his preaching so that others will not catch up on their sleep while he's in the pulpit. Come, dear girl . . . tea.'

'Thank you, Mrs Cooper. Thank you both, but really . . .'

'No excuses, Miss Ainsley. My husband and I are determined to have your company for a little while. Do you not realize that this is a momentous day in William's ministry?'

'Yes indeed, Miss Ainsley. Truly momentous. Why I had almost despaired of ever receiving anyone from Polmarran House in my church.'

'You see, Miss Ainsley! You are an answer to William's prayers. Oh yes indeed, for do you know that in the early days of his ministry, when he paid a courtesy call to Polmarran, that wretched old sea-dog . . .'

'Charity, Hester . . . charity, please.'

'Charity or no, that Captain Northwood is nothing but a wretched old pirate! Do I shock you, dear girl? No matter, be shocked if you will. I believe in speaking out. Is that not so, William?'

'Alas . . .'

'Wretched old pirate! Chased poor William off the property with a pistol or a cutlass or something like that . . . what was it, William? I cannot for the life of me remember.'

'Nothing of the sort. Please, Hester. Whatever will Miss Ainsley think of us?'

'A pistol, Miss Ainsley. Or a sabre. At any rate he chased my husband away with some weapon or other and a string of vile nautical oaths.'

'Gross exaggeration.' Mr Cooper clucked his tongue.

'It is not an exaggeration. Why, William, do you not recall how dreadfully disappointed you were when you returned after that visit?'

'Only because I failed to make contact with young Mr George Northwood.' The clergyman sighed, his eyes momentarily raised to heaven. He turned to me. 'As you probably know, Miss Ainsley, George Northwood was at one time seriously studying for Holy Orders.'

'No, I was not aware of that.'

'Oh yes. A friend of mine, a clerical colleague who holds a residential canonry to the north of here, and whom I meet every week, was once an undergraduate with young Mr Northwood before the latter's unfortunate breakdown.'

'Breakdown?'

'You did not know about his nervous disorder? Dear me, I am sorry. Yes, most unfortunate. His mind became unhinged, you see. Poor lad. Of course

110

I understand that he is now quite recovered. It all happened some years ago, when he was a divinity student. A singularly brilliant student too, I am led to believe. Unfortunate really. Some family tragedy . . .'

'A family scandal,' Mrs Cooper interposed.

'Please, Hester. We do not know that. Let us be charitable.'

With her lips pursed and a slight wink twitching the corner of her eye Mrs Cooper leaned closer to me; in a low tone she quickly murmered: 'A scandal. Something to do with his brother's death and that girl.'

That girl . . . Eliza?

'Eliza was wicked!' Unbidden, those words sprang to my mind, hinting at a corollary, a will-o'-the-wisp connection between John Northwood's death and his brother's derangement. I felt momentarily confused - yet curious to learn more. For just an instant I thought about putting some questions to Mrs Cooper, of mentioning some of those things which I had learned from Margaret Rebstock that night in the ball-room, but just as quickly I discarded the notion. I scarcely knew this woman before me, and suddenly to pour forth my ill-defined fears might require explanations which I could not give, and moreover must surely present me to the Coopers as an alarmist.

Yet something of the effect caused by Mrs Cooper's words must have shown on my face. Through the thinning ranks of a departing congregation, Margaret Rebstock was watching me. She was standing stiffly amongst her friends, her features taut and hostile. Almost immediately my attention was drawn elsewhere. Beyond her I could see Redmond Carne at the church gate, deep in conversation with Sir Arthur Rebstock and two other men. I wasn't sure, but I thought I recognized one of them as the landlord of *The Crown;* he was agitated and was pointing down

111

the street in the direction of the inn. Carne was nodding his head, grim-faced and angry. Sir Arthur had his arm on Carne's shoulder and even though some considerable distance separated me from them, I could tell with my first glance that it was a gesture of restraint. Something was wrong . . .

'I'm sorry. Will you please excuse me, Mrs Cooper?'

'Of course, my dear . . . perhaps next Sunday for tea?'

'Yes, that would be nice. Thank you.'

As I stepped from the porch Margaret Rebstock broke away from her friends and came to my side; she had been following my gaze.

'Something is the matter. Judging by the presence of *The Crown's* landlord and the look on Redmond Carne's face I would hazard a guess that Charles has been on the rampage again. Oh, don't worry, Miss Ainsley. Arthur will set things right. He is very capable, you know.'

At that very moment the 'capable' Sir Arthur had turned about and was starting up the pathway towards us. Redmond Carne followed, quickly overtaking Sir Arthur.

''Morning, Miss Rebstock.' Carne tossed off a blunt, perfunctory nod in her direction before turning to me. 'Beg pardon, miss . . . but there seems to be a spot of bother below at *The Crown.*'

'Good old Charles has run amok once again.' Sir Arthur smiled. 'But Jack Tregarron has agreed not to press charges if Carne will undertake to rid his shattered taproom of Charlie's troublesome person.'

'Sorry about this, Miss Ainsley, but I'll have to hoist him aboard and fetch him back to the house with us. He's drunk and ruffianly from all accounts but no cause for you to be alarmed. I'll see that there's no . . .'

'Good grief, Carne!' Sir Arthur protested. 'You cannot expect this young lady to travel alongside

Charles when he's in one of his moods. Where's your sense of delicacy, man? Utterly unthinkable!'

'Well, miss, it can't rightly be helped, but if you . . .'

'No 'ifs and buts' about it, Carne. I'll be most happy to take Miss Ainsley back to Polmarran. No, no, Miss Ainsley . . . I insist! I'm going in that direction shortly and it's the least I can do.'

The matter was settled without my having very much say in it. I was not displeased with the arrangement. I hadn't been particularly looking forward to the return journey with Redmond Carne in view of our earlier clash - but with a drunken Charles Northwood accompanying us! No, thank you. If the deep frown on his face signified anything, then Carne did not seem too happy with the new arrangement, but with more pressing matters to attend to, he said nothing. He took leave of us with that now-familiar sketchy salute of his, the big hand barely brushing the side of his forehead before he turned quickly on his heel and marched down the pathway to re-join Mr Tregarron of *The Crown*. We followed at a more leisurely pace, hardly a word passing between us until after Sir Arthur Rebstock had helped me into his curricle.

'Is your sister not coming with us?' I asked, surprised to see her still standing on the kerb and giving me a polite little wave of adieu as he took the reins and settled into the driving seat.

'Margaret always spends Sunday in Marrambridge with her friends. Stays overnight with one of them. Chance to catch up on, and exchange, all the tit-bits of gossip from the preceding week.' He smiled indulgently. He kept the horses to a brisk canter and presently we were approaching the little stone bridge outside the village. Not until we had crossed it and were turning sharply to follow the course of the rivulet did he resume. 'Yes, my sister enjoys her weekly visits to Marrambridge. The gossip too, I suppose. In a neighbourhood such as ours everyone sooner or later knows the next fellow's business and at times gossip and rumour in Marrambridge is like a fox let loose before a pack of hounds. It is a game, a diversion, for most, and without any real harm where my sister and her confidants are concerned. But for others it is something much more than a sport. Much more. Something deadly and vicious. Such people will not be happy until they have marked their hunt to the ground and then brought home every hound.'

What was he driving at? I couldn't be sure, but for a start I suspected he was being a bit too lenient where his sister was concerned. I shrugged, and my disinterest was more real than feigned when I added: 'Oh well, I suppose it's pretty much the same anywhere.'

'Uh-huh, but since your arrival here, there has been a considerable increase in the rumours and the gossip. Not a soul but knows of your meeting in *The Crown* with Charles and what took place there. Needless to remark, the incident has been enlarged and embellished beyond all recognition, and while I would not for the life of me pretend it to the Reverend Mr Cooper I suspect that the reason we had such an excellent turn-out for service this morning was simply because so many wanted to have a good look at you.'

'At me? Because of that incident?'

'That, yes . . . but more especially to see if you were really a newcomer, or Eliza returned. You see Miss Ainsley, quite a few people around these parts have reason to remember her.'

'Well, I hope they're satisfied now. I am not Eliza Northwood, and I'm growing just a little bit tired of being frequently confused, compared, or linked with her in some way. Indeed, I have grown rather weary of the sound of her name.'

'Because of the aura of mystery that surrounds it?'

'Because so many people here have an uncanny

trick of making frequent references to her in one connection or another and yet at the same time withdrawing from any direct straightforward question I make about her. Why, even your own sister, when she spoke to me the other night at Polmarran . . .'

'Oh come now, Miss Ainsley, surely you don't take Meg too seriously? Apart from the fact that she may have been just a teeny bit tipsy at the time, Meg likes to make a big show of her grief, her fidelity to the memory of John Northwood. It's as if she's publicly announcing that, if Eliza tricked her out of the role of wife, then she's certainly not going to be deprived of the role of widow . . . especially if the real widow cannot be found. Silly, girlish stuff and sentimental nonsense for the most part. Like the flowers each Sunday.'

'Flowers?' I echoed, not understanding.

'For John Northwood's grave. Every Sunday for the past seven years without fail. Indeed, if it hadn't been for my sister that plot would now be entirely overgrown with weeds. No one else visits it.'

'What about Captain Northwood?'

Sir Arthur smiled. 'That old sea-dog? I think, if he had had his way, John would have been buried at sea. Davy Jones locker, and all that sort of thing. A plot of earth with a slab of granite upon it means nothing to our good Captain.'

'What about Adelaide? Surely she would be allowed to attend the grave?'

'Why should she?'

'What . . . her father's grave?'

'Ah, but who can say with any certainty that the late John Northwood was in fact the child's father?'

The suggestion was no less nasty for being tossed off in such a light and flippant way. I dismissed it with a cool glance. I considered it unworthy of a gentleman and grossly unfair to my pupil.

'What's the matter, Miss Ainsley? Does that remark

115

shock you? It shouldn't, you know. As Charles said, Eliza was a most interesting woman. Besides, sooner or later you're bound to hear it from someone else. Meg probably. Her one consolation really . . . the knowledge that her beloved John never actually shared the marriage bed with Eliza.'

'I think I've had quite enough of this conversation.'

'Come, Miss Ainsley, I'm divulging no great secret. The whole county has had that story for years and without any reason to doubt the truth of it. It's generally held as the reason for John's "accident". Some fellows cannot easily accept the fact that the girl they married in secret haste was already pregnant by someone else. Myself, I take a much more civilized attitude on such things. A good thrashing might be called for, I admit . . . but for a chap to take it so much to heart as to blow out his own brains! It might be the done thing for a military gentleman and all that, but it's so damned messy and inconvenient, don't you think?'

'I think I should get out and walk. This sort of conversation is in very bad taste. I don't wish to hear any more.'

'My mistake. You really aren't very like her, are you? I mean, Eliza would have revelled in every squalid detail.'

'Would you mind stopping the carriage, please.'

'I'm so sorry.' His apology was accompanied by a wan smile. 'You're right of course. Maybe we should talk about something else.'

After that he was the perfect guide, never once mentioning Eliza or the Northwood family again as he pointed out everything of local interest or importance along the route. Not that there was too much to point out. The road soon left the peat-brown, turbulent river and took us up through richly wooded combes and on to the uplands. When I reckoned that we must be less than two miles from our destination we came to a fork in the road - one way leading down towards the coast and Polmarran; the other rising, steep and narrow, and with an untidy border of rhododendron and laurel bushes on either side. In the distance I could see a thick cluster of tall trees protecting a square stone-built country house on the side of a hill.

'Rebstock Grange.' Sir Arthur indicated the family homestead with a slight nod of his head. At the same moment he brought the horses to a halt in the centre of the forked road. 'Not much of a place compared with Polmarran, I admit. But I think you'll find it much more congenial . . . and intimate.'

There was no mistaking what he had in mind. He had moved imperceptibly nearer to me, one hand sneaking along the top of the back-rest, the other brushing against my thigh, and now trying to caress the flesh above my knee through the folds of my skirt. 'You don't mind if I call you Katherine, do you?' His hoarse whisper had a sudden, blunt candour about it. 'You have such a pretty mouth . . .'

My response caught him unawares. Even as he intoned his words, his face looming much closer to mine, I was already plucking his hand contemptuously from where it rested above my knee and pushing him away. At the same time I twisted out from under the other hand before it could pinion me against his shoulder. Before he fully realized what was happening I was out of the carriage and standing on the roadway.

'Mistaken again, Sir Arthur. I'm really not very like Eliza, am I?' I mustered up every shred of obstinate courage which I possessed and fashioned it into a scathing look.

His expression of feigned, tender passion wilted immediately. Poor Miss Rebstock - her man-of-the-world big brother was not nearly as capable as she imagined! His hasty attempt at seduction had been a crude, bungled affair, embarrassing for both of us; but

117

I at least was exacting some measure of retaliation with my raking look. I almost felt sorry for him as I saw his look of surprise gradually give way to an uneasy smile. He shrugged his shoulders and then spread out his hands, palms up, trying to adopt the pose of a gambler who had just wagered a trifle and who could therefore accept his loss with equanimity.

'All right, come along then.' He patted the empty seat.

'I'm walking to Polmarran.'

'Don't be ridiculous!' He was no longer smiling.

'Good morning, Sir Arthur.'

'Come back here! Did you hear me . . . come back here, I say!' He was standing up, frowning, undecided as to whether he should jump down and follow me on foot, or urge the horses after me.

I stepped out boldly, almost triumphantly, and walked straight ahead. Behind me I heard the flick of the reins and the steady clip-clop of the hooves. I didn't look round. When the driver's seat was just about level with me Sir Arthur leaned down.

'Come now, Katherine . . .'

'*Miss* Ainsley.'

'Come then, Miss Ainsley. Climb up here. I'll take you to Polmarran.'

'If you don't leave me alone I'll report this to my employer the very moment I arrive there.'

'Damn, girl, not that. You know, I'd rather looked forward to a pleasant afternoon with you, but I'll be damned if I'll go about attaining it by having to submit to a lecture from that superannuated old pirate!' He grimaced with vexation. Then with a leering sidelong glance he added: 'Maybe I'll have better luck next time, eh? Or is it a case of "finder's keepers" . . . with Charles having the honour and the pleasure of your favours?'

His words I found even more offensive than his recent attempt to take liberties. I swung round, my eyes blazing with anger. 'How dare you even suggest such a thing! Your afternoon might be much better spent in learning respect for others and the general tenets of good behaviour.'

'Oh, for heaven's sake, spare me all that rot. There's nothing quite so tiresome to a well-born gentleman as the moral self-righteousness of a prim little miss who needs to work for her livelihood.'

He turned the carriage about and lashed at the horses savagely. Well-born gentleman indeed! The only advantage of birth which Sir Arthur Rebstock possessed was that of being well removed in time from that scaffold-dodging old rogue who had founded the family fortunes by wrecking! Furious, I set off down the road. I didn't look back, but somewhere behind me the sounds of his departure were being gradually swallowed up by time and distance. Except for the scrunch of my shoes on the dusty gravel, all was silent, yet within my mind his words still echoed and rankled. What disturbed me most of all were his references to Adelaide's parentage. More than ever I felt consumed by a protective compassion for the child. Poor Adelaide. For how long could she remain the unknowing and uncomprehending object of local rumour and gossip? And once she moved outside the comparative security of Polmarran's precincts, what then? How would she cope with the sly whisperings, the smirks and nudges, the meaningful looks and innuendoes which must inevitably draw back the curtains of the past and reveal her origins?

Such questions - relentless and unbidden - dogged my footsteps. As if to shake them off I quickened my pace. But I hadn't reckoned on the rigours of a mountainous track (one could scarcely describe the twisting, rutted, pot-holed route as a road) for it was one thing to travel it when seated beside Redmond Carne, or Sir Arthur Rebstock for that matter, and shielded by a twirling parasol, quite another to walk

119

it with little or no breeze to temper the unremitting glare of the mid-day sun.

But I didn't remain on the road for very long. When I was just in sight of those dark, overhanging rocks that marked the narrow entrance to Polmarran I heard the sound of horses approaching from behind. They were still some way off but the steady drumming of the hooves bespoke great haste and when I stopped for a moment to listen I could just about make out the clatter of iron-tyred wheels over the rough stones. Sir Arthur hastening to resume his unfinished business under the pretext of returning my parasol? Or Redmond Carne with his drunken cargo?

I had no wish to meet up again with the occupants of either vehicle. I hurried across the dusty track and plunged into the nearest thicket just as the carriage and pair came thundering round the bend.

Chapter Seven

Where the foliage was darkest and thickest I crouched, hoping that I hadn't been seen, I kept my head down, so that I was unable to see out on to the lane as the horses raced past. By the time I had poked a tiny aperture through the leaves all I could see was a cloud of dust settling down again in the wake of the plunging and snapping hooves. I did not straighten up again until the last sound had died away.

I stood for a while, thinking. It was cooler amongst the trees. Above them the sky was still a deep and brilliant blue but all around me scattered shadows were burying patches of sunlight and dappling the ground. Why should I bother hurrying back to the house? The peace of early afternoon and the surrounding woodland, softly golden and russet with all the glory of autumn, made it ideal for a leisurely stroll. It would be pleasant to savour a rare period of solitude and freedom from the oppressiveness of Polmarran House and to be out from under the eye of that gloomy-looking tower.

I found a narrow, half-hidden animal track through the ferns and kept to it until it finally gave out. After that, the going became a bit more difficult. In some places I had to clamber over boulders, to skirt fallen trees and thick undergrowth. After nearly a half hour of this I soon found that I was not in any condition for mountain walking. I stopped once to sit on an old log, looking back idly over my shoulder.

There was no sign of the road. Indeed, I was none too certain in which direction it lay. As I turned away, there was a movement, a blur of colour in the trees over to my right. I switched my gaze back, but it was gone. Had there been someone there? I watched the place for quite some time but there was no further movement, only the close-standing trees and bushes. A bird probably. I dismissed it and started off again.

Progress was much slower now and I was less certain of my direction. The all-engulfing greenery of ferns and bushes, so enticingly cool only three-quarters of an hour before, now seemed to vibrate with the intensity of the sun. It had become a gold-white orb above me, blazing, relentless. My clothes were soon clinging to me with the heat of my exertions and I was beginning to discover that my shoes were really no protection against sharp, hidden stones. A greater urgency took command of my movements, over-ruling all considerations of discomfort. Just when I was beginning to debate the wisdom of pressing on (or trying to find a way back to the road, I wasn't sure which) I stumbled through the bushes and into a small, sunlit clearing. A narrow gap in the wall of trees at the opposite side disclosed a distant view of Polmarran Tower less than a mile away. Despite my feelings about that tower it was something of a relief to see it at that moment. My sense of direction had not been so bad after all!

Equal to my satisfaction in sighting Polmarran was my discovery of this secluded glade. I moved into it. Here, all around me, there was not one single sign that man had ever been this way. It was an oasis of tranquillity. Unspoiled, picturesque - and for the moment it was all mine. I was captivated by its wild beauty. Its centre-piece was a pool lying at the foot of a rocky projection to my left and fed by a minia-ture waterfall issuing from the rocks. A tiny streamlet, brown, silver and murky gold, leaped from the pool and coursed through the glade. The banks of the pool and the brook and the entire floor of the clearing was a blaze of colour - the fading yellow of gorse bloom, the odd purple splash of heather, green clumps of hart-tongue and tall, fronded wood ferns. Where some of the ferns had begun to fade the sun was now tingeing them a ruddy bronze. On all sides grey-white boulders acted as a foil to the colours of nature.

I went to the edge of the pool. The water was dark and cool, writhing and chuckling over the little stones at the edge. Kneeling, and with cupped hands, I drank from it. Then I moistened my handkerchief and dabbed at the beaded perspiration on my forehead. My clothes still felt heavy and clammy against my hot skin. On a sudden impulse I removed my outer garments. Here there was no need of vigilance or modest caution. This was my secret bower, my private haven. I laughed out loud and plunged my arms down into the sparkling water and scooped it up, dashing its tingling freshness over my back and shoulders. After that I quickly removed my shoes, my hose, then raised my skirts well above my knees and stepped into the pool. I paddled out for a bit, gently splashing the water from one leg to the other, dancing a little on the sandy bottom. I gathered my skirts about my hips and waded out into the centre. The water here was quite cold and it reached just above my knees. Shivering with a kind of breathless delight I remained there for - oh, I don't know how long! It was all so invigoratingly cool and refreshing!

Eventually I returned to the bank. I did not bother to dry myself or to dress. I wanted to enjoy every moment of it. I lay down in the sun, my head thrown back and my eyes gazing up at the wavering ribbon of water suspended from the rocks. Sunlight teased its way through every shimmering strand of the little cascade. A slight breeze flicked fairy handfuls of the spray into my upturned face every so often. I continued to lie there, calm, languorous, lulled by the water's unchanging pattern of descent, by its soothing murmur. It was all so peaceful. I closed my eyes . . .

. . . I must have slept for some considerable time. I woke suddenly, chilled, and for some unaccountable reason vaguely apprehensive. The sun had gone down behind the distant hills and the glade was being invaded by the long shadows of evening. A cold little wind had sprung up, rattling the dry leaves and sighing in the trees. I sat up, looking quickly about me. My secluded glade, now that it was deprived of sunlight, was no longer a peaceful haven. My being alone was no longer a thing to exult in. Quite the reverse. Maybe it was the sudden discovery of the trees as dark masses against a lighter medium, that the approaching dusk had shrouded the distant view of Polmarran Tower, or that I was wearing less clothes on me than were actually spread out on the grass beside me - but a cold little shiver once more ran up my spine. I felt vulnerable, nervous. With the corner of my eye I caught a brief flash of movement further up amongst the trees on the hill. I jerked about quickly, but it was gone. Was there someone there? No, I was being silly . . .

But I reached for my blouse, struggled into it, got to my feet - in one swift, continuous movement, too hasty and agitated to be anything but the action of a frightened person. Frightened? Why? It may have been my fancy, or a trick of the evening light creeping through the pattern of shadow amongst the trees, but suddenly I felt certain that someone was concealed there, silently watching my every movement. Perhaps had been there all the while, from the moment I'd

124

entered the glade, watching me disrobe, lying full out on the grass, half-naked . . .

I was afraid to look around me now. I pushed my feet into my shoes, rolled my hose and the remainder of my clothes into an untidy bundle, tried to appear calm and unhurried as I started to move off. Already the shadows and the stillness were deepening. Threatening.

My strained hearing caught a sudden noise! Somewhere behind me. Sharp, small, like a footstep on a dry twig or a stretch of shale. I looked back over my shoulder. Nothing. Only the trees, the shadow, the silence marred only by the faint gurgling of the brook. I hurried on, much quicker now, making no pretence at calmness. The stillness was broken by a piercing cry. 'Eliza!'

I spun round, startled, horrified. That haunting cry was repeated again but with even greater and frightening vehemence. 'Eliza!'

I recoiled from the sound, running, stumbling over the broken ground as I sought the shelter of the nearest trees.

'Eliz-zzzahh!'

I was in the woods now, tearing my way through the low-hanging branches, the tangled undergrowth clutching and snatching at my skirts. I flung the bundle of clothes from me. The tumult of panic inside me forced greater speed into my limbs. They thrust me forward, my arms clearing a path of escape - at one moment shielding my face from the trailing brambles, the next, pulling and hacking an opening through the screen of foliage bearing down on me from all sides. I ran blindly for some time, unable to tell if the thrashing noises in the undergrowth were caused by the chaos of my flight or were the result of a pursuer. No matter how fast I ran I felt that someone was gliding along just behind me, effortlessly keeping pace with my panicky stride.

Someone unseen, unhurried, eyes gleaming and gloating over my floundering fear. Someone unmoved, remorseless, ever-stalking . . . Sir Arthur Rebstock's words dinned into my ears. *'For some people it is something much more than a sport . . . something deadly and vicious . . . such people will not be happy until they have marked their hunt to the ground and then brought home every hound.'*

I don't know how long I kept at it, alternately stumbling and running, now walking for a bit and panting with near-exhaustion, then goaded into fresh effort by hammering fear as I heard the heavy rustling in the undergrowth just behind me. Some time later I found myself scrambling up a grassy slope, scratched and bruised and dripping with sweat. There was a stab like a knife in my side. My heart sounded like a heavy drum beat, blotting out every other noise. I was compelled to rest, to find new breath - above all, to try to keep down the panic inside me and to think with some semblance of clarity. I leaned against a tree until my breathing was almost normal again. I listened anxiously. If someone was still pursuing me, then he had the light, unhurried movements of a phantom. There was no longer any crackling of twigs or loose stones, no rustling leaves - none of the usual sounds that I would have expected of a pursuer.

What did that mean? Had I eluded him, or was he much closer, moving with a confident stealth? Slowly I backed away from the deep shadows of the nearest thicket, my wary eyes seeing each clump of foliage sheltering a menacing watcher. I caught a whisper of movement just to the rear of me!

'Eliz-zzzahh . . .' The ominous hiss could not have been more than a dozen paces from me!

Almost feeling the invisible hands about my throat I sprang away, my impetus sending me crashing through the bushes, tumbling, rolling back down the slope. Instantly I was on my feet, rushing off in some other direction - anywhere.

'Eliza! You are wicked!' The tormented tremor in the voice was hurled back and forth by the mountain echoes, not diminishing, drawing nearer!

'Help . . . help me!' My parched throat seemed to split and tear with the effort of screaming.

But there was no one to help. I was defenceless, stumbling blindly into a maelstrom of terror and physical exhaustion such as I had never experienced before. It wrenched from me all energy and reason. I had only a wild desire to escape - but already my limbs were giving out; perspiration and tears filled my eyes as they tried to pierce the composition of foliage and shadow, tried desperately to find a route of sorts along which I could force my straining body. Running, sobbing uncontrollably, walking, struggling to piece together the puzzle of shifting light and shade. Trees. Darkness. Movement.

A shadow sprang from the trees, huge, man-like in its swift menace. I tried to elude the outstretched arm. A deep rut snarled my footing. I tripped, pain shooting agonizingly through my ankle. With a scream I fell forward and tumbled headlong down through a briar-covered slope.

'Now, Eliza . . .'

I fell face down. As I tried to rise, to turn and see and match features to a voice which I knew, and yet did not know because of my terror, a big hand clutched ruthlessly the hair at the back of my neck. My face was pressed suffocatingly against the grass and the dry, hard earth. I tried again to turn on to my back, kicking and twisting in a violent frenzy, but my attacker's full weight was upon me, his hard thighs straddling my writhing body. A hand tore at my blouse and ripped it away. My back and shoulders were bare. My wrists were seized, first one, then the other, and then both were dragged behind my back and held together in the vice-like grip of one hand. The other hand, still deeply enmeshed in my hair, jerked my head up sharply. I sucked at the evening

127

air for breath. My sobbing, feeble cries were suddenly choked off by the pressure of the same hand as it quickly let go of my hair and slipped in under my chin and closed about my throat. The tiny diamond points of moisture in the grass glistened and grew and began to swirl drunkenly before me. Thunder assailed my ears and reverberated through my head. The pressure on my throat increased and for an instant there was a swirling chaos of lights hurtling towards me. I felt them crash against my skull, a thousand tiny fragments, but without pain - for all the pain was in my aching throat and my lungs - and the lights began to fade into nothingness, the throbbing pain to grow and build up to a bursting pressure. And then swiftly everything was plunged into darkness . . .

. . . I had one brief and lucid moment. Someone was carrying me. I was nestled against his shoulder, safe and secure, and gently rocked by the swaying rhythm of his walk. My eyes flickered at the sound of voices, half-opening to see who it was.

'Oh, good heavens! What's happened? Oh, the poor girl! What's happened to her?' I recognized the voice of Mrs Forrest. The words quivered with alarm and compassion.

'Got lost in the woods, I think.'

'Oh, but just look at her clothes, Mr Carne!'

'The brambles.'

I looked up through the flickering, half-veiled lashes, still moist with tears and perspiration and saw Redmond Carne taking in my wet, dishevelled hair, the scratches on my face and the bruised throat - and the nakedness still gleaming through my torn and shredded blouse.

'The brambles, Mrs Forrest. She must've taken fright at some animal noises and panicked. Good thing I was out searching for her.'

128

No! I tried to speak, to shake my head in denial of Carne's words. But the attempted movement brought a throb of pain and dizziness. The darkness came flooding back again, shrouding me with uncertainty and new fears . . .

When the darkness slowly dissolved again I realized in some vague and half-comprehending way that I was in bed and that all my torn and soiled clothes had been removed. The linen sheets were soft and clean and soothingly warm against my limbs. There was a dull, steady ache through my ankle and instep. The whispered buzz of voices was too far away to be real or wondered at - so I lay for some time without moving, without any clear recollection of what had happened or why I was here. Where?

My head lay sideways on the pillow. Misty and uncertain, my eyelids opened and gradually revealed crooked human shadows wavering gently on the opposite wall. The wall looked vaguely familiar. My bedroom? And there were voices, low and murmuring. Men's voices. In my bedroom. But the faint throbbing of my temples and the general feeling of lightheadedness left me completely outside the compass of either curiosity or fear. Besides, one of the voices seemed vaguely familiar, known to me - a soft-voiced echo from reality . . .

Very slowly I turned my head. Yes, men. A whispering trio standing close to the fireplace. The tall, broad-shouldered one with his hands supporting his coat lapels was the familiar one. Redmond Carne.

'Shush . . . I think she stirred, Doctor. Is she all right?'

'Should be. I gave her sufficient to make her sleep soundly . . .'

Through veiled, still misty lashes I watched a short, elderly-looking man with a black leather bag detach himself from the shadowy huddle and tip-toe over to the side of the bed. 'Ah, so you are awake. Feeling a bit better now, I'll warrant, eh? You had quite a nasty fall, you know. Still, no bones broken. Nothing to worry about, m'dear.'

I nodded my head gently, accepting his presence, his geniality, everything, without wonder.

'Still, you must rest now. I will call by tomorrow to see how you are. Take another look at that ankle. Bad sprain. A week or so before you'll be out of bed, I'm afraid.'

'What happened?' It didn't seem like my own voice. It was so far away and like a child's whisper that I felt certain he hadn't heard. I repeated my question. 'What happened to me? Why am I here?'

'You had a bit of an accident, m'dear.'

'Please, Doctor, leave her to sleep. Time enough for talk tomorrow. Let her rest easy now.' I savoured the concern in Redmond Carne's tone. He walked slowly around the side of the bed as he spoke. The movement placed him in the firelight's glow, sweeping the shadows from his face, showing him handsome and earnest, with his eyes dark and grave. 'I'll have Mrs Forest sit by her tonight . . .'

'Yes.' The doctor nodded. 'Back to sleep now, m'dear. You have nothing to worry about.'

I nodded submissively. I closed my eyes as the third man came over from the fire. I think it was Charles Northwood, or perhaps his brother George. It seemed too much of an effort to open my eyes again to make sure. They continued chatting quietly for a time, the voices drifting away, blending in a soft harmony of solicitude for my welfare and comfort. The gentle murmuring gradually retreated from my awareness and the door opened quietly and then closed. The only sound was from the tendrils of some vine tapping and sweeping against the window panes and the wind's sighing through the trees and the crackle of blazing logs in the fire . . .

A deep sleep. I stirred only once, half-waking in the grey dawn light and recalling only the comfort of Redmond Carne's arms about me, nestling me into his shoulder, carrying me. Nothing more - only his strength and protection.

It was much later than my usual time when I awoke next morning. I was immediately and acutely aware of my painful ankle. The sheets no longer soothed, but chafed my bruised limbs. My ankle throbbed violently - and instantly I was remembering how I had sustained the injury. I sat up in bed recalling all too vividly my foot catching in the rut, twisting, the ground tilting away from me - falling through the briars, downwards, and then my frantic efforts to rise. I looked down at my arms, at the tiny cuts and abrasions, and I shuddered as I re-lived every terror-filled moment of my flight through the woods. The huge invisible hands clutching at my hair, tearing my clothes, my face pressed ruthlessly into the ground, the unseen fingers encircling my throat. Someone had tried to kill me!

But who? Why?

The second question was only somewhat less difficult to answer; I had been pursued and attacked because of my resemblance to Eliza Northwood; that much was certain. Someone had mistaken me for her, someone who either feared or hated her enough to want her head and who believed that she had returned to Polmarran. Margaret Rebstock's words stabbed through my thoughts: *'If I could be certain that Eliza Northwood was dead I could be happy.'* And there had been an ominous ring to Sir Arthur Rebstock's words as well: *'Quite a few people around these parts have reason to remember her.'*

More than ever now I felt I should have heeded Charles Northwood's attempt to warn me of some threatening force. Perhaps I had been too hasty in spurning his offer of co-operation. But could I trust him now? Could I trust anyone here? Hardly. It was

131

strange, indeed there was a cruel and frightening irony in the fact that my assailant's voice (though thickened and distorted by demoniac emotion) had still seemed vaguely familiar and yet had remained unidentifiable. That could only mean that somebody here at Polmarran (or Rebstock Grange, perhaps?) might be waiting for another opportunity to attack me - waiting with ruthless patience, wearing a face I already knew, and at the same time did not know.

Calmly I tried to review everything which had happened and everything which had been said since my arrival in Marrambridge less than a week before: I had to seek some order, some pattern or motive, if I were successfully to reason things out, or else by midday I would find myself a mumbling, distraught wreck. But it was no use. I lay there for nearly an hour, disorientated by a sense of shock, more than a little frightened, and confused by the wildest of conjectures which led my suspicions everywhere and nowhere. Once or twice I tried to rise and get out of bed, but pain and an all-engulfing dizziness kept me shackled to it. I felt helpless and trapped.

I was so relieved when Mrs Forrest arrived. She came with a breakfast tray and she was accompanied by Redmond Carne who likewise carried a tray. This second tray was laden with a gigantic kettle of boiling water, a basin, clean white towels, rose water and various jars of ointment. He remained outside in the little parlour until after Mrs Forrest had helped me with my toilet and attended to all my minor cuts and scratches. She was the soul of kindliness in her ministrations, tender, full of concern and so obviously upset to find me in such a state. But all my questions about the attack came to nought.

'Hush now, dear child. Doctor Howard says for you to have absolute rest. You mustn't go distressing yourself with all sorts of imaginings.'

'I am not imagining things, Mrs Forrest. I was

132

attacked by someone. He kept calling me "Eliza".'

'Now, now, miss, you mustn't fret yourself with all this. You had a bad fright sure enough, but . . .'

'He tried to strangle me! Oh, please, Mrs Forrest, you must believe me. Look at my throat!'

'Hush now, Miss Ainsley.' She continued to chide me gently, infuriating me with her calm disregard of all that I was trying to convey. 'And it's that Sir Arthur Rebstock I'd blame for your mishap. To leave you to go walking off through those hills on your own. Most ungentlemanly, to say the least. Oh, my Jem is right . . . he says that, like all the high-and-mighty gentry, them Rebstocks are so upright and sure of what's right and wrong that they're downright bad! To leave a poor slip of a girl alone like that, lost and frightened and stumbling through that jungle.'

'I was not lost. Not at first. Only after my pursuer had . . .'

'My Jem says that Mr Carne should've taken a horse whip to that scoundrel, and I says it's a pity he didn't box Sir Arthur's ears. Oh yes, Miss Ainsley, soon as Mr Carne found you and fetched you back here to your room, he sent Mr Charles galloping off for the doctor - being as how Mr Charles, whether drunk or sober, is such an excellent horseman - and then after I took charge of you, Mr Carne himself went hell-for-leather across to the Grange to give that so-called gent a good lashing with his tongue. If Captain Northwood had not given strict instructions not to lay a hand on our fine Sir Arthur I think Mr Carne would've punched a hole in that fellow's head, such a temper was he in! To tell truth, Miss Ainsley, if there was ever once I saw Mr Redmond Carne fit to disobey a solemn order from the Captain it was last night. He can be very violent and quick-tempered when driven to it, can Mr Redmond Carne.'

'Did he see my attacker? Did he say who it was?'

'I'm sure, miss, that he said nothing about an attacker. Only what attacking he'd do on that well-bred whelp for leaving you unescorted.'

'Please ask him to come in'.

Carne, like someone who had been anxiously pacing up and down outside, came hurrying in at Mrs Forrest's call. He surprised me with his greeting - taking my hand gently in his, quite without formality or any embarrassment at the housekeeper's presence. 'You look a lot better this morning. Thank God for that! You had me . . . had us worried for a while last night.' He smiled. This time it was without the old watchfulness, as though the Captain was no longer hovering behind him and looking over his shoulder. I felt as though this powerful, awkwardly gentle man had reached out and touched me with some extra-ordinary quality of tenderness, enveloping me in warmth and a kind of tremulous excitement.

But that feeling didn't last very long, alas . . .

'Thank you . . . thank you for rescuing me.'

'I just happened to find you, that's all.' There was a subtle change in his smile, a hint of caution.

'My attacker . . . did you see who he was?' I asked, though I already anticipated his response.

'Attacker? I know nothing of an attacker, Miss Ainsley. I was out searching for you. I heard you stumbling through the bushes and I called out to you. You obviously had a bad fall, and when I found you, you were lying unconscious.' Carne looked at me in a kind of challenging manner, almost daring me to refute his statement.

And it was much the same when Captain Northwood and his son George paid me a visit shortly afterwards. When I tried to describe everything which had occurred Carne took over with the words: 'Easy enough to imagine all sorts of things and sounds when it's dark and you're scared. The important thing is that no harm came to you, Miss Ainsley.'

Captain Northwood nodded his head. 'An animal

nosing about in the bushes. Jem Forrest reported a stag in the trees a few days ago. That's probably what frightened you.' As though the final word on the affair had just been uttered the Captain stepped back from the bedside. I allowed his version of an animal in the woods to go unchallenged. It seemed the simplest, perhaps the wisest, thing to do. It was what they wanted me to believe. And if I was to survive here and safeguard myself against what was beginning to appear like some intricate conspiracy of silence, then I would have to pretend to believe whatever they wanted me to. That is, until such time as I could get away from Polmarran. That idea was already beginning to take root in my mind.

'I think we should leave Miss Ainsley to her rest now.'

Just before they withdrew, George Northwood sidled over to the side of my bed. All this time he had been standing in the background, staring vacantly out of the window. Now, for the first time, his troubled and compassionate gaze settled on me. 'I h-hope you will h-have a quick return to g-good health, Miss Ainsley. P-perhaps you might like to read this . . .'

He placed a small Bible on the counterpane beside my hand.

'Thank you. That's very kind.' I smiled wearily and then glanced down to find the Bible open and that his forefinger, with a kind of furtive twitch, was directing my attention to a passage already marked out with pen and ink in the margin.

As soon as they had all left the room I turned my attention to the page. The book was open at Chapter 4, *Philippians,* and the marked passages read:

> *Let your moderation be known unto all men. The Lord is at hand. Be careful of nothing; but in everything by prayer and supplication with thanksgiving let your requests be made known unto God.*

My instant reaction was something almost bordering on impiety. I was desperately anxious for some clue as to what precisely was going on here at Polmarran, what hidden forces posed some threat to me - and I needed something considerably more tangible and relevant to my predicament than these Bible verses. I read them a second time, slowly, word for word, trying to unearth some hidden meaning. There was none that I could see. Poor George. It was sweet of him of course, but so typically ineffectual. With a sigh, and my hands joined together, I tried to eradicate my sense of futility with a silent, half-hearted prayer. Oh well, I mused, my eyes looking down on the tiny demure little steeple of my pressed-together forefingers, I should at least be thankful for the fact that I had suffered nothing worse than a sprained ankle and a few scratches here and there.

Not long afterwards I was visited by the doctor, who came rambling in, to drop his beaver and medical bag on the foot of the bed and casually enquire after the same sprained ankle and the tattoo of criss-cross scratches on my arms. 'Well, well, sitting up and bright as a new penny, eh? Good, good. Feeling somewhat better this morning, eh?'

'Much better, thank you.'

'That's the spirit, m'dear.' In his triple-caped benjamin and dusty riding-boots Dr Howard looked more like a hearty squire than a country physician. A bluff garrulity seemed to be an integral part of his bedside manner and I quickly formed the impression that he placed as much confidence in its efficacy as he did in all his medicaments. 'No giddiness or mental confusion or headaches?'

'No, not really . . .'

'Good. Thought there might be a slight concussion last night.'

'I'm afraid I'm giving everyone a great deal of bother . . .'

'Bother? Nonsense! For my part I greatly enjoyed the ride over this morning. One of the great pleasures of a rural practice I always say. If only all my patients could be as pretty and bright as Polmarran's little invalid. A pleasure to be out and about on a morning like this, though there's a bite in the wind and a drop or two of rain in the offing if I'm not mistaken. And I seldom am. Still, it sharpens the appetite, eh? Now then, with your permission, I'll take another look at that ankle, m'dear . . . no, when you're ready, young lady . . . easy now, easy . . . ah, yes! Still badly swollen I see, but young bones mend quickest I always say. Not worried about the scratches? They'll heal up in a matter of days . . .' His eyes were more often on my face than on my injuries, studying me with kindly interest. 'The ankle still painful, eh?'

'Not very . . .'

'Something else bothering you, eh?'

'Well, Doctor, you see . . .' I hesitated.

'Come along. Out with it, m'dear. That's what I'm here for, isn't it?'

Rather foolishly I suppose, and with just sufficient nervous uncertainty to lend a faint note of incoherency, I started into an account of how I had received my injuries.

'The mind, young lady. All in the mind.' He interrupted me with an indulgent smile. His manner was amiable, incurious. It may have had something to do with his profession but I guessed him to be one of those men who accept without wonder whatever life sends along - in this case an over-imaginative, sensation-seeking female! 'All in the mind, m'dear. You see, miss, I have invariably found with the female that many of their maladies spring from the mind . . . mark you, sometimes with the male too. Take young Master George Northwood, for instance. And let me hasten to add that your bumps and scratches and your sprained ankle are very real ailments . . . no, what I question is the reasons which you put forward as having caused them . . .'

'I know very well what caused them, Doctor!'

'You were told that you look like Eliza Northwood, and it's true . . . you do look like her. But that idea took hold in your mind. Started to work in the imagination, you see. And then when you got lost in the woods, and with dusk coming on and all that . . . why, naturally you got frightened and confused. Devilish lonely place out there, I agree. Frighten old Nick himself, I wouldn't wonder. And then when you heard an animal coming through the brush towards you, or an owl hooting, or something like that . . .'

Physician, heal thyself! But I stifled my growing vexation and tried to put an end to his words with a quick nod of acceptance. 'Yes, Doctor. No doubt you are right. I must have imagined it all.' I hated myself for such abysmal surrender, but I found his matter-of-fact sincerity every bit as frustrating as the secretiveness of Redmond Carne and Captain Northwood.

'That's the spirit, m'dear! Once you toe the line with your fears and meet them head on you won't be long in giving them a finishing blow. And believe me, young lady, I can appreciate how a thing like this could play on your mind . . . if they weren't so damned reticent and evasive about their precious Eliza then people around here would forget all about her and her name wouldn't be invested with such mystery. Not that I ever considered her much of a mystery in spite of all her behaviour.'

'You knew her?' I asked, suddenly finding myself wholly attentive.

'Oh, everyone in these parts knew Eliza, or knew of her.' He smiled reflectively.

'What sort of a person was she?'

'Beautiful . . . beautiful to look at, at any rate. And when people tell you, m'dear, that you resemble her to a great degree then you are perfectly entitled to feel complimented.'

'Thank you, Doctor, but . . .'

'I know what you're thinking.' He checked my words with a forefinger jabbing bluntly in mid-air. 'But only in looks, m'dear. There the resemblance and the compliment ends. Eliza Northwood was wild and tempestuous. Sparkling wine in her veins instead of blood . . . deadly, poisonous wine.'

'Tell me about her. Please.'

Dr Howard nodded, smiled, sat down on the side of the bed and took out his snuff-box. 'Marec . . . Eliza Marec, or Marisch . . . that was her maiden name. Leastways that was the name she used hereabouts before her wedding. Foreign, I think. Of course to your natural-born Cornishmen everyone who hails from the east of the Tamar is a foreigner . . . a relatively insignificant river, I admit, but the Tamar cuts us off from Devon and the rest of England. But with Eliza I'm referring to real honest-to-goodness foreign. French, or Austrian or some such. A slight bit of an accent and all that. Just certain words, mark you . . . but it all helped to give her an air of mystery. We knew nothing whatsoever about her background. The usual rumours, of course.'

'Rumours?'

'Oh, you know the sort of thing . . . the daughter of an officer killed at Waterloo, or the mistress of some diplomat or other, a foreign countess living incognito, or a runaway opera singer from Italy. Oh yes, our little ma'mselle could sing and dance and play a tune as good as any of your fine ladies in London town. Sweet as a nightingale! And by the same token she could drink and swear like a dragoon when she had a mind to. My word, but what a woman she was!' He looked away, half-smiling, enjoying the memories. I couldn't help noticing how he kept referring to her in the past tense. Was Eliza dead?

139

'Where is she now?'

Dr Howard turned back to me, shrugging. 'Damned if I know . . . and for that matter I doubt if anyone else round here knows. Nobody knows except the Almighty or Lucifer - probably the latter, if you'll pardon my blunt talk.'

'Then you think she's dead?'

'I believe so.'

'I don't understand. If she was dead wouldn't you as the doctor know for certain? I mean, if you were called . . .'

'Let me explain to you about Eliza Northwood.' Dr Howard tapped the lid of his snuff-box before opening it. 'Brings a fine film of the best stuff to the top, you see . . .' He took a pinch and laid it on the back of his hand, then he brought it up to each nostril in turn. 'Ah! Mmmm . . . now then, yes - about Eliza Northwood. Splendid girl in most particulars, sound in wind and limb and the most accomplished horsewoman I've ever clapped eyes on. She could hunt a fox day or night, m'dear, through upwards of twenty parishes, then mark him to the spot, return with every hound yelping about her horse hooves, looking as pretty and fresh as when she'd set out in the morning, and then, without the least display of fatigue, she could laugh and dance right through until the next morning when she'd mount up and follow the chase again. She led a gay, whirligig existence. All part of an impromptu adventure that could whisk her off any place at a moment's notice in search of some new excitement. But there was another side to her nature, a less appealing side, I must confess . . .'

The doctor paused to raise more snuff to his discoloured nostrils. 'I have seen her standing by, laughing and shouting with delight as the dogs leaped to rip the flesh from their wounded quarry. Once, when we were working in a valley about twenty miles from here, we came upon a stag at bay under a bridge.

140

Fighting for its very life it was, a great big handsome beast that had already killed one hound and wounded another. Eliza was first to the bridge and already shouting like a madwoman when we rode up. We were in time to see her dismount and wade into the water and start lashing the stag across the face with her quirt. We could hear the blows striking off the animal's head. Between her efforts and the hounds the poor animal was dragged down by sheer ferocity and weight of numbers. Unbelievably cruel! And on another occasion . . .'

'Please, Doctor, I really do not wish to hear any more.'

'Just trying to illustrate my point, m'dear. Letting you know what sort of woman she was. You see, miss, Eliza crashed through life in the same manner as she took a hedge or a ditch or caught up with her quarry . . . head on and straight through. That was her style, and I hold that there is a logical inevitability to such a pell-mell mode of living. Sooner or later there has to be a fence which is too high, or a brick wall, or a ravine that's too wide . . . something that your impetuous madcap rider just cannot crash through or leap across.'

'And you think that perhaps that's the way she died?'

'I think so.'

'But you're not sure?'

'Nobody is. Had we found her body at the foot of a cliff or draped over a stone wall with her neck broken or whatever, why then we could have given her a Christian burial and been done with her. But, as was her custom, Eliza keeps us all guessing. She just seemed to leap into the unknown. And it's this confounded disappearance into thin air that's behind all the trouble hereabouts.'

'What do you mean by trouble?'

'With the local people, I mean. Why, there's never

141

a torn fishing net, or a crop failure or a hen that won't lay, but they attribute it to her! To Eliza Northwood. 'Pon my honour, miss, they have it that she's some kind of a witch still lurking about in the neighbourhood. Damned superstitious lot really, but there's no telling them otherwise. Her disappearance, you see. The not knowing for certain.'

'But how can you be so certain that she is dead?'

'Stands to reason, does it not? I mean, with that helter-skelter mode of living. I believe that she skipped off back to France or Italy or wherever it was she came from originally. Russia, I think. One of those damned foreign places, anyway. Got bored here, you see. After the birth of her child. Oh, she made no secret of the fact that she considered the baby a nuisance. Marriage, motherhood, widowhood, whatever . . . none of these things were allowed to stand in the way of her pleasure. The only thing that mattered to that girl was having whatever she wanted on the spur of the moment. Stands to reason that she went off on some other adventure, ran off with some other gay admirer.'

'Leaving no clue? Nothing of remembrance for her own child?'

'Nothing but rumours, m'dear. It's really no great wonder that so many of the simple and superstitious folk around here hold with all this nonsense about her being some kind of a witch and living at the top of Polmarran Tower with spiders and bats as her familiars.'

'The tower?'

'Aye, many of them believe so. Damned superstitious lot.' Without warning he pulled out his fob watch and glanced at it. 'So now, young lady, you know all there is to know about the mysterious Eliza Northwood. The facts and the nonsense . . . so there's no need for you to go imagining things any more just because you've been told that you look

142

like her. Remember what I said . . . all in the mind. Just toe the line with your fears and you'll soon give them a knock-out blow.' He stood up, stretched himself and then gathered up his hat and his bag. 'I'll be by again in a day or two to take another look at that sprain. In the meanwhile, your bed, young lady, and plenty of rest. That's the spirit. Good morning, m'dear.'

Chapter Eight

I was not finished with visitors, it seemed. Dr Howard had scarcely departed when Adelaide and Charles Northwood came to see me. Each carried a posy of wild flowers and Adelaide rushed towards me with outstretched arms.

'Oh, Katherine, just look at you!' She was on the verge of tears, her cry a tremulous compound of sympathy, awe, delicious excitement and distaste. 'Look at your poor arms! All those horrid scratches! If only you had taken me walking with you I would not have allowed you to get lost in the woods.'

'Yes, it was very silly and very naughty of me to go without you. It serves me right.' I feigned a look of the utmost penitence and won a smiling nod of forgiveness from her. Then, including Charles Northwood in a look that was full of meaning, I added: 'I assure you it will not happen again.'

Charles Northwood remained standing at the foot of the bed but said nothing. The noon light pouring into my room showed me the earnest set of his features. How youthful he looked, how like his brother George! So far I had always thought of him as a pleasure-loving libertine, undeniably handsome but sardonic and wilfully malicious too - now he surprised me. Something of concern and sympathy lit his eyes and with gentle sensitivity his fingers traced a nervous pattern on the side of the bed-post. Where was the customary jauntiness and truculence?

In that moment I found myself wondering if some finer feelings did not pulse deeply within him, a decency and self-respect that was locked in perpetual conflict with his passions.

I snapped out of my reflections with the words: 'The flowers are beautiful. Thank you.'

'Uncle Charles helped me to gather them, but I picked most of them for you. Didn't I, Uncle Charles?'

'Yes indeed, pet. So you did.'

'We went out early. Uncle Charles said you'd still be asleep and we did not want to disturb you. I rode on the horse with him, Katherine. Clip-clop, clip-clop, clip-clop. Her name is Empress. I picked all the little goldeny ones by myself, didn't I, Uncle Charles? Millions and millions and millions of them up near the little waterfall place.'

Charles came round from the end of the bed. 'How do you feel this morning?'

'Splendid.' I waved an ointmented arm airily. 'Should I not?'

'If I hadn't been drinking heavily and so determined on smashing up Jack Tregarron's counter, none of this would have happened. Whatever else about Carne he'd never defy my father by leaving you to find your own way home. But for the fact that I felt the most urgent matter last night was to fetch over Dr Howard, I would have gone to the Grange and called out that scoundrel Rebstock.' His eyes smouldered with anger. 'Be assured, Miss Ainsley, that I will challenge him at the first opportunity.'

'Not on my account,' I said, full of cool determination. 'I will not have it.'

'But he . . .'

'He said, and did, nothing beyond acceding to my request to be allowed to walk the last mile or so by myself. And, like a gentleman, he did so with some reluctance, but he respected my wishes in the matter.'

'But why?'

'Why did he respect my wishes or why did I want to walk back by myself?'

'The latter.'

'Simply because I like walking. I wanted to take the air.'

Adelaide, bored with all this talk, spied one of my bonnets lying on the chiffonier and danced over to it. 'May I, Katherine?'

'Certainly.'

She put it on and stood before the mirror for a few moments before turning once to the left, once to the right, and then executing a most elaborate curtsey.

Charles Northwood's gaze was still upon me. He seemed a trifle confused. 'I thought perhaps Rebstock might have said something, or tried to . . .'

'You are mistaken.'

With a kind of defeated shrug he said: 'I would have ridden over this morning and challenged the scoundrel, only I had a more pressing matter to attend to.'

'Yes, the posy is quite charming. Very thoughtful of you.' I smiled innocently as I watched the way his mouth tightened with exasperation.

Adelaide was a princess now, swaying before the long pier glass with that dedication to fantasy only a child can indulge in so delightfully.

'I'm sorry, Miss Ainsley, but I don't think I can accept that you just took it into your head to go strolling through the woods. Not just like that. There was some other reason, wasn't there?'

'Yes, perhaps there was . . .' I hesitated for just a moment as I tried to weigh up the effect my next words might have. 'I think I wanted a little time by myself so that I could take a final, farewell look at Polmarran and its surroundings.'

'Farewell?'

'I've decided to leave.' Instantly I knew that I

meant it. Adelaide hadn't heard, but I was afraid to look at her. I felt in some way that I was deserting her. Betraying her. I felt guilty.

'You can't leave, not now!'

'I can and I will. As soon as my ankle . . .'

'Why? Because they pretend not to believe you about being attacked?'

That took me by surprise. I looked up, no longer smiling, but peering into his face with a kind of desperate hope. 'Do *you*?'

'Yes.'

'Why should you when everyone else tries to convince me that it was nothing more than a lurking animal or my own imagination?'

'Because I rode up to the little waterfall early this morning and found signs - a man's footprints.' Charles Northwood leaned towards me, his voice lowered, so that the child might not overhear. 'While she was gathering flowers I poked around. In your panic you left an easily discernible trail. In point of fact, you were running blindly about in circles . . . bits and pieces of your clothing scattered here and there. And the footprints of your pursuer were clearly visible along your route.'

I lowered my gaze. It was a relief to know that at least one person believed my story, but the relief was hedged in by a swift return of last night's fear. Involuntarily my fingers went to my throat and gingerly traced the echoing weals of terror.

'Tell me, Katherine, did you see who it was?' He reached out with his hand and gently drew my fingers away from my throat. 'Who was it?'

I shook my head from side to side.

'You've no idea?'

'No.'

'Could it have been Rebstock?'

'It could have been anyone. I was far too scared to turn round.'

'Carne, maybe?'

147

'B-but why . . . why would anyone . . .?'

'Is this the only bonnet, Katherine?' Adelaide flounced back to the side of my bed, my broad-brimmed summer hat flopping about her ears. 'It's just a teeny bit too big, you see.'

'There's a little fur hat in the drawer beside the wardrobe, dear. And a lace one. You might also like to try on my blue shawl.'

'Oh yes! This time I shall be a countess from Austria!'

A countess from Austria. Eliza Marisch's daughter - I experienced an unwelcome pang of concern and sympathy for the child as I watched her depart, for at the same time I was recalling Sir Arthur Rebstock's words. *But who can say with any certainty that the late John Northwood was in fact the child's father?* Charles Northwood was following my gaze. Reading my thoughts?

'You have a way with that child. You're very fond of her, aren't you?'

'Yes, we have become good friends.'

'And yet you talk about leaving Polmarran?'

'Can you blame me after last night?'

'No, I can't.' Quite without warning he took my hand. 'But I'm asking you to stay. For Adelaide's sake.'

'Mr Northwood.' I said, retrieving my hand, 'I must remind you again that less than twenty-four hours ago I was violently attacked . . .'

'And if you leave now I fear that Adelaide will be similarly endangered.'

'Adelaide? Oh no!'

'Oh yes, Katherine. Look, I tried to warn you before - I wasn't sure of what exactly, and I'm still not sure - but I believe you were brought here because of your resemblance to Adelaide's mother, that you were attacked last night because of that resemblance, and that it's just possible Eliza's daughter may also be attacked.'

The effect of his words was one of numbing fear. It was one thing to flee from whatever danger threatened me, quite another to abandon the child to the same danger. No, I would have to remain. I had no choice, even if I was liable to some unknown calamity (and all the more frightening for being unknown!) But how long would I have to stay here?

Once again he seemed to be divining my thoughts. 'Only for two weeks. That's all.'

'Why two weeks?'

'Well, for one thing your injuries will put considerable constraint upon your movements for at least a week. Dr Howard says you must have plenty of rest.'

'And the second week?'

'I have to go away for two weeks. Three, at the very most. When I return I expect to have the answers to all our questions and to put an end to all the mystery.'

'How?'

'Please, you must trust me. I'm with you in this thing. And I promise that, when I return, you and the child will no longer be in any danger.'

'But when you say away . . . what then? You can't promise that we won't be in any danger then, can you?' I turned to him, a thread of irony woven into my anxious tone.

'Yes, I can . . . if you both stay close to each other and remain here in the house all the time. Be vigilant, Katherine, and don't let them suspect anything.'

'Them . . . suspect . . . vigilant! This is too much, Mr Northwood! If I am to remain here, vulnerable to some physical menace, to being watched or spied upon, or threatened in some way . . . and all because of my resemblance to a woman I have never met, then I think I am entitled to know more about it.'

'Yes, I know, but . . .'

'And if that poor child is in any danger whatsoever,

149

then why can't you take her away with you? I don't understand any of this!'

'Please, Katherine, it's better this way. You must trust me.' With a kind of desperate and impatient emphasis he smacked the closed fist of one hand into the open palm of the other, stood up, and then began to pace about for a few moments. He turned round again, calmer in his manner. 'Besides, Katherine, the child will be safe here with you, and you can't leave here for the present, can you? Not with that ankle.'

'We couldn't travel more than a few miles before they'd overtake us.'

'They? You mean your father and Redmond Carne . . . really, I cannot believe they would harm or upset Adelaide in any way. No, it's unthinkable!' I bit down on my lip, close to tears, confused, not knowing where to turn or what to believe or in whom I could trust. It must have been all there in my expression.

'Whether you like it or not, Katherine, I'm the only one here you can trust. Brother George is too far gone. They've already destroyed him. It has to be me, Katherine.'

'Please stop calling me by my Christian name!' It was a silly, unreasonable thing to say but I could not help myself.

'As you wish, Miss Ainsley.' He squared his shoulders with just a suggestion of the old arrogance. The swagger came back into his step as he turned again and walked back down to the foot of the bed. He looked back over his shoulder and smiled. 'Funny, really . . . yesterday morning I half-wrecked the taproom at The Crown and thrashed a loose-tongued drunkard for daring to use your Christian name in a careless and disrespectful manner.' His concluding smile was one of mockery - self-mockery.

'I'm sorry. I didn't mean to . . .'

150

But my words were cut off by the sound of voices from the parlour. 'Look, Grandpapa, I am a Russian princess! Katherine said I could . . .' Adelaide reappeared at the open bedroom door caparisoned in the fur hat and blue shawl. She swept into the room with all her make-believe regality, followed by Captain Northwood and Redmond Carne.

'Did I not say to you that Miss Ainsley was not to be disturbed? The doctor says she must have complete rest.' Captain Northwood confronted his son with a stern reprimand.

'No doubt, Father, but I'm equally sure that old Howard did not say I was to be prohibited from paying my respects to our charming invalid before I departed.'

'Pay your respects then, and be off.'

Carne added: 'Forrest has your horse saddled and ready.'

'Indeed, Redmond, my old salt, I'm deeply touched by these tremendous efforts to detain me. I regret, though, that I must be off and away on some very urgent matter.' He switched his meaningful look from Carne's face to mine, and then with a bow in my direction, he smiled. 'Good day, Miss Ainsley. I trust that on my return I will find you completely recovered.' He took Adelaide by the hand. 'As for you, my pet, I shall bring you a *real* princess's ball gown.'

Carne was the last one to leave the room. 'Well, miss . . . everything ship-shape and sea-worthy, eh?'

'No, Mr Carne. I am all at sea.'

'Aye?'

I lay back and closed my eyes - tired, retreating. He closed the door softly behind him.

I kept my eyes closed, trying to shut out thought and to clench them firmly against all my uncertainties. A short while later I heard the sound of horse hooves on the gravel outside, and then the steady drumming of departure, and my hope and confidence diminished with their sound. How I envied Charles Northwood his freedom! His estrangement, the absence of any real filial bond with his father, meant that he had no real ties here - neither Carne's loyalty and sense of duty nor George's dependence. Above all he was temporarily free of that unseen, imprisoning circle which seemed to be slowly moving around me, and which, like some dark web, might pull me into its horrifying centre . . .

Two weeks. Three at the very most, he had said. No, he had promised.

Those two weeks must surely have been the longest and most eventful of my whole life. Also, the most unnerving. Nights - when I was unable to sleep - were the worst. When the house was hushed. I would still lie there, listening for the sound of careful hands at a window, of footsteps slow and stealthy on the gravel below my window, of someone waiting outside my bedroom door. Sometimes even the most ordinary sounds - the distant sound of a door opening, or closing, or the night wind against the shutters downstairs, or a vine rasping across a pane of glass, any little sound at all - would be invested with the most dreadful menace. It was like one continuous nightmare, a twilight time of waking and dozing fitfully and sitting up in bed, horrified to see shadowy figures in my room. Too horrified to scream as my eyes burned anxiously with efforts to focus, only to discover that the spectral figures were nothing more than the curtains billowing as they let in the night air.

I would wake suddenly and in a cold sweat, my strained hearing trying to catch at voices muttering unintelligibly close at hand and then discover that it was nothing more than the windows rattling faintly in the breeze, or the wind like a sad piping echo through the trees, or the distant thunder of the surf against the rocks.

Had Dr Howard been right after all? Was I beginning to imagine things? Was it all in my mind? Or was Polmarran House moving slowly into life, gradually and by insensible degrees releasing that germ of malevolence which it had nurtured for so long, requiring only my presence here for its fruition?

Towards the end of that first week I forced myself to get up and I began to hobble and limp about my quarters; but to look from my window (which gave out on to the dark and wooded hills) was to be reminded constantly of how I had come by my present injuries, and my partial mobility in no way lessened the sensation of my imprisonment.

On the Saturday morning, despite the protestations of all my self-appointed nurses (or gaolers?) - Captain Northwood, Redmond Carne and Mrs Forrest - I made my way downstairs. For my foolhardiness in disregarding the doctor's advice I was punished by a stony silence from my employer during breakfast. Later, when I repaired to the library in a determined effort to take up my duties again where I'd left off, I was given yet another indication of just how much a prisoner I was. Jem Forrest joined me there and from the outset - for one thing he didn't trouble himself with a tap on the door or a 'by your leave' - his manner was clearly that of a fellow who still disputed a schoolma'am's right to take over what had once been his 'hide-away'. He came shambling in, wearing the inevitable makeshift livery on his bulky frame, and a derisive scowl on his features, as he surveyed the bookshelves.

'Yes, Forrest, what is it?'

'You meanin' to go to church tomorrow, ma'am?'

'Certainly. Why do you ask?'

'The Cap'n and Mr Carne sends me aboard with apologies in that case, and likewise sez for me to pass along their regrets on account of how there'll be no conveyance for you.'

'I'm afraid I don't quite understand.'

'Axle-box, ma'am. The carriage be needing a job of repair work that'll take me best part of a whole week to put to rights. Though where I'm to lay my hands on all the proper tools and such-like, seeing as how they've been a-shifted out of their rightful place . . .' He gave a sly little grin and rubbed his hand along one of the shelves.

'Thank you, Forrest.'

So, I was to be cut off from the outside world, from Marrambridge and the Reverend Cooper's church! I knew instinctively that someone was lying - the Captain or Carne or this butler with the lopsided manners, it didn't matter greatly who - and I knew too that any enquiries about alternative transport - a saddle mount, hay-wain, dog-care, anything - would almost certainly meet with a litany of pre-arranged and plausible excuses. For an instant I considered running down the list of possible alternatives just to see if I could fluster him, but a combination of pride, stubbornness and a flash of anger dissipated the impulse. 'Very well, Forrest. Will that be all?'

'Aye, ma'am. Pity about that there axle-box. Could have it as smart as new paint if I knowed rightly where to lay my hands on all my bits and pieces.'

'I take your point, Forrest. And now if you'll excuse me, I have some matters to attend to.'

'So-ho, ma'am. Attend away with your matters then. You'll find Jem Forrest knows his place and will be slipping off out of your way . . . same as did them high-and-mighty Rebstocks as came a-calling yesterday . . .' He uncovered his yellowed, tobacco-stained teeth with another leery grin. 'There's a thing now, ma'am . . . you could've gone churchwards to-morrow with Sir Arthur had the Cap'n bid them come aboard.'

154

'What do you mean?'

'The high-and-mighty, ma'am. Came yesterday to pay respects to yourself 'ccount of you being invalid-like. But the Cap'n fired one across their bows in a manner of speaking and then gives the order for them to turn about, seeing as how he holds Sir Arthur accountable for casting you adrift last time out . . .' He chuckled at the recollection and I caught the stale whiff of tobacco and spirits from his breath as he drew nearer. 'Oh, a handsome sight it were, ma'am! To see them two turning tail before our Cap'n. Clap them in irons our skipper would for such scurvy treatment to one of us here.'

'But if the Rebstocks called to see me, then I think I should have been at least consulted in the matter.'

'Consult, is it, ma'am? Ho-ho, our Cap'n is not much given to consulting when all hands are standing by to repel boarders . . . and them same boarders only supposing to be paying respects when all the time they be up to their old tricks of spying.'

'Spying?'

'Spying and 'grudging us Northwood people for capturing their prize . . . this here hulk of stones. Aye, ma'am, as I'm alive they'll never forgive us for that. Always skulking about the place at every chance they be, and fully laden with jealousy of what we have. 'Specially the child.'

'Adelaide?'

'Aye, ma'am. The young mistress. A bitter taste in the Rebstock mouths from knowing that Mistress Eliza's baby stands to gain all that ever was or is to be of Polmarran.'

Adelaide, an heiress - is that what Charles meant when he said that she might be in danger? And there was something else he'd said. What was it? Yes, that night in the dining-room when he'd arrived with the Rebstocks, something about being 'written back into the will' and then he had turned to Redmond

Carne to add: *'Well, Redmond my old salt . . . it seems that you have not entirely replaced myself and poor brother George after all.'*

Jem Forrest interrupted my train of thought; he was still muttering away, loquacious and confidential, convincing me by his manner that he was already partly drunk. 'Aye, your pupil, ma'am. Her as has taken a great fancy to your own good self stands to gain thousands and thousands, for the Cap'n fairly prospered in his voyagings.'

'Why are you telling me all this?'

'Why, ma'am? Why, 'cause you're a noticing lass and 'cause my missus says I'm to be civil with you at all times.' He looked sideways at me, no longer grinning, but advancing his bulky frame within a few inches of me so that the brass buttons of his faded coat almost touched my arm.

I moved uneasily to one side. 'Thank you, Forrest. I appreciate your civility, but I think we should now leave off this discussing of the Northwood family matters. After all, they really do not concern us.'

'Don't they, ma'am?'

'I think not. And now once again I must ask you to excuse me. I have so much to attend to here.'

'As you please, ma'am. You'll find I knows my place . . . and knows a lot more as concerns all the high-and-mighty hereabouts. And you may lay to that,' he said through his pursed lips as though wishing to show that, however great my curiosity or his own desire to strike up some familiarity, I had just forfeited an excellent opportunity of having both desires satisfied. 'Just trying to be civil as instructed and paying no mind to the fact that all of my fine things had to be scattered far and wide to make room for a worthless cargo of old vollums.'

'That will be all, Forrest. You may leave now.'

He walked over to the door, and then turned round for one parting shot. 'Can't rightly say how long that axle-box will take for mending . . . seeing as how I can't lay my hands on the correct tools. Might be upwards of two weeks or more.'

'I shouldn't worry about it,' I blithely returned, my nose already in a book. 'No doubt the Rebstocks will call on me again.'

The door closed behind him with a sound that was well on the way to being a heavy slam.

I had no way of knowing for certain if Forrest reported everything of our conversation to my employer. I rather suspected that he had. No doubt, with embellishments. Nothing was ever said, of course, but the feeling of being constantly watched invested the house with a great oppressiveness. I met with the Captain, Mr George, and Redmond Carne only at meal-times during the next few days. It was always with great reluctance, for what little conversation we had was neither relaxed nor cheerful. It seemed as if we were all engaged in some tense game of watching and waiting. The Captain scarcely ever looked directly at me and rarely addressed me beyond the minimal courtesies required at table. Even his occasional miniature lectures on nautical matters had ceased. To give Redmond Carne his due, he sometimes tried to maintain a pretence of affability but was more often than not inhibited by Captain Northwood's frowning aloofness.

But it was Mr George who most disturbed me. Why, I did not know. I could see that he was somehow afraid of the other two - afraid when in their company to make any worthwhile response to my forced casualness. Oh yes, I persisted heroically in maintaining a kind of supreme, yet dignified, nonchalance. I was deliberately - magnificently - unaware of anything being amiss, had put that silly little matter of being scared by an animal in the woods completely behind me. I was almost gay before them, trying to out-manoeuvre them with studied charm, to best them with all the armoury at woman's disposal. Yes please, I would appreciate some more wine. Just a drop, if you please. Oh, thank you, and is this a good vintage, Captain Northwood? I feel sure it is but I really know so little of such things. And do you think this fine spell will continue into next month, Mr Carne? You don't? Oh, what a pity! It would shorten the winter so, don't you think? Yes, Miss Adelaide is progressing admirably. My ankle? Much better now, thank you. Hardly notice it at all.

But I wasn't sure how long I could keep up the charade. All I knew was that the next move would have to be up to one of them. Which one? The Captain, perhaps. Or Carne, acting under the inevitable orders, naturally. Mr George? Hardly . . .

At meals he spent practically all his time with his eyes averted, trying desperately to remain outside that area which the rest of us warily contested with skirmishing looks. Poor George. He seemed quite confused and frightened of it all. Frightened? I wasn't sure, but whenever I looked across at him, I had the feeling that something from his past life was sunk deeply into his heart and soul and that it now stared vacantly from his troubled eyes. Once or twice I surprised him as he watched me covertly. Surprised him and alarmed myself a little at such times for he had such a rigid, ghastly stare. And yet he appeared to be looking not directly at me, but at something beyond me.

At what?

Yet another question, and by now I had so many of them that I was almost ready to concede victory in the uneven contest between my own uncertainties and the dark silences of Polmarran. The only thing that I could be certain of was that the Rebstocks had called on me yesterday and had been turned away unceremoniously, that Polmarran's one carriage was to be denied me for more than a week, that even had I the will to walk away from this place my injured ankle would be against me, and finally, that Charles Northwood (my somewhat dubious ally) would not return for at least a fortnight. Until then I was virtually a prisoner.

But in spite of the sensation of being trapped by the inexplicable I came almost to welcome those meal-time meetings with the other members of the household, for there were places here infinitely more disquieting than the bizarre dining-room with its voodoo masks grinning hideously in the wavering candle-light. I dared not venture out on to the front lawn or go near the orchard again with Adelaide; the surrounding woodland was dense and peopled with unknown terrors, and looking from the windows it appeared to be creeping closer to the house each evening. Nor had I any wish to go down near the cove, down to the dark rocks and the angry sea. I knew instinctively that, from the uppermost window of the tower, a glint of pale light would be shining in the dusk like a tiny, eerie eye - watchful and menacing as it regarded my every movement.

Chapter Nine

Towards the end of the second week of Charles Northwood's absence the weather finally broke. The rain was unremitting, shrouding the woods and the hills in darkness.

I don't know exactly how I got through that week. Each night I locked and bolted my door, and once, because of the noises, I found myself taking the heaviest of the fire-irons and placing it beside me under the counterpane. I'm not sure how to describe those sounds - voices, I think - muffled and indistinct and accompanied by other faint noises which suggested someone constantly pacing to and fro, and the creaking of a heavy door, opening, closing, cutting off the trailing echo of a person weeping in some distant corner of this sprawling house.

Only once did it appear as though the noises emanated from outside. It was past midnight when I woke suddenly from a fitful slumber to the unmistakable sound of footsteps on the gravel just below my window. The faint mumble of low-pitched voices drifted upwards. I had the momentary impression of someone outside, watching my room, then slowly moving away. At first, with the recollection of my being spied upon that day at the waterfall still so painfully vivid, I lay rigid, undecided, scared. But curiosity and the comparative security of a first-floor bedroom within sheer massive walls urged me to leave my bed and take a look.

I slipped out of bed, limped over to the window and edged my way to one side of it. The bedroom was dark and the flooring creaked in the night air, brittle with my fear. Concealed by the darkness and the heavy curtains, I peered out through a narrow opening. The rain had ceased, but black clouds hung over the night sky like an evil canopy. After a few moments, my vigil was rewarded by a glimpse of two figures moving among the trees at the end of the lawn as though circling the house and heading in the general direction of the tower. They were only in view for a few seconds. I could not make out who they were, but one was certainly tall enough to be either Redmond Carne, Sir Arthur Rebstock, or Captain Northwood. The other, furthest from me, and first to disappear among the trees, was much shorter, slightly built, and almost completely enveloped in a full-length topcoat or a cloak.

I remained at the window for nearly a quarter of an hour but did not see them again. Shivering, I returned to bed. But not to sleep. There were no further disturbing noises that night, only a hollow silence throughout the house which was equally disquieting. Lying there, unable to sleep, the heavy fire-iron within easy reach, I found it an all-too-easy thing to imagine Polmarran House being hushed like a living thing. Could a house brood and become embittered from long years of mute begging for noisy laughter, and music, and loud footsteps, for all the gaiety of the Rebstock years? If it had been desecrated by tragedy and gloom, would it repay its desecrators with a deeper oppressiveness, its heart hardening into granite while it waited for revenge? The first pale gleam of dawn was touching the window frames before I fell asleep.

It was the following night that Adelaide came to my room. During that week I had spent practically every possible daylight moment with her, alternating games and amusements with the more mundane stuff of tuteluge, and all the while trying to hide from her my own nervousness. In our separate ways we had come to depend on each other greatly. Even so, I had not expected a visit from her at night, though, looking back on it all, I realize now that there was an element of fate, a kind of logical inevitability, in that visit and its awful consequences.

'One moment, please.'

I arranged the collar of my gown about my neck and, as I hurried over to the door, I tied the belt in place, knotting it and smoothing it about my waist.

'Adelaide?'

'Yes.' Through the heavy oaken door her voice sounded far away, yet the whispered entreaty penetrated with all the stark clarity of a cry for help.

'Just a moment, dear.' I tried to unlock the door with a minimum of sound but the key scraped loudly and I was suddenly experiencing a mixture of guilt and silliness. Whatever would the child think? 'Well, well. This is indeed an unexpected surprise. And at this hour!'

Adelaide came slowly into my room. I watched her thin white legs moving hesitantly beneath the ruffled gown. Her eyes were fixed on the key still in my hand and her brows were drawn together, angled and tense with dismay. 'Do you always lock your door, Katherine?'

'Habit, I suppose.' I shrugged and smiled, trying to veer away from admission on the one hand and falsehood on the other. 'And now, my dear young lady, should you not be fast asleep at this hour? If your grandfather knew!' I held out my arms to her.

'I can't sleep.' Adelaide responded to my welcoming smile with something of relief, yet her lip was trembling, even after she had crept into my arms. 'Please,

Katherine, may I sleep in your room tonight?' There
was a faint flush to her cheeks and her eyes burned
brightly as she searched my face. 'Oh, please, Katherine! Nobody need know and I promise to be good.
Please may I?'

'Very well, dear, if you wish.' I closed the door
behind her, taking care not to lock it this time, and
I drew her over to the fire. 'Cold?'

She shook her head, the perfection of her pretty
mouth marred a little by the still quivering lip.

'What then?'

'I am so frightened.'

'Why? What frightened you?'

'Are you not frightened, Katherine?'

'No, what is there to be frightened of?'

'But you locked your door. Do you have to do
that every night?'

'It's not locked now. I'll show you.' I went back
to the door.

'Lock it then. Please, Katherine!'

'Very well, if it makes you feel better.' I felt
deceitful, knowing that it made me feel a lot better
too. 'Tell me, Adelaide, what has frightened you?'

'I don't know. The noises I think.'

'I haven't heard anything.'

'No, last night. And the night before.'

So, I was not alone in my uneasiness. Adelaide
too, I thought, with a kind of grim and melancholy
satisfaction. It strengthened the already firm bond
that held us together, making us allies and partners
in dread of the unknown. But for her sake it was
imperative that I conceal my own anxieties. I actually
laughed. 'I suspect it's Forrest poking about in search
of all his bits and pieces. You remember, when Captain
Northwood asked him to vacate the library . . .'

'No, Katherine, it's not that.'

'Your grandfather and Redmond Carne playing at
being sailors again, then? You know, "shiver me

163

timbers and splice the mainbrace, me hearties". . . '
I tried to mime a seafarer's rolling gait. 'Grown men
can be just like little boys at times. Play-acting and
marching up and down pretending that they're on the
poop-deck and . . .'

'They've locked poor Georgie in that horrid old
tower as well!'

Her words stopped me in my tracks. What did she
mean by *as well?*

'You mean . . . do you mean that there is someone
else in the tower?' I was surprised by the calmness
of my own voice. It seemed totally unrelated to the
sudden stab of horror caused by her words - words
urgently whispered as though the night might be
listening, full of menace. Poor George locked in the
tower! With whom?

Eliza?

No, I decided hurriedly while flinching before the
remembrance of Dr Howard's casual remark and the
enormity of my own suspicions. No, it was too un-
believable, too unreal! The only reality was the cold
fear in the pit of my stomach.

Adelaide was looking at me steadily now, unblinking. 'Is there something wrong, Katherine? You look
so pale.'

'Adelaide, you said just now that Mr George was
locked in the tower . . .'

'Yes.'

'And you said *as well* . . .' I was speaking as evenly
as I could. 'Do you mean that there is somebody
else in there too?'

'In the old tower? Who?'

'Oh, Adelaide . . . please!'

She looked confused and hurt by my exasperation.

'Oh, I'm sorry, my dear . . . but please, who's in
the tower?'

'Only George as far as I know.'

'But you distinctly said *as well!*'

'As well as all the old furniture and things. That's what I meant, Katherine. They've locked poor Uncle Georgie in there with all the old rubbish that they no longer have any use for. Ugh, it's horrible!'

'Have you been in the tower?'

'Yes, but never at night. I would be too scared, Katherine. But I could show you in the morning. When it's bright. And it could be our secret and they need never know. I know how to get in. At the very tip-top of the house there's a landing and a little wooden door and I could show you. They need never know. You wouldn't tell them, Katherine, would you?'

'Do you mean your grandfather and Mr Carne?'

'Uh-huh. Will you tell?'

'Of course not. But tell me, Adelaide, why would they put your Uncle George in the tower?'

'I don't know.' She shrugged her shoulders, her eyes full of innocent candour, incomprehension, resignation in the face of the unknown ways of adult behaviour. Good lord, I thought, what an unnatural and nightmarish existence her young life must be in this place!

I hugged her to me protectively. 'My dear child, I think you must be mistaken in all this. I feel sure your grandfather and Mr Carne would never do such a thing. Not to George.'

'They did it once before. I remember it. It frightened me, Katherine.'

'Well, I won't let anything frighten you.' I meant it. Gently I tilted her chin and read trust in her expression. 'That's better, my dear. I promise I will not let anything harm you. Ever!'

'And you promised that I could sleep here?'

'Yes.'

Her arms encircled my neck and she kissed my cheek lightly. 'And will you read to me, Katherine?'

'I'd love to. Come.'

I carried her to my bed and tucked her in. In a little while she was yawning, warm, secure, feeling fussed over, her fingers relaxed and playing with the satin border of the bedspread as I read to her. My mind was not on the fairy-tale, but revolving around the inexhaustible theme of Polmarran Tower and its secrets. If what Adelaide said was true, then George was a prisoner. And I had no reason to doubt my pupil. Had I not already seen Redmond Carne accompanying George as a gaoler would, a gun cradled in his arms? John Northwood's gun. And Charles had mentioned something about how they had already *destroyed* his younger, more sensitive brother. Also (though I knew how improbable and far-fetched the notion was in reality) I still had to contend with the growing suspicion that Eliza Northwood might still be alive and suffering some kind of incarceration or banishment within the seclusion of the tower. I tried to argue against it. How could Captain Northwood conceal the presence of such a prisoner for so long . . . what about food, linen, clothing? Mrs Forrest as housekeeper and cook would have to know, wouldn't she?

I arrived at no end of logical suppositions to explain away my fears, but yet so many salient questions remained. Why did they discourage all mention of Adelaide's mother, even to the child? Why had Captain Northwood been so insistent that I never go near the tower, and so anxious to convince me that I had not been attacked by someone who had mistaken me for Eliza?

If only Charles were here to make sense of all this! To advise and help us. All I had now was my promise to the child that I would let nothing harm her and my determination to find some way of aiding George Northwood.

When I discovered that Adelaide was sleeping soundly I put the story book aside. I paced about for some time, knowing that I would be unable to sleep. My mind was full of the child's disclosures and the conviction that the answers to Polmarran's secrets were only to be found in the tower. This conviction, and the knowledge that Polmarran and almost everything pertaining to it and its occupants had already exerted some strange and baleful influence over this poor child and her Uncle George decided me. I would go the the tower. This very night!

Stealth and secrecy were of the essence. For that reason I decided against taking a lantern with me when I slipped quietly from my room a full hour after I had seen Adelaide safely to sleep.

The night was admirable for my purpose. The rain had ceased and there was just enough pale moonlight entering through the windows and illuminating the route along the gallery to the back-stairs; then on up to the next floor, along another deserted and little-used corridor, and finally up a short flight of stairs turning to the left and opening on to a narrow landing which ended against the ancient brickwork of the tower. My progress to that point was painfully slow. For some reason, I failed to convince myself that all were sleeping; I kept imagining that the Captain and Carne and a half-drunken Jem Forrest were likewise creeping about the place, bent on heaven-only-knew what dark errand. I paused frequently to listen for footsteps behind me, or voices. Thankfully, there were none.

Very little light penetrated to the landing on which I now found myself, but there was still sufficient to allow me to discern the shadowy outline of a doorway set into the rough-hewn wall, and enough dust to the touch of my trembling fingers to indicate years of neglect. Yes, trembling - for I had always imagined the tower to be a place where bats roosted and rats scurried about undisturbed, a place of dank cobwebs and nameless insects. Now that I was actually here I found myself wondering if I would have the courage to try the door and to discover what lay beyond. Full of foreboding and the beginning of fear I hesitated, and yet I knew that tonight of all nights I could not afford to be timorous. So much depended on my exploration. *The Lord is at hand. Have no anxiety about anything* - with one deep breath to summon up the scant measure of courage still remaining, I reached out quickly for the door handle. I think it was with much more disappointment than satisfaction that I beheld it fall back from the pressure of my hand, for had it been secured, I could have returned to the comparative safety of my room with the feeling of having at least tried to get to the bottom of things. I could still turn back. But as I waited anxiously, listening to the echo of creaking hinges which seemed to reverberate through every corner of the house, I knew, that I might never have this opportunity again. Or the degree of folly and determination which had carried me this far.

The moment of truth had arrived - and I passed through into the cavernous shadows, easing the door back into position behind me but without actually closing it. I forced my eyes to survey everything calmly.

Before me an archway of sorts spanned a pool of dark shadows. The faint outline of some half-dozen stone steps rose from the shadows. I walked over and climbed them. Gradually my sight adjusted to the pervading gloom, but at first it was more through the sense of touch that I learned to distinguish the dark, derelict masses of old furniture strung out along the walls - broken chairs, tallboys, discarded picture frames, a couple of old sea chests, and various other items of household bric-à-brac. A mass of cobwebs spread their intricate patterns over the furniture and draped across the low ceiling. To my nervous state of mind each shadow was a giant spider and the scuttling noises ahead of me were rats moving off to some future place of ambush.

Only a burning determination to forge ahead and discover all there was to know kept my fear in check. I moved slowly and cautiously, only once crying out in fright when a giant black spider, its bloated body suspended malignantly just a few inches from my face, seemed to waver between retreat and attack. I helped the creature come to a decision by picking up a piece of stick and tapping the furthest place from me on the cobweb. I jumped back with alarm as the spider's body made an ugly-sounding plop on the stone floor. When the rustling sound of its retreat faded in the darkness I drew a deep breath and prayed fervently through it that I might encounter nothing more frightening.

I reckoned that I had entered the tower about midway up and that I was on some kind of winding staircase. From the thickness of the walls it was apparent that the original Sir Arthur, Rebstock the Wrecker, had no intention of seeing his massive tower wrecked by man or nature; his builder had the foresight to fashion a structure strong enough to withstand the ferocity of the worst possible gales and even a siege.

Forcing myself to think about such things and how in the old days the Rebstock smugglers must have hauled up their kegs of brandy and contraband lace from some entrance near sea level, I climbed up on one of the chairs and looked out from one of those narrow windows which were deeply embedded in the massive walls. I caught a glimpse of the dark, boiling sea below, and drew back with a shiver when I recalled that the tower was built right on the cliff's edge, falling sheer to the jagged rocks and the foaming white crests of the angry, swirling waters. If Captain Northwood and Redmond Carne were correct in their reference to fallen masonry and rotting timbers then I would have to proceed very carefully.

I continued my ascent for a few more minutes, slowly, nervously; then worked my way back down past the low-hanging arch which marked my point of entry, all the time following the flagstones down towards sea level - but not all the way, and certainly never straying too far from the doorway by which I had gained access. In this way I carried out my cautious explorations for nearly thirty minutes, discovering the interior of the tower to be made up of small, cell-like rooms, damp stone passages, low arches, the entire place constructed in what appeared to be a higgledy-piggledy fashion (as though different rooms had been added at separate times in its history) and all parts linked together by this spiralling artery of a staircase.

All about me the shadows lurked amongst the rough stones and forgotten furniture. What scant light there was to aid me came from those narrow little windows positioned at regular intervals along the outer walls, mere slits of paler shade amongst the black-grey walls. I peered into every dark corner, tried different doors, listened, continued on, searched, but I could find no sign of recent occupancy or use, nothing to substantiate Adelaide's story of George Northwood's imprisonment. Or anyone else's for that matter.

Had I, after all, been the victim of some wild imaginings? Mine, as much as the child's? I think I was eager enough just then to believe so and to find some excuse for quitting this dreary place and returning to my own room. Though I had not ventured to the furthest reaches of the tower (nowhere could I find the courage to go right to the very top, to that one, evil-looking window which looked out over so much of the countryside!) I had descended the staircase to a point which I reckoned to be level with the first floor of the house, and I now considered that there was nothing more to detain me. I turned about and started back up again with a strange commingling of relief and disappointment. The place apparently held no great mystery, no secrets. All my vague theories and suspicions were groundless. Vanquished.

I had scarcely covered more than a half dozen slow paces when I was instantly arrested by a sharp sound arising from the depths below me. The sound of a key grating in a lock! A door was being unbolted somewhere. A mumble of voices drifted upwards, then footsteps mounted the stairs, the staccato crunch of heavily nailed boots on the bare stones, coming towards me!

I knew that I could never make it to the doorway which led back into the house, not without being overheard or overtaken, so I immediately cast about for some place of concealment. On all sides I was hemmed in by a shadowy blackness. No, not complete blackness. There was a faint, spreading illumination, wavering, growing - the glow from a lantern swinging to the harsh rhythm of the scrunching footsteps. It reached out ahead of the walker, twisting round the curved wall of the tower immediately beneath me. At any moment now . . .

I pressed against the wall, my hands splayed out and flattened against the damp stones for support. Desperately I looked for a hiding place. But the unresponsive darkness diminished and was turned into a ghastly yellow-grey by the approaching light.

A blessing in disguise, that light! It revealed what had been hitherto concealed by the unfathomable shadows - another archway, and beyond that a short gallery or corridor with two narrow doorways facing each other from opposite walls. I ran through the arch and wrenched at the handle of the nearest door. Locked!

Would the second be the same? I dashed over to it.

Any noise which my panic may have caused was surely drowned by the series of alarming sounds reaching from the stairway just behind me. In quick succession, so quick, in fact, as to be all of a piece, I heard the scuffling of footsteps, the metallic ring of the lantern crashing against the stone, then a human sound, half-sob, half-groan, which was one with the sharp smack of a hand against flesh and bone as though a face had been harshly struck. With the corner of my eye I caught a glimpse of the lantern's glow jerking violently just outside the archway.

'No! Please!' The anguished sob was sliced in two by another slap. As it trailed off into a submissive whimper, and the sound of two bodies struggling just outside on the narrow twist of stairs ceased almost as abruptly as it had begun, the second doorway opened to my frantic touch. With a muted sob of relief I flung my body through the opening and into the protective blackness of a tiny cell. I stood there, panting, my courage shaken. I had the door almost closed again, when, through its narrowing gap, I saw the light flooding the area outside, heard the loud footsteps, the heavy breathing. All so dangerously close. Whoever it was had just entered through the archway.

Something deeper than terror stirred inside me. I dared not close the door fully for fear of making a sound. I stood stock still, holding my breath and trying to stifle the rising tumult inside, the unbidden cry which would surely betray me. I bit into my lower lip. My eyes were riveted on the bar of light showing through the narrow opening.

'No, don't lock it! Please!'

George Northwood's voice!

'Do as I say. Get in.' Carne's answering tone was harsh and brittle with anger.

'Please, Redmond. Don't lock me in tonight.'

George came into view. He was clad in a long,

black greatcoat; the lower part of his face was hidden by the raised collar, his shoulders slumped in capitulation. Then Carne appeared. His broad back was to me, suddenly blocking off the view of the younger man, and so close to me that I could quite easily have stretched out my arm and touched his shoulder. But there was no such impulse. I was too scared even to breathe.

'Come now, George. No more nonsense. In with you.'

I heard the jangle of keys and the door opening. Then Carne moved so that I could see past him. He was pushing George Northwood ahead of him into a small room which I guessed to be of similar proportions to my own hiding place. But there the similarity ended. Whereas I could scarcely move more than a few short paces in my cramped hiding place due to the haphazard pile-up of old and musty-smelling furniture and the like, the room across the way possessed every indication of occupancy. In the dancing light from the lamp which Carne held I caught a glimpse of a well-furnished and carpeted interior, a table and chair, a single bed, bookcase, etcetera - all neatly arranged and with glistening, well-polished surfaces. So, at least one room in this ancient tower was still in use. For what? Some form of imprisonment, that much was obvious from what I was compelled to witness. Could there be other such rooms?

The door opposite me closed. Now the only light was from a pale slant of moonlight coming through a slender, barred window behind me. It cast an eerie glow over the sprawling bulk of furniture. I still felt scared, but a certain defiance was beginning to infiltrate my mood. Carne had absolutely no right to treat anyone in the manner which I had just witnessed - the angry blows, the bullying, all the brutish behaviour of a callous goaler. In that moment I was certain that he was everything I most loathed in a man, and the feeling was sharpened by the remembrance of the sympathy which I had experienced as he recounted to me the circumstances of his childhood that morning as we were driving to church. What a fool I had been! Thank heavens, I had resisted that sudden impulse to reach out and take his hand in an effort to communicate something of the compassion and tenderness which his words had aroused in me at the time! And to think, too, that only a few nights past I had lain in bed recalling the comfort of his arms about me, nestling me protectively against his shoulder. Protectively? Ugh!

But I had to suppress my growing anger and my desire to make my presence known by challenging him there and then. It was not only the possibility that I might meet similar harsh treatment - though any such treatment would have been answered by a much more vigorous defence than George Northwood appeared capable of! - but the fear that any precipitous action on my part just then must surely destroy whatever chance I had to solve the mysteries lurking here. Indeed, the very least I might expect was instant dismissal, for had I not disobeyed my employer by coming here and committing the unpardonable offence of meddling in family matters? Clearly then, if I was to have any chance of helping George and Adelaide, I would have to bide my time and contrive to act at all times as though nothing untoward was happening about me. At least until Charles returned. Anything else would seem like a desertion of my pupil.

The door of the other room suddenly opened. Redmond Carne was silhouetted against the light from within. His huge fist wrapped about the iron door handle.

'I'll come for you in the morning as usual. Meanwhile, no more tantrums. We wouldn't want to disturb her, would we?'

Her? For one awful moment I had the feeling that Carne knew of my presence in the tower. At that moment his face was towards me, masked by deep shadow. He was standing perfectly still.

He closed the door behind him and locked it. Poor George was now securely imprisoned. Carne next removed a loose stone from above the lintel and placed the key in the recess. He replaced the stone beside the door for a few moments, peering at the occupant through a small grille. Then he closed over the grille, picked up the lantern and departed. I waited until long after the last echoing footstep had died away somewhere below the depths of the tower.

I'm not sure what I intended to do just then. The cold, my frayed nerves, and the mounting uncertainties dictated an immediate return to my own quarters but I think too that I was also on the point of removing the key from its hiding place and releasing George from his captivity. Such a decision was fraught with so many imponderables, and whether or not I would have had the courage to carry it out and thus bring matters to a head I cannot say - but just as I was about to tip-toe from my hiding place something behind me caught at my shawl. Startled, I swung round, jerking my shawl free. And in that moment I came face to face with the likeness of Eliza Northwood! My own likeness too!

My sudden action had dislodged a draped cover from her portrait. She looked at me, a beautiful girl in the pale slant of errant moonlight, a haunting half-smile reaching forward from the canvas, holding me. I never doubted for one moment that this was Eliza. It was like peering receptively into a looking-glass - the same golden-brown braids crowning features that were mine as well as hers. No wonder everyone had been so startled by the resemblance! It was not only Eliza Northwood who returned my gaze, but Katherine Ainsley as well. A much different

175

Katherine Ainsley admitted, as though I caught a will-o'-the-wisp glimpse of some other element in my character. What was it?

I reached out and touched the canvas, trying to lend it substantiality as my fingers traced the oval shape of the face. Was I this beautiful? I was vain enough to hope that I was, yet, paradoxically, also hoped that I was not; for Eliza's beauty, now permanently captured on canvas, had a quality of obviousness - direct, superficial, almost sensuous and wanton. I had the impression of a kind of attractiveness that might appeal to all types of men, from the shy and gentle George Northwood to the forthright, bold masculinity of his brother Charles. And those contrasts encompassed all types in between, the deep and powerful Redmond Carne, the austere Captain Northwood, the effete Sir Arthur Rebstock. Any one of them might have been her lover. And Adelaide's father. Little wonder then that my life had become so enmeshed in theirs! To each of them I was a constant reminder of someone else. We were so alike physically, yet whereas I had never felt that I had anything to offer as a woman (except perhaps love to the right man some time) this other me - this Eliza Marisch - had a disturbingly exotic magnetism. Whatever was provocatively feminine in Eliza was not present in my character. I was what I had always been - a rather prosaic residential tutor, perhaps obstinate at times, but not very brave.

I continued to stare at the portrait. The long crimson lips held the suggestion of a smile, as though, even now in these odd surroundings, Eliza was finding secret amusement in my perplexities. I peered into every line of her face, every shadowy tone; in the eyes was reflected an unnatural glow and in their bright flaring I sensed something of warning, a gossamer touch that reached out, as light and delicate as the dusty cobwebs clinging to the picture frame. Warning?

I can still recall vividly the numbness which came over me when my hearing picked up the faint sound of a footfall just outside. It was too soft and stealthy to be that of Carne returning. Who then? The door was still partly opened behind me but I dared not turn round or make even the slightest sound. I could only stand still, trying to quell the loud thumping of my heart, and hoping against hope that I was completely cloaked in shadows. The creeping footsteps came closer. When they came to a halt just outside the door, they were followed by the sound of the loose stone being removed and then the key being inserted in the lock. The door to George's cell (for thus I had come to consider it) opened and then closed quietly. I released my held-in breath, too slowly and painfully to be a sigh of relief. Eliza still maintained her look of secret amusement.

In a little while the indistinct mumble of voices drifted out through the door of the opposite room. I waited for perhaps five minutes, wondering if the mysterious visitor might soon depart, but the voices continued on in the same meaningless drone. I edged over to the door, turning from the painting with a strange commingling of relief and reluctance. For a little while Eliza with that warning look had seemed like an ally; yet her enigmatic smile could also be construed as a callous enjoyment of my predicament. Should I risk slipping out of here and try to make it back to my own room?

It took ages to ease the door back and leave just sufficient of an opening for me to escape. My hand shook and every nerve of my body was braced against the tell-tale creaking of old wood and dry hinges - and still I held back, too scared to venture out into that narrow stone passageway. I looked back over my shoulder at the portrait, barely resisting an appeal for advice from a few square feet of daubed canvas. Yes, I tried to tell myself that's all it was, but the partially opened door now permitted some illumination of sorts to invade the tiny room, a new pattern of dull light and shadows which once again made a subtle alteration to the expression on Eliza Northwood's face. There and then (and for some reason for which I can offer no adequate explanation) I sensed that she was, after all, dead, but that this canvas held, frozen for all time, the essential qualities of her living. The qualities of malice and mockery.

In that moment I wanted nothing so much as to be free of her taunting smile and the evil shadows of Polmarran Tower.

I took a deep breath and stepped out into the passage. There was no alteration in the pattern of human voices emanating from the closed door only an arm's length from me. I crept away as noiselessly, yet as swiftly, as caution would allow. My fear was no longer reserved for those scurrying little sounds amongst the shadows as I made it back to my own room by the same tortuous route.

I sighed with relief when I got back unnoticed and locked the door of my parlour behind me. It was with even greater relief that I found Adelaide still peacefully asleep in my bed. Too tired to wash or change, I lay down quietly beside her. But it was a long time before I could get to sleep. A new legion of questions stood sentinel-like around the great four-poster bed, relieving last night's squad with the same blank impassivity. A new array of imponderables. Why was it necessary to make a prisoner of George Northwood, and who was his mysterious visitor in the tower? Certainly not Redmond Carne. Of that I was certain.

But apart from Carne, who else would have access to the tower? Captain Northwood of course, or perhaps Jem Forrest. But why the stealth, and the secretive whispering behind the closed door?

How about the Rebstocks? Yes, Forrest had mentioned the fact of their frequently snooping about the place, and they would certainly know every nook and cranny of Polmarran's shadowy passages. If there was some little-known point of entrance down near the cove, a smuggler's cave or some opening that led up into the dank bowels of their ancestral tower, they would surely know of its existence. They might even have been the two figures I'd seen from my window last night, one tall enough to be Sir Arthur, the other shorter, more slightly built, both moving among the trees at the end of the lawn. Moving too in the general direction of the tower.

But why?

And why, for that matter, having first been struck by something intrinsically alive about Eliza Northwood's portrait, did I now sense intuitively that she was dead?

The sentinel-like questions closed ranks about me, challenging a stranger who did not have the pass-word.

I turned to Adelaide and took the sleeping child in my arms. That gesture - instinctive, tender, protective - seemed to break the stillness of Polmarran House. Somewhere a shutter creaked sharply in a sudden gust of wind, and there was a deep rumbling as though the old house stirred in anger. I told myself that it could only be the distant surf against the rocks but for one terrible heart-beat my fears were raised to the point of terror. Adelaide gave a soft moan and I drew her even closer to me, nestling her golden head against my shoulder.

In that moment I knew that, even more important than consideration of my own personal safety, was the necessity to protect this girl from whatever evils lurked here. Evils - past, present, or to come . . .

Chapter Ten

We were late for breakfast. For Adelaide the fact of unpunctuality, and the causes which gave rise to it, held all the delicious dangers of truancy. We had a secret; last night she had slept in my bed and nobody else knew! She stifled a nervous little laugh in the palm of her hand and hunched up her shoulders mischievously just before we entered the breakfast-room.

Morning, dull and cheerless, had come in through the mullioned windows, turning the napery bluey-grey and gleaming coldly on the cut-glass and silverware. It was neither dark enough for candles nor bright enough to be without them, but apart from the pale light seeping through the windows the only other illumination was from a dampish, sizzling log in the fireplace and the few coals heaped around it.

There were surprised expressions all around when we entered - the gentlemen's presumably due to finding both teacher and pupil unpunctual for the very first time, while mine was occasioned by the sight of George Northwood seated at table as though nothing unusual had occurred in the tower on the previous night.

The surprise must have shown on my face. Redmond Carne gave me his appraising smile as he stood up. 'Morning, Miss Ainsley. Nothing wrong, I hope?'

I deliberately avoided his eyes and contrived to take my place as though unaware of his continuous action in rising, offering a chair, and hovering behind it with sinister politeness until I was seated. When he had taken his place again, opposite me, our eyes met once more. I knew that my colour was heightened, but remembering all that I had witnessed last night and the suspicions which I harboured, it was essential that I maintain my distrust of him.

'When you were not down on time we naturally wondered if you might not be indisposed, Miss Ainsley.' Captain Northwood seemed inordinately civil. The creases at the corners of his thin mouth might even have been intended as a smile.

'My apologies, gentlemen.'

'No need for apologies.' Like a flag of truce the table napkin fluttered in the Captain's hand. 'Just so long as there is nothing wrong.'

'Wrong?'

'Your ankle.'

'I have quite recovered, thank you.' And now it was my turn to be pointedly solicitous. I think I startled poor Mr George with my direct question: 'And you, Mr George, I trust you are recovered?'

'M-me? Recovered?'

'Well, as you seemed to be confined to your own quarters quite a lot of late I assumed you were unwell. Or if there might not be something the matter.' My questioning look moved back to Carne's face.

'Not a trace of bother on Mr George from what I can see,' he said blandly. 'Indeed, it's good to know that we are all in fine fettle and shipworthy condition, eh?' His smile was just a shade too casual. Nothing in it could quite disguise the old wariness.

'Still, if I may be allowed, Mr Northwood, I really do think you should try to get more fresh air. Too much solitude is . . .'

'Solitude is necessary for the foundation of character,' he replied coldly.

'Perhaps so, Captain Northwood. But surely not too much of it?'

'George likes to be alone,' Redmond Carne said. 'Don't you, George?'

The young man seemed to flinch from the question.

'I don't like to be alone. Especially at night time,' Adelaide put in, giving me such an obvious we-have-a-secret-but-we-won't-pretend-to-them look that I immediately wanted to veer away from the subject.

'That reminds me.' Carne looked at me, and then at the Captain. 'About tomorrow, if you're meaning to go to church again, Miss Ainsley.' He paused, giving the Captain enough time to add a comment, or take over, if he so desired.

Captain Northwood looked straight ahead and said nothing. Carne resumed. 'If you want to go to church you won't have to fret about transport or worry about a long hike back. I'll see to it that Forrest has the carriage fixed up by then, even if it means working till midnight.'

'Thank you, but I thought the axle or something was damaged.'

'Not nearly so bad as Jem Forrest made out. Don't worry, Miss Ainsley, the carriage will be available. And I hope I'll have the honour to drive you there and back.'

'And if you wish, you may have my granddaughter to accompany you,' Captain Northwood offered.

'Oh, may I?' Adelaide exclaimed. 'Isn't that wonderful, Katherine? All the way into Marrambridge!'

'Yes indeed. And we must not forget to thank Captain Northwood.'

'And Redmond and Forrest for repairing that nasty old axle thing! Oh, thank you so much, Grandpapa!'

'Thank you,' I felt bound to add. What was the matter with me? Last night I had been anxiously praying for just such an opportunity to get away from this house, even for a few hours: now I had

182

to conceal an involuntary shudder of apprehension. Both the Captain and Redmond Carne seemed far too eager to have myself and the child out of the way. Why? Did it have something to do with George Northwood's detention in the tower?

'And will you be coming with us too, Mr Northwood?' I asked on impulse, although I already guessed the answer.

They must have had great confidence in the power which they wielded over him. He was allowed to answer for himself! 'To ex-examine one's conduct in p-prayer and meditation be-before the Almighty it is not always necessary to be in c-church.'

'No, but . . .'

'George is one of those who requires solitude,' Carne interrupted.

'Such a pity.' Adelaide pouted sympathetically, and then signalled a swift change of mood by clapping her hands together. 'Oh, I so look forward to to-morrow morning . . . I shall wear my blue bonnet. What will you wear, Katherine? I know! You shall wear your Russian princess hat, the fur one.'

The infectious nature of her enthusiasm took over and almost dominated the remainder of the table talk. Oddly, I was relieved that the references to her Uncle George's penchant for solitude had not drawn from her some mention of his 'being locked up in that old tower'. I did not want them to know of Adelaide's sleeping in my room or anything about how I had spent last night. Nor did I want matters brought to a head just yet. I entered fully into the ensuing conversation. George alone was out of it, retreating into that shell of silence from which he rarely emerged. He looked slightly bewildered, dazed, not quite belonging in time or reality as the rest of the breakfast party knew it. There and then I resolved on seizing the earliest opportunity to speak to him on his own. I had to try to break through

183

that shield of frightened bewilderment, to let him know that he could depend on me and trust me. Above all, I would have to convince him that, until his brother Charles returned, he could count on at least one friend at Polmarran.

Immediately a plan of sorts began to take shape in my mind. Anticipating his customary habit of being the first to withdraw from the dining-room, I pretended some reason for returning to my room and asked to be excused. I hurried upstairs and positioned myself just inside the door of my little parlour. I deliberately left the door open. My stratagem was rewarded with the sound of his light tread on the stairs a few minutes later. I timed my exit to coincide with the moment of his passing by my door. He was alone, his head lowered, the eyes dull and vacant as he shuffled past.

'Mr Northwood . . .?' I had to repeat his name and step into the passage before gaining his attention. He turned round slowly. 'May I have a word with you, please?'

'W-with me?'

'Yes, I think that it may be of some importance to both of us . . .' I paused, my fingers still on the door handle, uncertain as to whether or not I should invite him into my room. How did one broach such a subject as last night's discoveries? Boldly, and to the point, I quickly decided. 'Forgive me for being so blunt, Mr Northwood, but . . . well, you see, I know about the tower. About your being confined there against your will. I went there last night. I saw what happened.'

His eyes dropped, eluding the intensity of mine. I had the impression that it was not from unwonted shyness or embarrassment, but from some kind of veiled defensiveness.

'You can trust me, Mr Northwood. I want to help.'

'I am af-fraid . . . I am afraid I do not quite understand.'

'I was there, Mr Northwood. In the tower, last night. I saw how Carne behaved towards you . . . his bullying attitude . . . imprisoning you . . .'

'B-bullying? But . . . but Redmond is my friend. He would never bully or ill-treat m-me! I don't understand you, miss. I'm sorry.'

Was his look of incredulity feigned?

Mine certainly was not. I could scarcely believe his disavowal of last night's mistreatment! To do so would have been to doubt my own reason. Had I not seen and heard the whole thing? Or was it that his fear was so great that he could not trust anyone here? Especially a near-stranger. Yet there had to be some way to reach him.

My next enquiry was desperately casual. 'Tell me about Eliza then?'

'What?'

'Eliza Northwood. Your sister-in-law. What happened to her?'

'Don't you know?'

'No, of course not.'

'What have they told you, my father and Redmond?' His features contracted with suspicion.

'Nothing. They avoid the subject. Everyone does.'

He nodded his head slowly. 'P-perhaps it is as well.'

'Why?' I enquired bluntly, gathering myself to approach him, to meet his tortured eyes. 'Why, George? Because she is dead?'

'Eliza . . . dead?' He shook his head, the dark curls falling over his pallid brow and adding to the impression of boyish vulnerability and confusion. 'Eliza? No, John is dead . . . my brother. I found him there, all that blood on his face . . . poor, dear John. And the gun . . . Redmond's gun now . . . and they said she had gone away, Eliza Marisch . . . John's w-wife . . . said they'd sent her away . . . b-but she did not go . . . Charles told me . . . he will h-help me . . . the Almighty will s-send Charles

185

b-back to us . . .' He went on and on in a hushed, abstracted voice, as if I was not present or only merited a tiny fragment of his attention; his random words were those of a young man disorientated by present tension and the propinquity of past events. 'The L-lord is at hand, have no anxiety a-about anything . . . Charles w-will return to s-succour us. He knows that they lied when they told m-me that she had gone away!'

'But . . . but where is she now then? Please, George, I want to help you and Adelaide. You must tell me everything you know.' I laid my hand on his arm in an involuntary gesture of entreaty and compassion.

He jerked away from me as though seared by my touch. 'W-why are you asking these q-questions? Are you p-part of this t-terrible conspiracy?'

'What conspiracy?'

'The evil which p-permeates the whole world . . . wickedness that h-has now p-penetrated into m-my father's house! A con-conspiracy of vile iniquities!'

'Oh, please, George. I only want to help. Please believe me. Trust me!'

'I t-trust only in solitude and p-prayer. Only in this way can one avoid the wrath of the L-lord!'

'No, I can help you . . .'

'Help yourself! Take care or you too w-will become a victim of their w-wicked conspiracy.' His eyes were fiery orbs, blazing windows on a troubled soul, no longer flitting away from mine but holding them in a kind of hypnotic challenge. 'Place all your trust in the Lord and let all men know your forbearance!'

'George, listen to me . . .'

But even as I said it I realized we were both listening for something else - a footfall sounded on the stairs.

Redmond Carne rounded the landing, striding easily at first, then almost pulling up short at the sight of George Northwood and myself in earnest conversation. By the time he reached us he had regained control and was adopting an easy matter-of-fact attitude. But behind the smile his eyes were still sharp and watchful. 'Ah, so here you are, George. Wondered where you'd got to. Hope Miss Ainsley has been repeating her advice to you . . . a brisk walk over the hills and a good mouthful of sea air is like a tonic. That right, Miss Ainsley?'

'Yes indeed.'

'Hear that, George? Sound advice, by all accounts. Coming then, lad?'

'Y-yes . . .' George nodded his head and looked away, the recent fervour and the confusion in his eyes fading slowly.

'Better look lively then, mate, if we're to get a mile or two before the rain comes on.' He turned to me and made a little salute with his forefinger touching his temple. 'Will you excuse us so, Miss Ainsley?'

'Certainly. I hope you enjoy your outing, gentlemen.'

'Enjoy it?' Carne gave me a quizzical smile. 'Aye, I suppose we might enjoy it at that. Ready, George?'

Puzzled, I watched them walk away, side by side and without a backward glance. George Northwood's gait was slow, his shoulders slumped dejectedly; and Redmond Carne, towering over his companion, looked every inch the gaoler.

What was I to make of George Northwood? What had prompted him to spurn my offer of help and trust? Fear?

Was he the sort of person who, through some peculiarity of temperament, viewed the 'love of God' as a euphemism and to whom the only stark reality was the 'Almighty's wrath'? Yes, he'd practically said as much. And if so, then to this ingrained conviction of sin and retribution must be added whatever shock had originated during his student days and

187

the subsequent discovery of his brother's dead body -
all of which must have unhinged his mind at the
time. Was it thus that his view of life had become
distorted? Undoubtedly, I thought, it was the oblique
angle of that distortion which now held him captive
to Redmond Carne's schemes and made the hapless
young man guess at and fear a vast conspiracy of
evil. And for him I was now part of that conspiracy.
Poor George. There was no one he could trust. How
well Redmond Carne, or Captain Northwood, or both
of them in concert, had completed the work of the
past. They had fastened on to the tragedy of John
Northwood's death and the mystery of Eliza's disappearance and were now trading on this young man's
fears and his half-shattered mind.

For what end? Something to do with the child,
of that much I was certain. And I too had become
involved. Either through accident or design I had
been drawn into the intricate web of mystery which
spread its impenetrable patterns through the dark
recesses of Polmarran.

If only Charles were here!

We were early to church the following morning.
Adelaide was first down the steps, pulling away from
my hand and skipping forward with impatient joy.
She stood first on one leg, then on the other, twisting her slim young body from side to side, unable,
because of her impatience, to take any delight in
Carne's fussing about with harnessing and reins and
what-nots.

'Oh, please, Redmond . . . *please!* We'll be too
late and they will all have gone home.'

'Won't be a minute, Princess.' He smiled easily,
and over her head he winked at me. 'Can't have a
real princess travelling in a coach that isn't sea-
worthy in all particulars, can we now? Come along

then, ladies. Steady as she goes, and uppsy-daisy, your royal highness.' He lifted the child up into the carriage.

At last we were on our way. The gaunt, watching tower, and the trees, and narrow lane slipped away under the turning wheels. Adelaide and I sat in the back. For her it was more fun to stand and sway with each merry bounce, balancing precariously each time she raised a hand to point out something to me. I tried to show my interest, but my thoughts were of George Northwood locked away in that dark little cell. I looked out at the pearl-grey sky and the twisting ribbon of road. Like my forebodings the roadway diminished, yet paradoxically and inexorably, continued, all the way to Marrambridge.

After Service it became apparent that some of the motives attending on our church-going were encountering mixed fortunes. Adelaide (who not unnaturally viewed the visit to Marrambridge as something between a picnic outing and a social event) was of course thrilled with her success. She captivated the Reverend Mr Cooper and his wife and those of the parishioners to whom she was introduced. But for my part, Carne's presence inhibited any attempt to confide even the least of my recent discoveries at Polmarran to the Coopers. Not once was he out of hearing, or out of view. He remained close by our sides at all times, holding Adelaide's hand like a proud uncle and clearly exhibiting his pleasure that all were so taken with the little girl's charm and comeliness.

He stood, knowingly or unknowingly, as a smiling barrier between myself and the Coopers. By neither a whispered hint nor an oblique gesture could I communicate with Mrs Cooper. Everywhere I turned I was met by Carne's open, assured smile - and it came as something of a shock to realize that he was not just pretending to be cheerful with the Coopers.

He was cheerful! His polite and rough-hewn amiability baulked me at every turn. Worse, the Coopers seemed to have entirely forgotten, or overlooked, Carne's brusqueness on the occasion of his last visit to the precincts of Marrambridge Church. Christian charity at work, perhaps. Or the fact that the clergyman and his wife were not burdened with the mysteries which I had come upon at Polmarran House.

I knew, or suspected, another side to Redmond Carne's nature. The gaoler side. They did not. So, assuming that I could get either the vicar or his wife aside, would they believe my story? Would it do any good to pit my word against the combination of Carne's ingratiating charm and their gullibility on the one hand, and on the other, the improbability of all my theories and suspicions? I had to admit that mine was a slender case. The one person who might corroborate my findings, George Northwood, had already demonstrated his unreliability and fear. His brother Charles had vanished into thin air for the time being. I was alone and without an ally. Mine would be like a voice in the wilderness of shocked disbelief - a woman's voice, a stranger's, without a tittle of proof. And to what avail? To be sent from Polmarran on the instant, leaving poor Adelaide and her Uncle George at their mercy . . .

No, I decided, as I watched Redmond Carne perform before the Coopers and the parish elders with all the graciousness of a candidate for a deaconry, this was not the time. Just to listen to him! Already he was confessing candidly that he had not been inside a church in more than ten years but that he had found this morning's service, and the sermon particularly, most edifying! No! Clearly then I would have to wait for some incontrovertible proof before approaching the Coopers or the local law officers. Where to find the proof?

We were joined by the Rebstocks in the porch.

Margaret was quick to commiserate with me on my recent mishap. I really shouldn't have gone off on my own like that, especially after Sir Arthur had offered to drive right to the hall door of Polmarran! Arthur was so capable and would have fended off any threat from a wild animal. Really quite foolhardy of you, Miss Ainsley, to dismiss the protection and courtesy of a *real* gentleman and to go wandering off through the woods on a whim like that. Sir Arthur hung back a little during all of this, nervous contriteness shimmering all over his features like rain on a window pane; eventually he edged forward and managed to silence his sister with a gentle 'shush'.

'Please, Margaret, the fault was entirely mine and you must allow me to make my own apologies . . .' He turned to me, his fingers nervously working round the brim of his hat. 'Dear Miss Ainsley, I cannot expect or hope that you will easily forgive me . . . I should have insisted that you allow me to see you safely home that day. I own myself a cad, ma'am, and as I cannot find the means to forgive myself, how then can I expect you to pardon me?' With his sister temporarily, yet adroitly, manoeuvred out of the line of vision, Sir Arthur subjected me to a most pleading look, begging me to make no mention of that incident which had caused me to quit his carriage. His grave expression was much more eloquent than his words. He seemed genuinely distressed and apologetic. I believed him.

'Please, Sir Arthur, no apologies. The greater fault was mine. It was very silly of me to insist on walking home. You must forgive me for not accepting your kind attentions.' I lingered meaningfully on the last words and Sir Arthur took my message. The matter was now settled between us two, and I knew intuitively that I would have no further trouble from Sir Arthur Rebstock.

Of his sister I was by no means quite so certain.

Margaret Rebstock construed my words and attitude to be the obeisance due from an employed tutor to the scion of the neighbourhood's most illustrious family. 'Of course Arthur accepts your apology, my dear. The matter is settled then. And now, Miss Ainsley, if you will be good enough to come with me . . .' She linked her arm in mine and quickly propelled me from the church door. 'I would like to show you John Northwood's grave. I'm the only one who ever visits it. Have they told you that?'

'They tell me very little, I'm afraid.'

'Too much to hide, I'll warrant.' Clutching my arm, she quickly led me around the side of the old church, almost dragging me bodily along the narrow pathway which was flanked by a variety of tombstones. But for his lengthy stride Sir Arthur might never have kept up with us. 'We called on you, my brother and I. To enquire after your health.'

'I know. That was kind of you . . .'

'But that old pirate . . . that upstart . . . had the effrontery to turn us away. The Rebstocks! To be ordered off what had once been our own land!'

'I think old Northwood holds me responsible in part for Miss Ainsley's unfortunate accident . . .' her brother tried to explain.

'Nonsense, Arthur, you cannot take blame on yourself. Miss Ainsley has already confessed to some degree of foolhardiness in the matter. No, we were turned away from Polmarran because they do not want us to know what's going on there.' She pulled up so abruptly that I almost collided with her. 'Here it is . . . John's grave.'

She knelt down before a slab of granite and drew back a small curtain of green leaves to uncover an intaglioed cross and the name JOHN WILLIAM NORTHWOOD. Her fingers traced the shallow incisions in the stone and lingered fondly over the beloved name. Without turning to look at me, or her brother, Margaret Rebstock said: 'He never loved her. He was infatuated for just long enough to be tricked into a marriage and he quickly grew to hate her. Can you imagine that, Miss Ainsley? John and that Marisch woman tied together in wedlock, and devoting all their emotional energy to despising each other?'

'Hush now, Margaret.' Sir Arthur bent forward and placed his hand on her shoulder in a restraining gesture. 'You must not distress yourself.'

'Did you know, Miss Ainsley, that your pupil is not John's daughter? Adelaide is not a Northwood!' she continued.

A shadow fell suddenly across the lettering on the tombstone.

'Are you ready to return to Polmarran, Miss Ainsley?'

Startled, I looked up into the face of Redmond Carne. He stood over us, taller even than Sir Arthur Rebstock and, aided by a slight rise in the ground upon which he took his stance, he loomed over our crouching figures with all the menacing authority of a gamekeeper who had just happened on a trio of poachers. The Rebstocks were equally surprised, though I doubt if they started guiltily as I did. Inexplicably I felt detected in some form of rebelliousness. Why? I had every right to be here with the Rebstocks.

'Ah, good morning, Carne,' Sir Arthur said. He moved towards Carne who contrived by a swift shift of position not to see the proffered hand.

'Ready, miss?'

Sir Arthur stepped back, undecided, looking in turn at all three faces, his sister's, mine, Carne's. His extended and futile hand fluttered about for a moment before making a vague gesture towards the gravestone. 'We, er - we were just showing Miss Ainsley the grave. John's grave.'

Carne never even looked at him. His eyes were on me, eyes narrowed with controlled anger. And there was something else in his look - a kind of muted appeal.

'Yes, I'm ready, Mr Carne. Please excuse me, Sir Arthur. I think I have detained everyone far too long. Good morning, Miss Rebstock.'

'Next Sunday?'

'Yes, I expect so.' I could not help looking at Carne for confirmation.

He said nothing. We walked back in silence. I think his mood of ill-humour had diminished by the time we collected Adelaide from the Reverend Mr Cooper and his wife. Still, on the return journey I was glad to be seated in the back listening to Adelaide's triumphant chatter; it precluded the necessity of making conversation with a very solemn-faced Redmond Carne.

By the time we reached the two overhanging and close-standing rocks which marked the entrance to Polmarran the weather had changed. For the worst. The distant tower looked down on our return through a dark curtain formed by diagonal sheets of rain, its one eye glistening coldly between windswept folds.

'We're in for a bad storm for sure.' Carne said, his narrowed eyes reading the sky and the grim set of features presaging some new threat.

Adelaide and I hurried up the front steps. A wall of rain swept in from the sea and drove hard against us.

'It frightens me, Katherine.' Adelaide said.

'Hush now. There's nothing to be afraid of. It will probably blow over in a few hours.'

But I too shivered with some kind of fear. I don't know what it was. I felt as though a cold breath of evil had just been swept in through the open doorway with us and that when the hall door slammed behind us that chilling presence remained to permeate every part of the house.

George Northwood was absent at the mid-day meal. His father and Carne scarcely spoke throughout the entire meal. Frequently their eyes wandered to the windows to watch the rain spattering the glass and falling darkly across the lawn. An air of gloom hung about that bizarre dining-room with its weird trophies, and the candles and rushlights which tried to replace the feeble daylight failed all too miserably in the matter of cheery illumination.

I spent the early afternoon in my own room trying to read. It was an impossible task. I had only to raise my eyes from the page to see the broad rivulets coursing down the window panes. The wind had increased in fury so that it now violently bent and twisted the young saplings at the far edge of the grass. With each passing hour the weather grew worse, and, with it, my mood. I became restless. If only there was someone I could turn to, I thought, putting down my book! It was two weeks since I had seen Charles Northwood; over the past few days I had tried to comfort myself by inwardly repeating: *'In a day, in two at most, he will surely return.'* But there was still no sign of him. And what, if anything, would his eventual homecoming mean?

Pray heaven it would signify an end to whatever threatened Adelaide and George! And an end to all the mystery! For my own part I desired nothing more than to be free of that constant feeling of vulnerability and helplessness. That's all - because Charles Northwood was not the sort of man I would normally permit myself to become attracted to. And yet here I was, counting the hours for his return. How hopelessly muddled my thoughts had become . . .

But if my thoughts were a vortex of confusion and depression, what agonies of loneliness and terror

George Northwood must have been experiencing just then. He was alone in his bleak cell with the storm raging outside, his mind all fragments and scattered fears, his very existence mocked by a phantom of what it once had been. Should I go to him?

How long I remained by the window, peering out at the wind-driven rain and pondering that question, I cannot say: nor can I be certain that I would have ever plucked up the courage to re-visit the tower had I not witnessed from my vantage place the unusual sight of Redmond Carne and Forrest, each clad in sou'westers and oilskins, setting off down towards the cove. Between them they carried a heavy coil of rope and what appeared to be some sort of grappling hooks. I formed the impression that they were bent on some errand of repair or salvage work and that they might possibly be away from the house for quite some time. Coupled with this notion was the knowledge that Captain Northwood would be having his customary mid-afternoon nap in the study just about then, and therefore if I so desired - no, if I had the courage - the upper part of the house, and the tower, were all mine. I might speak to George, undisturbed, for at least a half an hour or so. Suddenly determined, I threw a shawl about my shoulders and hurried from my room.

Minutes later I was at the door on that deserted top landing, opening it carefully, and slipping into the uneasy shadows beyond it. I descended the winding staircase with cautious steps, my nervousness fortified by determination and compassion for the tower's lone inhabitant. I found the place no less depressing in the feeble daylight than I had on my previous visit. The storm continued to howl about the building, and through the little barred windows almost as much darkness as light seeped through. It pervaded the interior with that chilling eeriness peculiar to certain old and near-deserted structures. Still,

196

there was at least one advantage: I could see where I was going on this occasion. Also, by now I was reasonably familiar with my surroundings and I had little difficulty in locating the particular landing, or gallery, and the door to George's cell.

There was no sound from within - only the wind, or the leaves, or some angry tendrils scuddering viciously across the outside stones. It took only a few moments to find the loose stone above the door. I quickly removed it and then groped about in the dark cavity in search of the key. My hand settled on a glass bottle first, then the key. I withdrew both, bringing the bottle round to the light. Laudanum!

I was afraid to conjecture the purpose of the drug, but all the old suspicions were aroused. Was this Redmond Carne's method of rendering his prisoner submissive?

I thought I heard a low moan, or sob, from behind the door. I returned the bottle to its hiding place and then placed the key in the lock, but before turning it I knocked on the door. 'Mr Northwood? George?' I called.

I received no reply. I turned the key and opened the door.

The storm had imposed its own curfew and the tiny room was almost in complete darkness - no fire in the grate, no candle glow, no worthwhile light through the barred window on the opposite wall. With infinite straining my eyes discovered the figure of George Northwood huddled in the farthest, darkest corner; he was half-sitting, half-crouched, on the edge of the bed with a heavy blanket about his shoulders.

'George . . .'

'Eliza?' Silhouetted in the doorway I must have seemed to his tortured fancy like some apparition from the past. 'Eliza . . . is it you?'

'No. I'm not Eliza. Don't you recognize me? I'm Katherine Ainsley.'

I came in, but did not shut the door behind me. Stepping to one side I tried to let as much of the pale light from outside fall into the room and bridge the shadowy area that separated us. Thus we confronted each other across the narrow room. For an instant I was at a loss to recognize the thin, haggard young man crouched amongst the tangled bedclothes. It took me a moment to be certain that it was George Northwood. His face was deathly white, the eyes bloodshot and like those of a demented soul. A day-old stubble of beard blurred the delicate outline of his jaw, giving to it a slack, indecisive line. It seemed to be all apiece with the troubled, yet vacant look in his eyes. He did not appear to recognize me, or at least not to recognize me as Katherine Ainsley.

'George, I want you to trust me. You must let me help you.'

His head rolled slowly from side to side. 'Are you not frightened by the storm?' he asked.

'No, there's really no cause for fear.'

'I was frightened by the storm before. Do you remember?'

'Then if you are still frightened you mustn't remain here. It's inhuman. You must come with me, George.'

'Did Redmond say so?'

'No, but . . . well, you just can't stay here, can you?'

'Where is Redmond? He would never permit you to come here alone . . .'

'He's not in the house now, so . . .'

'Redmond away?' Did I discern some covert glint in his eye? Oddly, too, I noticed the absence of his habitual stammer. George Northwood had changed in some way. Uncertain, and with just a tiny pang of alarm, I moved closer to him in an attempt to read his expression. His eyes were averted. 'And where is my father?'

'In his study. Resting.'

I took his arm, gently, nervously, half-expecting

some resistance. He offered none. Instead, as though responding to the grave sympathy which I so keenly felt, he rose to his feet. 'I can just remember you, Eliza. It has been such a long time.'

I did not know what to say. He stood perfectly still. Seeing him thus, the woollen blanket still about his shoulders, the gleam of his pale hands as they clutched it tightly about him, his body slumped forward dejectedly, cowering a little, I wondered if he was still perhaps under the influence of the drug - or if, because of it, the dark broodings and the tragedies of the past were now crowding back on his consciousness. 'You should not have come to my room, Eliza. You are John's wife.'

I steeled myself for the necessity of truth. 'John is dead. And I am not Eliza. Look at me! I am Katherine Ainsley . . . Adelaide's governess.'

'The storm, Eliza . . . I was so frightened. But you had no fear . . .' His random words grew out of the dark solitude of the cell and the past. 'Do you remember? You said you'd comfort me, Eliza. I didn't understand what you meant . . . I knew nothing of those things. It was a sin, Eliza! You are a wicked woman!' He turned sharply, his staring eyes blazing and shimmering with tears of anger, remorse and shame.

A surge of alarm engulfed me. I stepped back and realized that I was trembling.

'The wrath of the Lord shall smite the evil-doer!'

His hand was raised, the fist clenched. I think he was about to strike me, but the arm remained poised as I backed away, then simultaneously the fist unfolded and the arm drooped and his eyes flared brightly with fear as a bar of dark shadow from the open doorway fell across his face.

'What are you doing here?'

Startled, yet relieved too, I swung round. Captain Northwood was standing in the doorway. 'Get back,

George! This is Miss Ainsley . . .' He turned to me as his son crouched back against the dark outlines of the bed. Even in the shadows Captain Northwood's eyes shone with cold hostility. 'You have deliberately defied my orders.'

'Captain Northwood -' I was still trembling, but I tried to control my voice, to make each syllable precise - 'I am here, sir, because I believe your son is . . .'

'I want none of your explanations!'

'I believe we both owe each other some sort of explanation. You, sir, as much as I.'

'I owe you nothing save what money is due to you. Mr Carne will see to that. As of this moment you are dismissed.'

'No . . .'

'I insist that you leave Polmarran as soon as Mr Carne can make arrangements for your departure. Now leave us!' His long arm was flung out, imperiously pointing the way. 'Out!'

'I have certain responsibilities towards my pupil.'

'Not any more. Get out.'

'She is an adulteress! Iniquity and fornication are her . . .'

'Silence, George!' There was grief in the sharp words which tried to halt the unravelling of George Northwood's mind with all its dark peculiarities. His eyes were no longer slitted with rage but glazed pain. 'Oh, my son, my poor boy!'

He was no longer aware of my presence. I stepped to one side as he advanced. Despite having been startled to the point of terror only seconds before, I now stood watching the Captain and fascinated by the sudden transformation. Gone was the air of harsh command. All I saw was an old man, faltering in his steps, his hand trembling. Not really certain of my purpose I placed my hand gently on his arm. 'Captain Northwood . . .'

His eyes remained on his son, prolonging the silence.

I shifted uneasily. 'Captain Northwood, I want to help . . .'

'Please leave us.' The hard timbre was absent from his tone. It was almost tender, soft, wavering with deep emotion and great age. His dry, hard hand closed over mine. I took it that he was responding to the sympathy which I was now experiencing. For him, and for the sobbing, distraught young man huddled against the dark wall.

'I want to help in any way I can.'

'You . . . help? You are dismissed!' He exclaimed, turning round to find me again, to be reminded of my bungling interference. A spark of anger came back into his eyes. His hand closed over my wrist, pinioning it, the sharp fingers biting into the flesh. He led me to the door. 'Out! Do you hear me? I never want to see you again!'

'Very well. I'm going. But this is by no means the end of this matter. That young man is virtually a prisoner. It's inhuman, it's . . . it's by no means the end of this matter!' I finished, squaring my shoulders and trying to salvage some dignity with a hollow threat.

He slammed the door on my inadequacy.

I felt close to tears as I picked my way back up the spiralling steps. But tears seemed too futile after what I had just witnessed - futile and inane amidst these surroundings; the dark, compacted brickwork and the uneven shadows, which by their irregular shimmering seemed to sense my helplessness.

Chapter Eleven

I hurried back to my room, and spent the next hour or two packing, unpacking, then packing everything once more. It was no use: I was thwarted at every attempt by my own conflicting moods - humiliation, confusion, seething anger, fears for my pupil. Thoughts and emotions whirled round in wild disorder. I was leaving, not leaving; anxious to be away from it all, then determined to stay and fight them. Who? What did I know of these people anyway? Their affairs were not mine. The fact of being thrown so much on each other's company in this dreary old house had affected the inter-relationship of the household to a marked degree, and all existence here was bound up or hedged in by whatever had occurred here in the past. But it was no concern of mine!

Even so, I experienced a sinking feeling, a sense of futility and disloyalty. What would become of Adelaide? For her sake I would have to stay. Once again I emptied the contents of one of my valises on the counterpane, and yet . . . and yet I had no choice. The Captain had issued a stern command: Get out!

Still worse was the knowledge that I had brought all this on myself by a stupid imitation of my predecessor's incautious meddling. Like her, I was deserting my pupil. Adelaide, poor child. My role as her self-appointed protectress was ending before it had really ever begun. The thought of how I would take my leave of her was like the final twist of a knife in my heart. I pictured her before me - nervous, bewildered once more by the odd caprices of the adult world, and bright-eyed with the beginning of tears and wistful reproach. How could I possibly explain to her?

The futility of this conjecture and the bundling of personal effects in and out of my portmanteau was interrupted by a knock on the door. Rapid, loud and impatient.

'Come in.' My invitation was equally loud and impatient. The door swung in almost immediately. Carne entered. I was suddenly alert, hostile. 'What do you want?' I asked.

'I've just heard. You mustn't leave, Katherine.' He was clearly agitated and ill at ease. I experienced a kind of triumph; it was generally the other way round in our rather complex relationship.

'And why must I not leave?'

'You're needed here.'

'Captain Northwood doesn't think so.'

'The Cap'n . . . well, he's no longer in command.'

'Ah, so the first mate is joining the mutiny, is that it? And what of the Captain's son . . . have you bullied him into joining the mutiny?' I couldn't help adding as I reflected on Carne's attitude towards his prisoner.

'Yes, I suppose I deserve that.'

I affected not to hear. 'Well then, Mr Carne, please come to the point of your visit. I have packing to do.'

'You can't leave. Not now!' He came towards me; quick, urgent paces that brought us face to face. 'I need you here, Katherine.'

'You?' My attempt at swift and scathing rejection faltered. Abysmally. Losing out to a silly gasp of surprise.

'For God's sake, girl, can't you see? I need you! For too long I've had to hold this family together. I can no longer do it alone. Not after all this.' He laid his hand on my arm, full of appeal, helplessness. 'Please, Katherine, I'm begging you. For the child's sake above all!'

'But . . .?' Had he the power to countermand the Captain's order? Yes, it was just possible. Anything was possible for Adelaide's sake. We were certainly allies in that respect. 'If I agree to stay then - only for the child's sake, mind you - then you will have to explain why you keep George Northwood locked up. You'll have to tell me what's going on here.'

He nodded. 'Yes, but not now. Later perhaps when . . .'

'No, it has to be now, Mr Carne. Look, almost from the start I've been drawn into all this because of my resemblance to Eliza Northwood. I came here to do a job, but since I came I've been chased through the woods, attacked, spied upon . . . oh, why am I telling you all this? You know how it has been for me here. I want to know why.'

'All right.' Carne's voice was surprisingly agreeable. The withdrawal of his hand from my arm was like a gesture of capitulation. 'What do you want to know?'

'Everything, I suppose . . .' I shrugged uncertainly. 'At least everything that you think I should know.'

He remained silent for a few moments, looking at me from under heavy brows. I made a guess at his thoughts - could he trust a woman he had only known for a few weeks with all the secrets of the past decade? He came to a decision.

'Fair enough, then. Ask away. I'll do my best with the answers.'

'I don't know where to begin . . .'

'Then I'd best go back to the beginnings. It's a long enough story. You might like to sit down for it . . .'

He indicated a chair next to the fireplace. When I was seated he paced about for a few moments and then finally took up his position before me. Seeing him thus, his feet firmly planted on the hearth-rug, his expression grave, his lean and sinewy hand clutching the collar of his coat as though it were his only hold on his determination to speak, was to view a curious combination of story-teller and suppliant. He began, exhaling a deep sigh: 'Understand me rightly, Katherine - er, Miss Ainsley - that this family, Cap'n Northwood and Mr George I mean, were not always like this - you know, moody and strange. Indeed, none of us was.'

'Is it this house?'

'Partly, I suppose. The house and the tower and all the things that have happened here since the Cap'n took over.'

I waited for him to go on, giving him time to settle into a mood of pensive reminiscence. 'The place wasn't always run-down like it is now. Like the Rebstocks before him, the Cap'n had a fair number of servants and maids and the like. And there were flower gardens and what-nots, and acres of fine farmland inland from here and a whole crew of yokels to work it. The Cap'n bought the place after the death of his wife, when he'd done with the sea. In those days he had the notion to sort of set himself up as a country squire, though neither of us knew the ropes of managing an estate' - a wry smile puckered the corner of Carne's mouth - 'still don't, I'm bound to say. Not that it mattered much then, or now. The Cap'n had fairly prospered from all his voyaging and could well afford everything in the way of a land-lubber's luxuries. And where the children were concerned he spent lavishly . . . nothing but the best of tutors, music teachers and drawing masters. Everything to fit them for their proper station in polite society.

'John, the eldest lad, was for a military career. His father bought him a commission in one of the best regiments when John declared for soldiering, though I reckon the Cap'n would've liked him to go down to the sea and have his own command. Cap'n Northwood hoped young George would go into the shipping business likewise. As an owner in dry dock, mind you, for straight off we could see that the lad never had it in him to be a ship's master. You see, the Cap'n had the majority shares in a company working out of Southampton and also in another in Bristol, so the sons would've been nicely catered for on that score. I mean, what with the Portuguese wine trade and tobacco from the West Indies . . .'

'And what about Charles Northwood?' I asked.

'How do you mean, miss?'

'Did his father have the army or the sea in mind for Charles?'

'Hard to say what the Cap'n had in mind for him.' Carne shrugged. 'Even in those days Charles was never one for staying put. A good horse and a pack of hounds and he'd be off. Days on end, aye, and weeks too. Though there was no real harm in him then, I suppose . . .'

'And there is now?'

'Well now, Miss Ainsley, you'd best make up your own mind on that score. But I don't recall Charles offering you a dainty handshake at your first meeting.'

'They were unusual circumstances.'

'Nothing too unusual about seeing our Mr Charles drunk.'

'That's not what I meant.'

'No, miss?'

'No, I was referring to the fact that he mistook me for his sister-in-law.'

'Still no cause to manhandle a lady,' he snapped.

I was again reminded of that first day at *The Crown Inn*. Carne's eyes glistened with the same deep anger. He had come to my assistance then - and now, anything which smacked of a defence of Charles

Northwood's character seemed to be a retrospective spurning of Carne's protection. Having broached the subject I now veered away from it: 'Tell me, please, Mr Carne, about George. I understand from the Reverend Mr Cooper that George once studied for ordination.'

'Aye, and it's to the Cap'n's credit that, when he saw the lie of the land in that regard, he didn't stand in the young master's way. Maybe he was hoping for a Bishop's berth for the lad eventually. Or a seat in Parliament some day if George was to change his mind from one class of preaching to the other.'

'Why did George not complete his studies?'

'The fact is, he was holding too hard a course to all that studying. Steering straight into it without ever a let-up for relaxation. He was always a delicate-natured lad and it took its toll on his strength. Mind more so than body. You could see it whenever he came home to us for holidays . . . becoming tense and indrawn. Worried the Cap'n quite a bit, that did. Then on top of all the book-learning, George picked up some story at college about how the Cap'n had enriched himself by running slaves to the American plantation owners.'

I did not try to disguise my abhorrence. 'Was it true?'

'Maybe.'

'You mean you don't know?'

'He certainly had no hand in the slave trade during all the time I shipped with him.' Carne's tone was reassuring. ''Course I can't rightly speak for the time before that. Heard a rumour of it once in Port-au-Prince . . . but only a rumour, mind you. And I don't hold much with rumours.'

'But George did?'

'He did, worse luck. And he let it get right inside his mind so that his reasoning foundered and went under. Great pity, that. And it was the start of all his trouble. The Cap'n sent for some of the best London doctors, but to no avail. Oh, he'd be all right for a short while, then something else would set him off again. Poor George, he became like a drowning man clinging to a piece of driftwood . . . you see, miss, he held fast to this notion of his father being a slaver and that therefore the Lord would come with a sword of vengeance to strike down all the family in His wrath. Said there was a curse on the Northwoods, and was doubly convinced of it when John . . . when his older brother was found dead with the gun alongside him.' Carne half-turned from me and was silent for some considerable time.

I cleared my throat, intending it as a reminder.

'It wasn't just the death of his brother that put George's sanity over the side. No, miss, it was John's widow put the lad's mind in irons for sure.' Carne paused. He stood motionless and stared into the fire. When he eventually turned to me and resumed, there was curiously little tone in his words. 'You were in the tower just now - did you see her picture?'

'Yes, I . . .' but I was by no means certain of how I should bring up the subject of my first visit to the tower.

'That painting doesn't do her credit. Not by a long shot. I don't mean just about her beauty . . .' He paused as if remembering. 'But paintings don't show the real nature of a person. I don't rightly know how to describe her. Never could understand her, and then, as now, I didn't possess the know-how of dealing with shifting moods. For ever changing about, she was, like a vessel taken short by contrary winds. Smiling and sweet and innocent one moment, then veering round to every point of ill-temper and anger.' He swung round and stood facing the fire. There was a moment's silence which I saw no reason to break. Then he began speaking again: 'If I'd known the ways of her, I might have been able to warn the Cap'n and poor John. Warn all of them. But the fact is,

Miss Ainsley I was taken in by her ways too . . .'
He turned to me again, his huge hands spread out before him in a gesture indicative of helplessness.

'You see, miss, I was the very first of the Cap'n's
household to set eyes upon her. I'd heard from Cap'n
Northwood's legal gentlemen about Polmarran being
up for sale and so the Cap'n sent me here to take
soundings. First time I saw this place, Sir Arthur
was throwing a big party for all his friends, including
Miss Eliza Marisch. I'd never seen the like before . . . a
summer's night, it was, and I came riding up through
the trees . . . I could hear the music more than a
mile off. Then I watched them moving past the open
windows, dancing . . . gentlemen in dark evening
clothes and lacy white shirt fronts, and the scarlet
and blue and fancy fol-de-rols on the officers' dress
uniforms, all the young ladies in satin and silk . . .
and Miss Eliza queen among them all, up for every
dance and whirlabout, and always in the arms of
some young beau . . .' Carne said it as though he
wished it had not been so. For just an instant he half-
bowed his head. I had the impression that his eyes
were closed momentarily, but it was difficult to be
sure as his face was partly hidden by shadows.

Had he loved Eliza too? I thought so, as I watched
him, and at the same time I experienced a certain
tenderness for him as I imagined him, shy and awkward with his unsophisticated sailor ways, amidst
Polmarran's fashionable guests that evening; or later
perhaps in the role of loyal employee, a family
retainer carefully watching over the interests of Captain Northwwod and his children and never voicing
his secret affection for the young mistress of Polmarran. Had it been like that?

His silence was prolonged. I wondered if he was
waiting for my comment.

'May I ask if you also were numbered amongst
Eliza's admirers?'

'Me?' His immobility and silence was broken by a

short, humourless laugh. 'A rough and ready tar with nothing more to his credit than twenty years before the mast was no fit suitor for *her* hand. Leastways not in her eyes.'

'But you did admire her?'

'Everyone did.' His next words were accompanied by a deep sigh: 'Yes, I did admire her then. Very much. And I believed myself to be in love with her at first . . . before I knew her to be spoken for with Sir Arthur, mind you. I think, too, that I could be forgiven for thinking she felt something of the same for me during those few days when I was in Marrambridge. For you see, Miss Ainsley, when she learned the purpose of my visit to these parts she assumed that I was to be the new master and owner of Polmarran. I'd never before met a girl like her, and I don't mind admitting now that I was raw and unschooled in such matters. And that I was damned flattered and bowled over by her sweetness. How was I to know that she had been betrothed to Sir Arthur and that she threw him over as soon as she knew he was about to sell the place? And what if I did love her for awhile . . . she took it lightly and I was fool enough not to know the difference!' His eyes, tight and crinkly at the corners with pain and memories, had lost their tough, appraising look.

Watching Redmond Carne in that moment I knew something I had always sensed - that he was capable of deep feelings and great loyalty. And that he had been hurt once. By Eliza. Remembering all the suspicions which I had harboured since coming here, I nonetheless found myself relenting as I looked at him now.

'Anyway,' - he shrugged, the palms of his hands turned outwards - 'when I took my leave of her and left Marrambridge, it was with the firm belief that she and I had an understanding. I wasn't to see her again for the best part of a twelve-month. The Cap'n sent me back out to Jamaica on a final voyage and to

210

wind up some of his affairs in those parts. I was reluctant to go, and I told him as much. The first time I ever really spoke up to the Cap'n and tried to argue him down. Still, I owed it to him to go, and besides, I stood a good chance to improve my own finances on that outing and thereby be in a better position to present myself before Eliza on my return. I put it all down in a letter which I sent to her before embarking. And I wrote to her three or four times from Jamaica. Never a reply to any of them. And when I returned to England and made my way here, I found she was married to John Northwood.'

He paused. Then, seeing the look on my face and catching my nod of sympathy, he said: 'No, Miss Ainsley. I soon got over it . . . and accounted myself lucky when I saw how she treated her husband and George.'

'George? What do you mean?'

'Oh, you know what I mean . . . ogling, flirting . . . No, it was much more than that. Tormenting him. Every new conquest raised her self-esteem. Eliza was that sort of woman.'

So, even poor George! I thought. With his timidity and innocence, what a glorious challenge it must have been to Eliza! The blend of religious fervour and purity must have added a new and exquisite flavour to her desires, the swift temptings, the subtle advance and retreat. Yes, how it must have tormented and tantalized someone as sensitive and highly-strung as George Northwood. And what of George in all of this? His so-recent words came surging back with an awful clarity: *'It was a sin, Eliza! You are a wicked woman!'* To him it must have seemed like utter sacrilege. His brother's wife! Overwhelmed with violent longing, and yet at the same time, with loathing - could the twin elements of lust and repulsion have coalesced into a blinding rage . . .?

I glanced up, and was unprepared for the long look

that Carne bestowed upon me. 'George's mind is a blank on the subject. Or leastways it was until recently.'

'What do you mean - *recently?*'

He shrugged off the question. Too quickly, I thought. For just the fraction of a second the old wariness was back in his eyes, but his words contained a matter-of-fact tone. 'We got a special doctor once for George. All the way down from London. He said that some people, nervous, highly-strung people, can lose all memory of particular events, or persons, when they experience some violent shock.'

Violent?

'Where is Eliza Northwood now?' I asked.

Again his massive shoulders made an eloquent shrug. 'I wasn't here when she disappeared.'

'But you must have some idea . . .'

'Aye, lots of ideas and notions, but no hard facts. My own preference is to agree with Dr Howard . . . that she returned to the Continent. At any rate, it is the most convenient version to hold to.'

'And leave her baby here . . . no, I can hardly believe that.'

'Motherhood meant sweet damn-all to that woman!' His tone was sharp and brittle with scorn. 'Nothing was allowed to thwart her whims, neither husband nor child. She quickly became bored here. After John's death she was bitter with anger and disappointment when the Cap'n declined to settle a handsome annuity on her, or buy her off, or whatever. She talked frequently of quitting the place. With or without the child. Besides, Adelaide is better off without her . . .'

'But still, to disappear without any trace . . .'

This time there was just a hint of impatience in his gesture. 'Well, all I can tell you, Miss Ainsley, is that I wasn't here at the time. We had a fierce storm that winter and a great number of ships were lost along this coast. Like any other right-thinking man, I had duties to attend to. For one thing, the wreckers were out on the hills with their false beacons . . . aye, Sir Arthur Rebstock included, ever ready to try his hand at repairing his fortunes in the same manner as his ancestors had founded it, no matter what his sister may say to the contrary. For two days and a night I rode these hills with some good fellows, trying to douse the cliff-top fires and to disperse each crew of wreckers. When not at that work we were trying to get shore-lines out to some of the ships not already dashed to pieces, or we were tossed about in the long boats as went to pick up survivors.

'It was a sad time, Miss Ainsley, with nothing much to see or think about than the furious waves and the wrecks of once-proud ships and many a dead man washed ashore. I had little thought for the happenings at Polmarran for those few days. When I got back here, Eliza was gone. For good . . . or ill, I'm not sure which. All I know is that wherever she'd gone she'd taken George Northwood's last shred of sanity with her.'

His silence then, deep and prolonged, bespoke the awesome nature of what he'd found here on his return. He turned round and stared into the fire. The wavering flames gilded the grim and handsome face. In a taut voice he took up the story again. 'I got back here just in time to help the Cap'n disarm him. He had a knife on him, George had. Tried to slash his wrists. the Cap'n said. The lad was raving . . . crying out that the Cap'n had profited from slavery and that the sins of the father would be visited on the children, and about John's death and how Eliza was wicked and about Eliza's baby . . .'

'What about Adelaide?' With a surge of alarm I was recalling the child's account of a night of terror, of the storm and a man in her room, of the howling wind and the shutters banging and a man shouting angrily - raving! 'What did he mean?'

'The lad was out of his mind. Raving. Didn't know what he was saying . . . all that biblical stuff about hell and damnation and the wrath of the Lord, and how he must wipe out the curse on the family and atone for his father's crimes by sacrificing his own life. That's when he'd attempted to cut his wrists.'

'Oh, how dreadful!'

'So that's why the Cap'n has me lock him every time he starts acting a bit odd. For his own protection. Normally that boy wouldn't harm a fly. It's not in his nature. And that room of his in the tower . . . well, he can come to no mischief there. There's nothing lethal in it.'

'I feel so sorry for him.'

'We all do.'

'Then why did you treat him so harshly?'

'Harshly . . . me? Why, I never . . .' Carne stopped abruptly. He frowned, puzzled at first, then searching his memory, he quickly and unquestioningly found corroboration of my remark. 'Yes, there was one occasion. And that was quite recently. In fact, just a few nights ago.'

'I know. I was there.'

'What?'

There and then, and because a tenuous strand of trust now linked us together, I told him of my first visit to the tower and what I had witnessed there. He looked quite abashed and ill at ease.

'I'm sorry, Miss Ainsley. I'd no idea you were there. I would never have struck George, only he tried to escape from me, and because . . .' Carne looked at me with sudden tenderness. Then he shook his head quickly.

'What were you about to say?' I prompted.

'Nothing, it doesn't matter . . . except that I apologize. A lifetime at sea does not equip a man for

214

the niceties of life, I'm afraid. Perhaps I was too quick-tempered and harsh with the lad.' His powerful shoulders seemed to have slumped with the dual burdens of contrition and entreaty. 'I've told you everything I know, Kath . . . Miss Ainsley. Now will you stay on here as I ask?'

I hesitated, wondering whether after all my earlier distrust of Redmond Carne had not been seriously misplaced. Certainly he had just now seemed sufficiently assured of my sympathy to speak his mind openly on the subject of the Northwood's tragic history. I felt also that, with just a few more questions and answers, what little remained of that residue of distrust would be wholly eliminated.

'Will you stay?' he repeated.

'First, one or two more questions . . . please. I must know.'

'Very well.'

'You said that George had lost all recollection of Eliza until quite recently . . .'

'That's right.'

'And am I right in assuming that my presence here played a major part in jogging his memory?'

He nodded affirmatively.

'Is that why I was selected for the position of tutor?'

'I don't follow your meaning, miss . . .'

'The coincidence of my resemblance to Eliza . . . was it deliberate?'

'No. How could it be?' My suggestion obviously surprised him. 'No one here ever set eyes on you before your arrival in Marrambridge. No, miss, you can rest easy on that score. You were signed on solely on the strength of your qualifications as set down in your letter of application. Even Miss Rebstock gave you her vote . . .'

'Miss Rebstock? I don't understand. What had it to do with her?'

215

'The Cap'n asked her advice in the matter. Couldn't quite make up his mind between two or three of the letters of application, and felt that maybe an educated lady's viewpoint might be of benefit. Miss Rebstock picked out your letter after just one reading. Then too from her visits to Exeter she had some knowledge of the good reputation of that school where you were at the time. She vouched for it as a good establishment . . .'

Not Redmond Carne - but Margaret Rebstock - could have journeyed to Exeter for the purpose of seeing me at close quarters, without my being aware of it, and then, after noting the resemblance to Eliza Northwood, returned here to encourage the Captain to offer me the vacant post. But why? Was Charles right? Was I brought here for the sole purpose of fitting into someone else's carefully-laid plans? If only Charles Northwood would return now! He had promised an end to all the mystery, the answers to Polmarran's riddles . . .

And yet Redmond Carne was manfully meeting my questions as best he could, standing before me, frank, expectant, ready for my next query. And I still had so many. Could I rely on him to answer all of them?

'Tell me, Mr Carne. Was it George who pursued me through the woods that day? Who attacked me?'

This time there was a decided pause before replying. 'Yes, I think so . . .'

'You *think* so! You mean you don't know?' I looked up, my surprise tinged with irony. 'You were there, weren't you? You came upon him, found me lying there unconscious . . .'

'Yes, I was out searching for you. I was worried when you hadn't shown up. I heard the noises in the bushes, sure enough. And I heard your cry for help . . . but when I discovered you lying there, you were alone. My approach must've scared off your attacker. I might have caught up with him, true . . . but I was much more concerned about you.'

216

'Yet you suspect George?'

'Well, it looks that way, doesn't it? I mean, if he was wandering about and somehow mistook you for Eliza . . . you know, with the way his mind is all to pieces, with the past and present all of a jumble . . .'

'And because of your suspicion that he may have been the one who attacked me . . . was that suspicion responsible for your single outburst of anger with him that night in the tower?'

'Yes, it was.' He lowered his eyes, and spread his hands again with that same air of embarrassment and helplessness. 'I need you here. I can steer a course, Miss Ainsley, but I need a hand in setting it. Will you stand by me for the sake of this family?'

He came to me and surprised me by placing his hand on mine - appealing but clumsy, and somehow inadequate in view of my one remaining question.

'One more thing, Mr Carne. That night in the tower . . . who else was there?'

'What?' His surprise was obviously genuine.

I had to repeat my question and explain. 'I didn't leave the tower for fully thirty minutes after you departed, Mr Carne. During that time someone else visited George in his cell . . .'

'Who?'

'I have no idea. I couldn't see. But I distinctly heard the stealthy footsteps, the key being removed and then the door being unlocked. Whoever it was stayed for some considerable time, conversing with George in low tones . . .'

'Did you recognize the voice?'

'No. It was just a mumble. Calm, but indistinct.'

He stepped away from the fireplace and paced about for a few moments. Grim perplexion sculpted his weathered features into a deep frown. 'But who? Why. Who else would . . .?'

'Captain Northwood?'

'No.' He shook his head quickly. 'He was in his study. I know that for a fact. And Jem Forrest wouldn't venture further than the wine cellar. No one else knows the lay-out of the tower or how to enter it . . .'

Our eyes and our thoughts met in swift unison. 'Rebstock!'

'Or his sister? Whoever it was had a very light step.'

'But why? That's what I can't fathom. What would their purpose be?'

Neither of us had an answer, only the shared puzzlement of a long silence. With a final shake of his head Carne turned to me. 'I don't know what's going on, but I'm more convinced than ever that you're needed here. For Adelaide's sake as much as the Cap'n's.' Catching my questioning look, he added: 'Aye, Miss Ainsley, the Cap'n's ill.'

'Ill? When I left him he seemed all right . . .' But did he? Suddenly I was recalling how the Captain had looked just before I had hurried from George's cell - an old man, ashen-faced, his hand trembling, his steps faltering.

'I went there when I didn't find him in his study. He was poorly, miss. The shock of discovering you there . . . not that you must take blame to yourself, Miss Ainsley! No, his heart is poorly, you see, bound to come upon him sooner or later. But the shock of finding you running such a risk, then, after you'd gone, having to restrain his own son by physical strength . . .'

I got to my feet quickly. 'If he is ill then we must go to him.'

'Stay a bit, Miss Ainsley. Nothing more we can do just yet. I carried him to his room and attended to him before coming here. I've sent Forrest for the doctor.'

I experienced a pang of guilt. 'I must see him.' I insisted.

'Yes, but not now. Later, when he's rested. Mrs

Forrest and myself can do what's necessary. Leastways until I can speak up for you, though it doesn't much matter now, I suppose. I'm in charge, in a manner of speaking.'

I considered this for a few moments and then agreed reluctantly. 'Very well, if you think it best.'

'I do.' He stood for a while in silence, uncertain. 'Well then, I seem to have taken up a great deal of your time . . .'

'You have been most kind, Mr Carne. You've answered all my questions and helped me towards some sort of understanding of the position here. I am obliged to you.'

'And you'll stay?'

'Of course. That was our agreement.'

'Then it's I who am obliged to you . . .' He smiled, relieved and awkwardly appreciative. 'I'd best let you get on with your unpacking then.' He walked slowly towards the door, then turned to face me once more. 'With respect, miss . . .?'

'Yes?'

'May I . . . that is, would it be all right by you if . . . I call you by your first name?'

'If you wish.' I tried to say it without enthusiasm, but I sounded much more friendly than I had intended.

'Good night, Katherine.'

'Good night . . .'

'Good night Redmond,' I said silently.

When the door closed behind him I sat on the edge of the bed and absently surveyed the scattered personal effects and clothing which was neither packed nor unpacked. I was staying here after all. But what exactly had been achieved?

Well, for one thing, the rather uneven conflict between my questions and the dark, ubiquitous silences of Polmarran was drawing to a close. I still felt uneasy, but Redmond Carne's answers, his entire narrative in fact, had contained the unmistakable ring of truth. As unmistakable as the new elements of trust and mutual reliance which now linked us together.

Or was it something deeper than trust?

Later that evening I went with him to see Captain Northwood.

I was quite taken aback by the change in the Captain's appearance. No longer was he the stern and powerful master of Polmarran; in a matter of mere hours I discovered suddenly a frail old man with the flesh of his face sunken below the level of living - stark and frightening evidence of a much greater shock than Redmond Carne had first supposed.

I cast an anxious sidelong glance at my companion as we approached the bed. It was obvious from his expression that Carne was likewise appalled by the terrible change in the Captain's appearance. A casual enquiry attempted to disguise his concern: 'Feeling a bit better now, eh, Cap'n?'

Captain Northwood turned his head slowly, letting it loll to one side of the pillow. He looked at me, narrowly at first, his eyes half-closed against the glare of a solitary rush-lamp battling with the pervading gloom. Heavy, storm-laden clouds pressed against the dark window-panes; an angry blast of wind rattled the shutters. I shivered. Was it the room's dreary light and the chill air, or the glint of the old imperiousness in my employer's stare?

'So, you have disobeyed me.' His voice was hoarse and low. 'You refuse to leave.'

'Yes, I'm afraid so.' I was uneasy, but not apologetic. 'Mr Carne thinks it necessary that I should remain - at least for the present.'

The Captain's gaze slowly swung round to settle on Carne's face.

'I need her here.' Carne took my arm protectively, as though I was suddenly of personal value to him. I no longer hated myself for feeling appreciative of such a gesture. 'The child too. Adelaide needs her.'

There was no other sound save a petulant stutter of wind at the casement. The room darkened. Captain Northwood continued to stare at us in silence. We stood before him, for all the world like a young couple seeking his approval. The silence was finally broken by the old man putting a direct question to me.

'And are you determined to remain here in defiance of my command and . . . and after what you've seen here, this afternoon, in the tower?'

I think he expected me to flinch at that. Surprisingly, my refusal to do so, and my reply, did not appear to anger him. 'Not in defiance. I wish you had not put it that way, sir . . . but if Mr Carne considers I should stay on for the sake of my pupil and until you are returned to good health, well then, I hope you will give your consent. After all, Captain Northwood, I do feel responsible . . .'

'Come here, young lady.' His hoarse tone still retained an echo of the afternoon's stern authority. 'You are loyal, I see. It's a virtue rarely found in the young these days.'

Carne released my arm. I went across and stood beside the bed.

'Your former employer was a fool to let you go. What was it he said in that letter? Something about your being "a self-assured young lady with an independent spirit of mind" . . . wasn't that it? Yes, you have backbone, Miss Ainsley. I'll grant you that.' His words were cut off by a violent fit of coughing.

'Captain Northwood, I believe you should rest now. We can discuss all of this tomorrow if you like, after the doctor has . . .'

'Doctors, bah!'

'But your health . . .'

'My health, or ill-health, is my concern. Now be so good as to go to your pupil, Miss Ainsley. She progresses well under your tutelage and is quite taken with you, I am glad to say. She will need you more than ever now . . .' His eyelids fluttered and then closed. It was as if they had closed over on that thought, and as though he had some secret way of looking into the future. What exactly did he mean?

I turned to Redmond Carne, who merely nodded, whether in agreement with the Captain's reference to Adelaide, or to indicate that I should go to the child, I could not tell. The Captain's eyes were still closed. I wondered if he was beginning to fall asleep. Or pretending to.

'We'll leave the Cap'n to rest for a while.'

The old man spoke. 'No, you stay. We have certain matters to arrange.'

'Aye, sir.'

'Good evening, Miss Ainsley. Mr Carne will see you out . . .' He began to cough again. In search of a little ease he moved his head about on the pillow.

Carne took my arm and led me to the door. 'What do you think?' he whispered, indicating the figure on the bed with a troubled frown.

'He's obviously quite ill. We must do something . . .'

'Aye.' He bit down on his lower lip, thinking hard. 'What the hell is keeping that laggard Forrest . . . he's been gone these four hours!'

'Try not to worry. Perhaps Forrest and Dr Howard will be here in a matter of minutes. We can but wait and pray.'

He pressed my hand appreciatively and then stepped back into the Captain's room. The door closed softly behind him. They had matters to arrange. What sort of matters? Did the Captain know or suspect that he was on his deathbed?

I walked away slowly, disconsolately, not knowing

exactly what my feelings were. Through some cruel irony I owed my continued presence here to Captain Northwood's grave and sudden illness - an illness which I felt in part responsible for. And now there was nothing I could do about it but wait and hope and pray. I almost envied Redmond Carne his presence beside the old man's bed. He at least had some positive role. For my part I don't think I ever felt more wretchedly incapable.

Chapter Twelve

With each passing moment the weather grew steadily worse, and with it, the Captain's strength. Mrs Forrest, who was back and forth with hot broths and a variety of medicaments, said that he was like a man who no longer had the will to recover. Less than an hour after I had left the Captain's room Redmond Carne came to tell me that he was going for the doctor. He was already attired in his oilskins and top-boots.

I went with him to the hall door. 'Please take care,' I said.

'And you too, Katherine.'

'Me?'

'Just stay with the child. Continue as usual and you'll have nothing to fret about. When I get back I'll attend to everything.'

I wasn't too sure what he meant by 'everything' but I nodded. 'Very well. Be careful on the road. And God-speed, Redmond.'

His eyes lit up momentarily at my use of his Christian name. He pressed my hand gently in his, looked at me searchingly, then turned quickly and hurried down the steps. I watched him ride off, grim-faced and determined, awkwardly tall in the saddle. I remained standing at the door. I was rigid with anxiety and a strange, new sense of foreboding. I seemed unaware of the wind-driven rain slashing at the portals and splattering my face. Before he disappeared amongst the trees Redmond turned and waved to me. I wondered if he observed my answering gesture, for already the wavering sheets of rain were forming a dark curtain between us.

'Hurry back!' I called in vain. A long trembling wail of wind snatched the words from me and sent them echoing back through the house. With some difficulty I forced the door shut. He would be gone for at least two hours, I reckoned. It was now just a little after eight o'clock.

Though it was now well past Adelaide's usual bedtime I allowed her to remain in the kitchen with Mrs Forrest and myself. It was by far the brightest, warmest and most cheerful place in the house. Mrs Forrest was already rehearsing the sharp scolding which awaited her erring husband when, and if, he ever returned. From her and the child I hid my own uneasiness and tried to invigorate them with a feigned comportment. It took considerable effort. The glowering storm was everywhere; it shrieked about the house and with each blast the feeble flames of our candles lent to the surroundings a grim luminosity. My eyes were already accustomed to the gloom, but not my feelings.

'I wish Redmond did not have to go,' Adelaide said suddenly.

I shared Adelaide's wish but thought it better to say, 'He won't be long. You'll see. Another hour or so, that's all. Now then, shall we think up a word game or some riddles in which all three of us can participate? Any ideas?'

'What about Georgie?'

'What do you mean?'

'If Redmond should not return . . .'

Uncertainty pared my words down into sharp points of irritability. 'You must not talk like that. He will return presently with Dr Howard.'

'But Mr Forrest hasn't returned, has he? He's lost in the storm.'

'That's quite enough, Adelaide! Come now, drink your milk.'

'Don't fret yourself, child. As for Jem Forrest being lost in a storm . . . more likely he's trying to find his bearings in a taproom. I'll fetch that lop-sided wastrel a hefty wallop soon as ever he dares show his nose into this here kitchen of mine after the way he's deserted his post and neglected his duties this day! God's truth, I will!' The housekeeper sounded as though she meant every word of it. 'Neither should you go fretting about your uncle, Miss Adelaide. Mr Carne took a full tray of vittals up to the young master before he rode off. So there's nothing further to worry about. And even if Mr Carne and the doctor are held up awhile by the weather, Miss Ainsley will know what to do.'

'But supposing they get lost . . .?'

'Adelaide, I forbid you to continue like this!' I ordered her, frightened by the possibility.

But the child was right! What if Redmond was delayed, or ran into some difficulties - a bridge washed away by the torrent, or a rockslide, or a fallen tree - what then? I exchanged my troubled glance for Mrs Forrest's questioning look. Would I really know what to do? A rapid series of images flashed through my mind: George, alone in that dreary cell, and terrified by the storm; a spear of lightning shattering some part of the old tower, trapping him; a further deterioration in Captain Northwood's strength, or worse, his sudden demise! I was becoming morbid in my thoughts. I'd have to snap out of them for all our sakes.

'Very well then, if nobody wants to play riddles or think up some word games I shall read to you.'

I took down Mr Lamb's *Tales from Shakespeare* and read to my companions for the next forty-five minutes. But neither of them displayed any great interest. Mrs Forrest went on preparing tomorrow's

226

bread and Adelaide pursed her lips and tried to look attentive at first, but her mind was not on Shakespeare. Nor was mine for that matter. The child's bright, nervous eyes searched my features with a relentless insistence: *What will happen if Redmond too should be delayed?* Already a kind of fear was becoming part of our anxiety over his absence and the Captain's illness.

'I think that is sufficient reading for the present, my dear.' I closed the book.

'Yes, the light is bad and your eyes must be tired. Thank you, Katherine.' She gave me a sweet smile, but her eyes were still anxious.

'And now you must excuse me for a little while.'

'Where are you going, Katherine?' Adelaide's eyes dilated as though stretching imagination to a conception of some lurking horror.

'Pray do not look so solemn, young lady. Why, I'm sure Mr Newton must have deduced the Law of Gravity from just such an expression. I'm only going to see how Captain Northwood is, that's all.' I maintained the illusion of supreme ease and nothing-to-worry-about airiness by pirouetting at the door.

That mode of departure contrasted greatly with my journey up to the front hall. The front door creaked and rattled with the rising wind that now whispered eerily down the hall to meet me; on the stone flags my footsteps rang out with a lonely distinctness. There was little or no illumination, only the gaunt paleness of the great walls on either side of me - silent, watchful, closing in. Overhead the blackened oak beams spread their heavy shadows across the ceiling. Somewhere an open door swayed back and forth, a forlorn sighing through the dark recesses. A loose shutter tried to keep time with it as it clattered intermittently against an outside wall.

I hurried on - then paused, disturbed by a faint rustling as if something small was slithering along the floor behind me. I stepped quickly to one side and looked down. With relief I discovered that it was nothing more sinister than a sheet of paper. It slid along, wafted by a low whistling draught, stopping, twisting about, rolling over the broad flagstones. A second, and then a third sheet of paper came drifting towards me from the shadows. I bent to pick them up, found some more strewn along the way, followed them, gathering them up, and soon found that they were coming from the half-open door of Captain Northwood's study. I pushed the door and entered.

It was only my second time to be in that room. A steady draught of cold air was riffling the collection of papers on the desk, the topmost ones sailing to the floor, some tumbling out to meet me, others settling against the base of the waist-high globe or the legs of the chart table. The hanging shutter was close by and, suspecting an open window to be the cause of the disarrayed papers, I hurried over with the intention of closing it. But that odd-looking window, with its crowded lattice-work and deliberate tilt to resemble a vessel's stern window, was secure. Each pane of glass was intact. Then where was the strong draught coming from? Puzzled, I looked about me. With some degree of straining, my eyes made out a break in the otherwise regular arrangement of those dark wood panels which were modelled to give the impression of state-room bulkheads - a peculiar distortion of shadows, a narrower, deeper tone set against the wall - something told me that one was either different, or loose, or slightly open, like a concealed door. I went over to it.

The cold air was seeping through an aperture between two of the panels, breathing its musty chilliness into my face through a six-inch gap. I tried it with my hand. It *was* a door. I opened it and peered inside. As soon as my eyes became accustomed to the new degree of darkness I perceived a small passageway. And the unmistakable brickwork of Polmarran Tower.

I knew now how Captain Northwood had earlier made his entrance and thus surprised me in George's cell. And through this same door Redmond Carne must have carried the stricken old man back into the house, forgetting to close it behind him in his anxiety. I stood with one hand on the panel, wondering just how close this cabin-like room was to George Northwood's cell, but I had no intention of venturing through the connecting passage to find out; the darkness, for one thing, and the musty odour of - no, not just mustiness! There was something else, some faint, familiar scent that came to me with each new gust of stale air from the interior - known to me, yet not known, subtle, vague, a will-o'-the-wisp aroma that didn't linger in the air long enough for identification. I opened the door further and leaned in, sniffing. Laudanum? Was I that close to George's cell?

Opening this secret door to the tower caused a more intense draught to rush out and close the other door behind me with a loud crash. I jumped with fright, spun round, and hurried over to it, oddly dreading the possibility that it might not open to my touch. It did, as I should have known it would, but the fact that only a moment before I had half-expected it to be locked revealed to me just how frayed my nerves had become. I left the study without a backward glance, all thought of the wind-blown papers swept from my mind, and went on up the stairs to the Captain's bedroom.

I tapped on the door and waited. I tapped again, then opened the door, and tip-toed into the unresponsive stillness. The light from one single candle touched the marble-like pallor of Captain Northwood's face. His eyes were closed in their hollow sockets. For just an instant I thought he was dead, so acute had my nervous sensibilities become. But, thankfully, his gaunt features flickered into life at my approach.

'Redmond?'

'No, Captain Northwood . . .'

'Where's Redmond?' The eyes opened - the only live thing about him - and settled on me.

'He's gone for the doctor. Forrest still hasn't returned.'

'Redmond shouldn't have gone. Not now . . . not in this weather. Besides, there's no use . . . no need to . . .' The voice combined resignation and mild reproof.

'Is there anything I can do for you?'

He shook his head. 'Just send Redmond to me when he arrives.'

'Certainly. He should be here shortly,' I said, trying desperately to sound convincing though inwardly imagining Redmond Carne's riderless horse trotting into the stable at any moment.

Captain Northwood was also trying to sound convincing; for my benefit, I think. 'Yes, Redmond is an old hand. He will come to no harm in this storm. In the meanwhile, Miss Ainsley, I must request you to take charge of everything until his return. The road might be bad and he may be held to some delay, so . . .'

'Delay? What do you mean?'

'Be so kind as to hear me out,' he muttered testily. Then, in combined explanation and apology, he resumed: 'You see, Miss Ainsley, I doubt that there is much time left.'

'No, surely if you rest . . .'

Again that weary wave of his hand. 'You must stay with your pupil all the while. You and Mrs Forrest. Then if Redmond has not returned - say within the next hour - you must take the pony and trap. Mrs Forrest should know how to hitch it up. And you must take the child to Sir Arthur Rebstock's place, the Grange. Mrs Forrest knows the way . . .'

'And what of my responsibility to you, sir, a sick man, and to your son? What would become of you if we were to leave at a time like this? No sir . . .'

'I am of no importance . . . and my son is . . . well, he is not your concern.' There was no admonition in his words, none of the old authority. I was seeing the Captain as an old man, helpless, close to pleading.

'I'm sorry, Captain Northwood, but we shall wait here until Redmond comes back with the doctor.'

He succeeded in raising himself into a half-sitting position in the bed. His pale hand made a vague, half-beckoning motion. 'How much has Redmond told you?'

He was watching me closely, troubled, without hostility, as though sympathizing with my hesitancy. 'Please, Miss Ainsley . . . I feel certain that he has told you everything. Or rather, that he has told you as much as he knows. So do not be afraid to speak. For, believe me, I have come to share Redmond's high opinion of you as a person to be trusted and relied upon. Please, Miss Ainsley.'

I still wasn't sure, and so chose to be evasive. 'Well, naturally there is a great deal which I have guessed at . . .'

'Please, young lady. No hair-splitting. I have little time left.' The lone candle cast its wavering light over a face that was momentarily lost in the past. When he spoke again the strength had gone from his voice: it faltered for just an instant. 'It must be quite obvious to you that my son is hopelessly insane.'

'I'm not sure I would use quite so strong a term, Captain Northwood. That your son is disturbed, and lonely, and of an extremely timid and sensitive nature has been quite apparent to . . .'

'He is insane!'

Despite the father's grief I was not completely successful in eradicating a note of recrimination from my tone. 'Then it is hardly to be wondered at when your son is compelled to spend so much of his time in that depressing place.'

'It is precisely because of his insanity that we must keep him there at certain times. Such as now, with this storm. His mind can snap at any moment.'

In the flickering light Captain Northwood's eyes looked at me with tragic anger and my only response was to half-shrug my shoulders and murmur ineffectually, 'Still, it does seem so cruel to keep him locked up like a criminal.'

'Cruel, yes! Cruel on my poor boy and equally cruel on the father who must do it out of necessity! But can't you see . . . the boy is dangerous!'

'Dangerous?'

'Yes . . .' He paused, a man on the brink of some desperate decision. When he resumed his words had the impact of a physical blow.

'My son once attempted to kill his sister-in-law. Yes, Miss Ainsley, a long time ago, and during a storm just like this . . . poor George, with his twisted sense of right and wrong, and believing himself to be an instrument of Divine wrath and retribution. Oh, he is not responsible for his actions at such times. How could he be? The blame is mine for not watching him more closely in those days, for not fully understanding . . . and for not sending that woman away from here.'

I was listening now, not only to the Captain's awesome words, but to another noise which rang out with sharp clarity above the howling storm - the noise of a door slamming somewhere downstairs, and then of footsteps hurrying quickly along the stone-paved hallway.

'And once before, on a night like this, he attempted to kill Eliza's child. So you see why we must . . . what is it, Miss Ainsley?'

'Downstairs . . . the door to your study was open. And also a panel door which led into the tower . . .'

232

'Open! But that door is always locked. No one knows of it but Redmond Carne and myself.' His face was blank with shock and incomprehension. 'Someone must . . . George?'

A chilling clutch of terror seized me and impelled me towards the bedroom door. 'Good God, no!'

I was at the door, wrenching it open, fear spreading through me.

'Quick! Go to the child!' Captain Northwood's last order was a hoarse cry, something pulled together from the habits of a lifetime and the shadows of his dying. 'Please hurry . . .!'

I had a fleeting impression of him trying to rise, to follow and assist me. But my concern was not so much for his plight as for the innocent and unsuspecting Adelaide - and the nemesis of a suppressed, half-dead evil which might at this very moment be surfacing to threaten her!

I dashed along the dark corridor. By the time I reached the top of the stairs my sense of George Northwood's proximity was acute; the past had become frighteningly vivid, the echo of my wild panic through the woods and the whispered menace of close pursuit. In panic it now flashed through my mind that, mistaking me for Eliza, he had intended to kill me. And now Adelaide?

I hurried down the stairs and stumbled into the hallway. Turning sharply I raced to the kitchen. Fearful anticipation had become a source of courage. But how to weigh my own feeble resources against the unpredictable strength of a madman should I find George there with the child?

I flung wide the kitchen door, guillotining with swift urgency whatever had been in progress. He was there!

They stood stock still, close to each other, wordless for the moment, all eyes riveted on me in collective surprise. But what contrast in their expressions!

The alarm on Mrs Forrest's face broke and was flooded with relief at the sight of me; Adelaide's features were so taut with confusion and fear as to be incapable of sudden readjustment. But George Northwood's face sent a fresh quiver of panic through me - his look was of such extraordinary hatred that I could actually feel it. I *was* Eliza.

In desperation I broke the silence. 'Did you have something to eat, Mr Northwood? Mrs Forrest, perhaps you will be kind enough to prepare something . . . ah, Adelaide! Long past your bedtime, I'm afraid. Come, we will say good night to your grandfather. You too, Mrs Forrest . . . the Captain would like a word with you . . . we shan't be long, Mr Northwood . . .' My words made little sense. They were not intended to, only to dispel the hypnotic stare which held me captive. 'Come along now, Adelaide . . .'

'Your child, Eliza. I remember now,' he said, following my gaze down to the frightened child. 'You sinned, Eliza. This child is the fruit of your corruption.'

All the time he was speaking I was edging imperceptibly towards the child, inching one foot forward, then the other, ready at any moment to snatch Adelaide from his side . . .

'Stay where you are!' He moved with cunning adroitness, placing himself between me and the girl.

'Mrs Forrest, be so good as to take Adelaide to her room. Mr Northwood, I would like you to come with me to your father's room . . .'

'My father condones your wickedness by allowing you to remain here. He should have cast you out . . . you and your bastard.' His body had the tense litheness of something ready to spring forward at any moment. I fought down an impulse to step back.

'Look at me, George. I am not Eliza. I am Katherine Ainsley.' I knew that it was too late to convince him of my true identity; the past was tearing his mind to shreds in a paradox of hate, guilt, and twisted righteousness. But by confronting him thus, and making him focus all his attention on me, I was playing for time. Precious seconds. Over his shoulder I could see Mrs Forrest in the act of sidling closer to Adelaide and reaching out with one hand to take the child's. Not until she had secured the child's hand in her own and was stealthily tip-toeing with her towards the door could I risk speaking again.

'Look at me, George. Who am I?'

'Eliza.'

'No. Eliza is dead.'

'You are Eliza! You came back . . . I recognized you that day at the pool. You, Eliza . . . lying there half-naked and unashamed!' He was now my accuser. He flung a torrent of wild denunciations at me, the words running into one another so that I could distinguish nothing but their fury. 'You must be punished for your wickedness!'

I tried to elude the swift grasp of his hand. He clutched me fiercely by the wrist.

'Let go of me!' I twisted and struggled, with only anger as a weapon. Anger and fear.

His free hand streaked towards my throat. Adelaide screamed. The piercing cry distracted him for just an instant and deflected the movement of his hand. He swung round, seeing Adelaide again, remembering . . . 'The fruit of your wickedness! She too must be punished!'

'Run, Adelaide!' I cried out a desperate warning. At the same time I swung my hand up sharply, the open palm crashing against his jaw and drawing his attention back to me.

He caught me by the hair and forced me back against the wall. The hand still pinioned in his fierce grip was twisted upwards and behind my back. With his other hand he clawed through my hair and found my throat. The fingers splayed out, the thumb hooked under my chin. Our straining, writhing bodies met and he held me close to him in some horrible travesty of an embrace, crushing me, forcing me back, overpowering me. My eyes became misty with tears of pain. My throat ached, seared with a breath-robbing agony. His white face was almost touching mine, a passion scarcely human suffusing every feature. Blood showed on his lower lip where he must have bitten deeply into it. It showed, too, in three tiny parallel streaks along his cheek where I must have clawed at him - for I had never in my life felt so possessed of violence. With a sickening dread I realized that I was fighting for my life, for each diminishing gasp of breath . . .

Just when I thought that I must surely succumb his hand lost its hold on my throat. I cried out and I sensed him falling away from me. I opened my eyes to see Mrs Forrest behind him. With both hands she was pulling at his hair. He lost balance in turning so quickly to meet her attack. As he fell against the table we somehow managed to push him to the floor - and then, miraculously, I was free of him and Mrs Forrest was pushing me towards the door.

'Adelaide . . .'

'Outside. Quick!' Grabbing my arm, she hurried me ahead of her. As we stumbled from the room together, I cast a swift, frightened glance over my shoulder. George Northwood was in the act of rising, clawing at the table for support, his hand tangled in the hanging folds of the table-cloth, dragging it down and toppling its contents to the stone floor. The big carving knife struck the ground with a sharp, metallic ring and lay there amidst the broken crockery, only inches from his hand. I slammed the door, knowing it to be futile, but desperately anxious to blot out the sight of his fingers settling on the knife handle.

'Quick now, miss,' Mrs Forrest urged me.

We raced up the hall together and found Adelaide crouched in fear at the bottom of the stairs. She rushed to me and my arms closed about her instinctively.

'Oh, Katherine!' She clung to me, sobbing, on the verge of hysteria.

'Hush now, my dear. It's all right.' I prepared to mount the stairs.

'No, not that way,' Mrs Forrest called. Her hand reached across the banister and drew me back.

'But Captain Northwood . . .?'

'There's no time. Listen!'

We heard the kitchen door opening.

'This way.' Mrs Forrest indicated the shadowy outlines of the doorway to the old ballroom. We ran swiftly towards it. From the pocket of her apron she drew forth a key. I prayed silently that it was the correct one.

'Eliza . . . you are wicked!' His voice came hissing from the darkness somewhere behind us, the anguish and hate sounding above the storm and reverberating through the lower regions of the house. We made the ballroom door almost in one bound, dragging the child with us, and slammed the door on the sound of quick-gliding footsteps further along the hall. I threw all my weight against the panel while Mrs Forrest fumbled with the key and the lock. Was it the wrong key after all?

Thank heavens, no! It clicked home just in time - and George Northwood's beating fists made no impact on the enormous thickness of the oaken panels. Once inside the great room, I realized that I was still trembling. I locked my hands together, forcing one to steady the other. Tremors of fear still raced through my body. Mrs Forrest and poor little Adelaide were in a similar state. The three of us stood huddled together in the dark, our shoulders still pressed against the door as though distrusting the strength of the lock. We dared not make a sound even though the hammering of his hands against the wood had ceased. Was he still outside? We remained listening with bated breath. The gale continued to shriek and howl about us. It rattled the shutters, the casements, even the stout door, striking everything with all the demoniac fury of some evil thing seeking entrance. How long we remained thus I cannot remember, but it seemed an eternity. A horrible time of waiting and listening fixedly for a noise just on the other side of the door.

'Do you think he's gone?' Mrs Forrest whispered.

'I don't know.'

'What'll we do then?'

I had no answer to that either. My mind was still incapable of concentration. Yet clearly some course of action would have to be decided on. We couldn't just remain here, helpless, listening to our own heart-beats ticking away the handful of moments separating us from the next terror.

'If only we had something, some weapon . . .' My eyes searched the shadows. The panelled walls offered no metallic gleam, only the dull specks of peeling gold-leaf. Dust covers still shrouded the furniture and John Northwood's portrait continued to look down on the darkened room with unfeeling timelessness. There was nothing here.

'In the dining-room, miss. All those fearsome swords hanging on the wall, and there's the pistols. But I don't know about powder and shot and such-like.'

'Would you know how to fire a pistol?'

'Merciful heavens, Miss Ainsley, 'course not! Would you?'

'I'm not sure, besides . . .'

I had no wish to handle a gun. To overpower, or render harmless in some way, yes - but deliberately to shoot at him! No, it was absolutely out of the question. There must be some other way.

I began to regret the panic which made us flee the kitchen such a short while before; had we been less frightened, and more resolute, when George Northwood had fallen to the floor, together we might have successfuly held him and bound him. My mind was starting to function again. I moved away from the door, trying to think out the next move. Mrs Forrest remained in the same position, rigidly vigilant, like a sentinel by the door, but Adelaide clung to my arm, her panic gradually subsiding.

'Everything will be all right, dear. I promise.' Removing my shawl, I draped it comfortingly about her narrow shoulders and led her to a large armchair.

'Katherine, listen . . .'

'What is it?'

'Listen . . .'

I obeyed, suddenly aware of a relative stillness. It was as if the storm had died away on the instant, only to be succeeded by a strange silence - no, not really silence, for there was still the steady pit-pit-pit of the rain outside the windows. But the wind was gone for the moment, the last howl sinking to a whimper somewhere out on the hills. After eight hours of shrieking gales this change was too swift. It left a sinister echo.

'Yes. Thank heavens the wind has died down!'

'No, Katherine, not that. Can't you hear it? Listen . . . it may be Redmond returning.'

'Redmond!' I flew to the window, my strained hearing seeking out each faint sound. Was it only the steady beat of the rain that I heard, or the distant thud of approaching hooves? Or something else? The scrunch of hurrying footsteps on the gravel path just outside?

I threw back the dusty, moth-eaten curtains and discovered too late that it was the latter - the figure looming up from the darkness on the opposite side of the pane was that of George Northwood! I sprang back in fright, and jumped to one side just before the knife handle struck the centre pane. A shower of broken glass flew past me. The long wet slivers gleamed menacingly on the floor and snapped beneath my feet as I swung back again to confront him. Already his arm was thrust through the jagged aperture, the fingers deft and busy with the clasp. I struck wildly at his wrist and knuckles. Scarcely six inches separated our faces - his streaked with rain and sweat, mine flexed with fear, our eyes locked in a deadly duel. Our hands too were engaged in a frantic contest, tearing, twisting, slashing and pulling at the window clasp. He almost succeeded in wrenching it and flinging open the window, but somehow I thwarted him. My nails left ugly marks across the back of his hand. I saw his free hand - the one clutching the knife - raised outside the window, preparatory to delivering another strike at the glass. I would surely have received the full impact of the flying glass, or worse, the knife, had I not broken off the struggle on the instant and thrown myself to one side. Another shower of glass fell about me. I stumbled and fell.

In all this time I was vaguely aware of the fact that Mrs Forrest had unlocked the ballroom door and hurried away with the child, now I was only partially aware of the fact that she had returned and that she was dashing to my side and trying to help me to my feet, for my eyes were riveted on the horrifying spectacle of the window, now almost devoid of glass, swinging open and George Northwood's head and shoulders leaning into the room . . .

'Your beauty is evil and corrupt, Eliza. Like a pestilence on all whom you touch . . . it must be destroyed!'

Mrs Forrest reached him first. I leaped to her side. We struggled and pushed with concerted effort. For just a moment it seemed likely that he would come tumbling in on top of us, but with one desperate lunge we forced him off balance and sent his thrashing body falling back into the night. He lay spread-eagled in the churned mud of a flower bed with the rain streaming over his upturned face. Yet all we had succeeded in doing was gaining a brief respite. There was still no bolted door, no secured window, no barrier, between us. Together Mrs Forrest and I stood transfixed, peering through a curtain of rain with a kind of horrible fascination as he got to his knees and started to grope about in the mud for the knife. It came up, ugly with damp earth, firmly clenched in his hand.

'Here, Miss Ainsley . . . you take it!' From her apron Mrs Forrest drew forth a heavy pistol.

'Oh no!'

But George Northwood was already on his feet and hurling himself at the shattered window once more, the knife held aloft. Mrs Forrest raised the gun, using both hands. With her arms outstretched, holding the pistol as far away from her as possible, she took aim.

'No, Mrs Forrest, don't . . .!' Even as I uttered the words I knew that there was really no other way. Our assailant was half-way into the room again, his face pale and malevolent, and seemingly oblivious of the weapon pointing at his chest.

'Stand off, Mr George . . . for pity's sake, or I needs must fire!' The gun barrel wavered, but not Mrs Forrest's voice or her tense features.

'Don't fire!' The words came from behind us, an urgent command splitting the darkness.

I spun round, surprised - and oh, so relieved to discover Charles Northwood in the doorway.

He ran towards us, sweeping his cloak from him, taking in the entire scene in a thrice. 'Give me the pistol, Mrs Forrest.'

'Gladly, sir.' She thrust the weapon into his hand.

'Get back, George. Do you hear me? This is Charles. Get back! You've made a dreadful mistake, brother. This girl is not Eliza . . .' Charles pocketed the gun and walked steadily towards the window.

Casting a final glance in my direction the demented young man drew his head and shoulders back through the window.

'Wait, Georgie. Listen to me . . .!'

But George Northwood wasn't listening. He turned sharply and ran back along the side of the wall. Moments later we saw him hurrying off across the lawn towards the trees with a darting sideways gait as though hurt by his fall a short while before - or as though his twisted and tortured mind had wrought its work right down through every fibre of his body. The rain swirled about him, gathering him into its drenched folds and concealing him somewhere in the night.

'Poor George.' Sighing, and grim-faced, Charles turned away from the smashed window. 'We'll let him go for the moment. I'll know where to find him. It would appear that I arrived just in the nick of time. Are you all right?'

He came towards me with one arm extended, as though about to place it about my shoulders. For my part it took a supreme effort of will not to throw myself into his arms from sheer relief. 'Yes, we are now. Thank heavens you're here, Charles!'

Mrs Forrest said, 'The child was right. She said she heard a horse coming.'

'When I found the hall door closed I rode round to the stable-yard and came in through the kitchen. I knew then that there was something amiss. My word, Mrs Forrest, but your good crockery is a shambles.'

How wonderful it was to see someone who was actually smiling, if only for an instant! Charles was in command of the situation now, protecting us, relieving us of the burden of decision. I sat down

242

wearily on one of the covered chairs, heedless of the little cloud of dust that rose about me. I felt drained of all energy and purpose. Adelaide had returned and was huddled and cowering in the deep well of the big armchair, my shawl clutched tightly about her. She was bravely attempting to stifle her sobs. Her face - still angelic, but withdrawn and older now - gleamed with the most recent tears. Charles went over and knelt down beside her.

'Hush now, little girl. Everything is all right.' He picked her up in his arms, cradling her golden hair against his jaw and gently caressing her. 'Hush now, my pet. I won't let anything harm you.' He continued to soothe the child in this manner but his eyes were on me, silently conveying the same message of protection. When Adelaide was calmer Charles turned to Mrs Forrest.

'Take her up to her room. And stay with her all the time.'

'Very good, sir.'

'Where are you going?' I asked him.

'To my father.'

'Wait, Charles. You don't understand.'

'Yes, Katherine, I think I do.'

There was that in the manner of his saying so which told me that he knew, or suspected, everything. Perhaps it was that fear and grief were so vividly emblazoned on our faces that he could not avoid knowing the worst. He gathered up his cloak and led us from the deserted ballroom. It was no longer quite silent: the wind, with a plaintive wail, crept in through the shattered window and billowed the frowsy curtain. It breathed a kind of dank, chill life into the deserted room for just a moment, then Mrs Forrest closed the door.

Charles was already half-way up the stairs. I followed him, but paused at the first step until I had ascertained that Mrs Forrest had locked the door behind her and that she had the child safely in tow. Even with Charles's presence in the house now and the sound of his footsteps - quick, clear and reassuring on the landing above - I experienced a new tremor of fear. What would he find in his father's room?

'Wait here, Mrs Forrest. Just in case. I'll join you in a moment . . .' I hurried after Charles.

I met him coming from Captain Northwood's room. I knew immediately that the Captain was dead. The son's face told me everything - it was around the grim set of his mouth and the sadly staring eyes. If I needed further proof, I had only to look past Charles and through the partly opened door. Captain Northwood was lying on the floor, his feet shrouded in the tangled and trailing bedclothes. He must have died within moments of my hurrying from the room! My hand rose involuntarily to my mouth in a vain attempt to stifle a sobbing intake of breath. Very gently Charles took my arm. As he led me back to the top of the stairs his eyes, full of deep pain, strayed back to the now-closed door.

'Oh, Charles . . . I feel so responsible, so desolate!'

'You mustn't. His time had come.'

'He was trying to help us . . . Adelaide and I. Oh, I feel so much to blame for all of this.'

'Stop that, Katherine.' He did not have to speak loudly: his half-whispered words were full of quiet authority.

'Forgive me. It must be so dreadful for you. Your father, and your brother.'

'It was inevitable. I should have returned earlier. Perhaps I could have prevented this.'

Mrs Forrest and Adelaide, seeing us at the landing, started up the stairs towards us.

'This was all Carne's doing.' Charles said without any change of expression touching his handsome features. 'A deliberate, well-thought-out scheme to get the entire inheritance for his daughter.'

244

'What . . .?'

There was just a fleeting instant of incomprehension - then I turned to look down at the approaching child and for the first time I saw something in her face which had been there all the time but which I could not until this moment apprehend. I saw the elusive, fugitive resemblance to Redmond Carne!

Chapter Thirteen

'I still can't believe it . . .' Too much terror and tragedy had been compressed into this one day, forcing out all sense of reality. I still felt numb with shock, confused and exhausted.

'Well, there's the proof. What more do you want, Katherine?' For the second time in less than three minutes Charles placed the sheet of paper before me. 'There it is . . . Eliza's signature, her own handwriting naming Carne as the father of her child.'

Once again the paper shimmered before my eyes; the writing was a blur. I pushed the sheet away, again without reading it, and looked up at him.

'Yes, I accept that. But I cannot accept that Redmond Carne would deliberately expose his own daughter to such danger . . . to such a frightful experience.'

'Not the child, Katherine . . . but *you!* You were the victim.'

'But why?'

He shrugged; there was just a hint of exasperation in the gesture. Then he turned from me and went to the window again and looked out. The rain continued to beat steadily on that odd, ship's stern window. Dark, desolate rain that formed crazy erratic patterns on the small panes. The rain patterns held for a short while on the glass, only to disintegrate with each fresh gust of wind. Like my thoughts, holding together for just a little while and then breaking up, running into each other, losing themselves in nothingness.

We were in the Captain's study. The room already had a forlorn, derelict look despite Charles's valiant efforts to get a fire going in the grate. I had gathered and tidied up the strewn papers and charts, but their arrangement on the desk only served to emphasize the fact that they would never be used, or cared for, by Captain Northwood again.

Frowning, Charles came back from the window. He bent down and picked up another log to place on the fire. 'I want you to go up and stay with Mrs Forrest and Adelaide.'

'Why would Carne want to harm me, Charles?' I persisted, probably because I could not bear to think he would.

'Look, Katherine, I do not as yet possess all the answers. Why, if I hadn't found Jem Forrest swilling rum at *The Crown* I might never have stumbled on to any of this.'

'What has Forrest got to do with it?'

'The wretch was drunk when I found him, and he had sufficient money in his pockets to remain in that condition for at least two days. Carne gave him that money. I had to clout Forrest into some semblance of sobriety before I could discover that much, or make any sense of his mumbling. But this much I did learn: that Carne had given him the money, had told him to enjoy himself at Jack Tregarron's and that he was not to report back here for at least twenty-four hours. There had been no mention of seeking out Dr Howard. Can't you see, Katherine? Carne wanted Forrest out of the way, and with that achieved he was then free to absent himself on the same pretext. Before he left he must have opened the door to George's cell and this hidden door . . .' Charles indicated the dark panel in the bulkhead-like wall. 'Before skulking away he must have worked on

247

George's mind, convincing the lad that you really were Eliza. Not that George needed much convincing on that score . . .'

'But I still fail to see the reason for such a scheme.' *It couldn't be, could it?*

'No, Katherine, allow me to correct you. The fact is you do not want to see the reason for it.'

'What is that supposed to mean?'

'Simply that you've allowed yourself to be taken in by Carne . . . by his well-acted role as the loyal and trusted servant of my late father. Indeed, I do believe you are actually in love with the fellow.'

I looked away. There was more than a modicum of truth in what Charles was saying. I *had* believed Carne. Earlier today, in my room, when he had begged me not to leave, I had trusted him, and withal had discovered myself to be on the brink of loving him. That which I had half-feared and half-expected from the moment of our first meeting had come to pass. Memory moved swiftly back to that evening outside *The Crown Inn,* to the picture of Carne emerging from the taproom, his broad shoulders almost filling the doorway and his reddish-gold hair brushing the stone lintel; something in our respective personalities had sparked off an instant awareness of that kind of personal immediacy from which either deep affection, or animosity, can grow. I had been lured into the former. How quickly too I had discarded my long-nurtured suspicions of Redmond Carne's motives - and how eagerly I had accepted his version of things!

For that matter was I not now being too eager in accepting Charles's version? True, he had arrived just in time to rescue us . . . or George? No matter. He had arrived in time to avert another tragedy. But he still hadn't satisfactorily explained the purpose behind Carne's scheme. Or perhaps he had, and I hadn't been listening. He was talking now, looking intently at me, his words coming in a quick, urgent rhythm, ignoring my puzzlement, my reluctance to accept. I tried desperately to concentrate, as though the task itself would be a link with reality and coherence. In what way would Redmond Carne have profited by my death at the hands of a deranged youth, or by exposing his own daughter to the same danger?

Charles, with that unique quality by which he seemed to be able to divine my innermost thoughts, provided one answer: 'Has it never occurred to you that Carne's loyalty and service over the years might have turned into rancour and jealousy? Think of it, Katherine. Devoting the best years of his life to being the Captain's lackey, and nurse-maid to a sickly, mentally disturbed lad. Giving up his own chances of a command at sea, of making his way in the world as the Captain had, of amassing wealth from his voyaging. And then to discover that the woman he loved, who was carrying his child, was nothing more than a fortune-hunter who married into this family behind his back, while he was acting as errand boy for the Captain at the other side of the Atlantic. Think on that, my girl, and see what a fine fellow your Mr Carne is!'

Was that the answer? Were Redmond Carne's actions today the result of a powerful impulse actuated by bitterness and revenge and all the more violent for having taken possession of a character formerly loyal and grateful? Seeing the Captain so close to death, and free at last from the burden of service and duty, had Redmond Carne succumbed to a passion so long and so consistently held in check? I still wanted to hope that it was not so. But because conjecture held so many emotions for me I needed some sense of reprieve - a chance to avoid a confrontation with Carne until I had sorted out my thoughts and feelings.

I realized then that I needed to get away from

Polmarran, to take Adelaide and Mrs Forrest with me. But was that possible? Yes, if Charles could be persuaded to escort us to Rebstock Grange, or to the Reverend Cooper - anywhere, even through the storm, just so long as we were free from Polmarran's baleful influence!

That idea swiftly took hold of my thoughts, dispelling much of that blank and utter exhaustion which had been steadily overtaking me. I stood up.

'Yes, Katherine, go to Adelaide and stay with her. She needs you right now. It's better that I deal with Carne alone when he arrives.'

But Charles was mistaken this time.

'No, I want you to take us from here. All of us. Please, Charles . . .' I picked up his cloak and began to move towards him.

As I did so he froze for a moment, staring hard at me, then, with deliberation, he stooped down to the fire and, using a taper, lit a cigar. 'That's nonsense. You'll do as I say. Go up to the child.'

His voice was brittle with growing anger.

A cold fear, without meaning, took hold of me. Not his voice, but something to do with the cloak. What was it? I had been absently smoothing it out, my hands moving slowly down the warm, dry folds. Then I knew - the cloak was perfectly dry! Yet it was still less than a half hour since Charles had hurried into the darkened ballroom with the claim that he had ridden from Marrambridge.

And his boots! The firelight gleamed on the well-varnished leather - no mud-splatters on the polished surfaces, no rain streaks - nothing to indicate that he had ridden through the storm. He was standing with his feet apart, one hand behind his back, the other hanging loosely by his side and holding the cigar. Something about the trailing wisps of cigar smoke completed the shock of discovery. Yes, a tobacco scent, faint and elusive, had been mingled

250

with the smell of laudanum and musty air which met me earlier as I'd drawn back the panel door and peered into the passageway leading into the tower and George Northwood's cell. These disclosures, swift and accidental, shifted into balance with each other . . .

'You!' In the shock of the moment I stepped back. 'It was you!'

'You know, Katherine, you are just as much a meddling nuisance as Eliza was. More so, in fact . . . for Eliza could at least make some claim to being one of the family. Ah-ah . . .!' He moved briskly, stepping round the chart table and cutting me off from the door. It closed behind him with an ominous click. He remained with his back to it, a sardonic smile on his lips, his voice just as quiet and self-contained as before: 'Strange to think of Eliza as one of the family, isn't it? Of course from the point of view of the Captain's will she was a Northwood. Think of it, Katherine . . . a free-and-easy trollop and her brat, each with the Northwood name, and each helping to further erode the Northwood inheritance. 'Pon my honour, Katherine, at this rate of going there would have been precious little of the old fellow's fortune for the only member of the family who had any real need of it.'

'Meaning you?'

'Naturally. Good lord, woman, what use has my simpleton of a brother for money? One can only buy so many bibles.'

'And you killed Eliza?' It was all fitting together. My heart was pounding with fear.

'Naturally. She had to die. All that greed for pleasurable living had to be stilled. Even the family fool, George, could see that, though he was only concerned with her moral shortcomings, whereas I had to contend with the much more important business of the deep inroads into the Captain's riches that must inevitably accompany Eliza's continued existence. So . . .' Charles shrugged; his laugh was a mocking cadence. 'It was for Eliza's own good, really. How she would have hated what the passing years would have done to her beauty. Oh, I can assure you that she made a very pretty corpse . . . just as you too, Katherine, would have made a pretty corpse if I'd had a little more time to arrange things.'

'Arrange? What do you mean?' I had not expected my fear could reach even greater depths than before. But just as before, with George, I had to keep him talking; I had to hang on to, and extend, every precious second in the hope of a rescue. 'How long have you been planning all this?'

'I'm not sure really. Do you know, m'dear, at first I felt certain that your precious Mr Carne and the old fellow had some scheme afoot - what exactly I couldn't for the life of me guess - but your resemblance to Eliza struck me as far too much of a coincidence. I'm damned if I could come up with any reason! But then, as it became obvious both from my conversations with you and my own investigations, that they hadn't after all got anything up their sleeves . ... that it was nothing more or less than a complete accident, your likeness to Eliza, I mean . . . then it came to me that I should turn the whole thing to my own advantage. Damme, if it wasn't a stroke of fortune that might never repeat itself again in a hundred years!' He looked like a man in triumph, rocking backwards and forwards on his heels and gesturing magnificently with his cigar. 'All I had to do was work on George's wreckage of a brain, convince him that you really were Eliza.'

'So it was you who visited him in the tower late at night?'

'Uh-huh. Meg Rebstock showed me how to get in and out. Great girl, Meg. Knows every stick and stone of this old place, and so easily enlisted in any enterprise which might win back Polmarran for the Rebstocks. My word, but what yarns I had to spin that woman!'

'Did she know that you were contemplating murder?'

'Ah no, m'dear. Meg Rebstock might be an embittered and jealous old bitch, but I reckon her to be a bit squeamish on that score. No, I merely picked her brains with the utmost charm and delicacy. She was only too willing to show to the brother of her dear, beloved John a hidden entrance to her ancestral tower.'

'And all this time you have been lurking and hiding there, waiting and plotting . . .'

'Not all the time. It's such a confoundly miserable place, don't you think? No, let's just say that over the past few weeks I've had my entrances and my exits while I was waiting for my scheme to bear fruit. I had only to wait for the right moment . . .'

'And tonight your chance arrived. Your father's illness, and the storm . . .'

'Precisely. Yes, Katherine, it was I in fact who filled Forrest's pocket with cash and told him to dally at *The Crown* while I'd ride over for Dr Howard. It was only a matter of hours for the old chap, from what Jem Forrest told me, and then with Carne out of the way . . . well, it required only the release of George, and Eliza's brat would be a goner. Devilishly hard luck on you, of course . . . but then, every worthwhile bit of slaughter usually claims an innocent victim or two, doesn't it? Mind you, I felt sure your time had come in the kitchen. I must compliment you on your tenacity. And then again in the old ballroom, when George was at the window . . . but that damned Forrest woman was too quick! Good lord, I thought she would have done for old George with that damned horse pistol . . . and, as you can imagine, that would have spoiled everything for me. You see, I need George alive. I mean, when

253

Carne comes back, he'll have to find someone who is responsible for all these dead bodies, won't he?'

'But George is . . .'

'George is wandering around in the dark. He'll be found in the morning, raving mad as usual. The obvious culprit. Everyone knows he's insane.'

'No, it is you who are insane.'

'Perhaps, but as the last of the Northwoods - for by the time this mess is cleared up poor old George will be gallow's meat for certain - and I, as the last of the Northwoods, will have the bulk of the Captain's fortune to help me cure whatever degree of madness you impute to me, won't I? Also, to pay off an increasing horde of creditors. And not before my time, m'dear, for let me assure you that there is very little stands between me now and a debtor's cell.'

'You cannot expect to carry out this monstrousness without discovery!'

'Can't I? Who is to discover me? Poor old Forrest will meet with a fatal accident as he returns from *The Crown* in the small hours of the morning. No one else will know that I was here while all these horrible things were happening, for you see, my pretty governess, there's a certain tavern wench in Bristol town with morals as soiled as her apron who'll willingly swear on a stack of bibles that I spent the night in her bedchamber. And she will be well rewarded for calling down the Almighty as witness to the fact. So, as your precious Redmond Carne would say, everything is ship-shape and Bristol-fashion, aye?' He came towards me then, slowly, with menacing triumph. 'Indeed, my only regret is that you refused to go upstairs when I told you. It would've saved all this unpleasantness for you, and you might even have retained a good opinion of me as the flames engulfed the upper floors, trapping you and Eliza's brat and that damned Forrest woman.'

Numb with dread, I backed away from him. The window ledge halted the futility of my retreat. He didn't come any closer, but paused with one elbow lightly resting on the mantelpiece. The fire which he had been so assiduously attending when I'd entered this room such a short time before had caught on. With a now-frightful brilliance the flames were leaping about the logs. The spurting and crackling noises were drowning out a faint background sound, steady, drumming sound, muffled by distance and the night the continuous downpour of rain, perhaps, or my pounding heart-beat?

'Yes, my dear. That Forrest woman is a plucky, resourceful jade, I will admit, fetching the gun like that . . . why, it came very near to upsetting all my plans. Still, this hasty improvisation has considerable merit, don't you think? A jolly honest-to-goodness bonfire might look a lot more convincing in the long run . . . more accidental, so to speak.' With all the casual ease with which he might select one of his cigars Charles Northwood picked up the fire-tongs and began to poke about amongst the blazing logs. 'Of course one can't be sure that an *accident* will result in Georgie's dangling from a gibbet. But an asylum for the criminally insane must amount to much the same thing, I should imagine.' The wavering flames highlighted his features, cruel and arrogantly handsome. Was there no escape from the deadly mockery in his eyes?

I turned in desperation to the window.

'No, Katherine, I'm afraid there is no escape. In the morning there will be nothing left of this place but a mound of ashes . . . What is it?'

We were both listening, hearing and simultaneously identifying that sound which had been drumming relentlessly and increasingly in the background. I recognized the unmistakable approach of horses and the iron-tyred wheels of a carriage travelling with urgent haste up the drive. Redmond Carne? Pray God that it was!

'Get back from that window, damn you!' Behind

255

me I heard the fire-tongs fall to the ground. Charles Northwood reached my side just as a fast-moving curricle swayed into view through a gap in the trees.

Flanking the carriage were two mounted horsemen - and there could be no mistaking the tall figure in the lead! Every line of Redmond Carne's body was taut with an urgency that seemed to mirror my own. He was urging his steed on, his whip-hand rising and falling across the animal's dark rump. As the cavalcade came wheeling around by the front lawn I experienced a tremendous surge of relief.

'Back, I said!' Charles Northwood grabbed my shoulder and tried to wrench me away from the window.

The palm of his hand struck hard against the side of my face. I fell against the desk. I was momentarily dazed, but otherwise unhurt. Charles Northwood appeared more confused than I. Confused and violently enraged. He pulled at one of the drawers in the desk with such force that it fell to the floor and spilt its contents. Then he pulled at a second one, with less force this time, and plunged his hand into it.

'Where the hell is that key?' He swore.

With the corner of his eye he caught my movement towards the door. In one lightning bound he came around the desk and hurled himself at me. 'No, I'm not finished with you yet!'

We struggled for an instant. His hands were like steel bands about my wrists. I tried to break his hold, to twist out from under the painful clasp of his fingers, but I had nothing to pit against his strength. With animal-like ferocity he forced me back, the powerful thrust of his body slamming me against the edge of the desk once more. He spun me round, so that my back was to him. The rim of the desk bit sharply into my thighs as he forced the upper part of my body forward. In some desperate, half-comprehending way I knew now that it was Charles who had pursued and overtaken me that evening in

256

the woods - the same savage tactics were being employed; first, one of my wrists was seized, then the other, and both were wrenched up behind my back and held there by a combination of his body-weight and the vice-like grip of one hand. My face was almost touching the surface of the desk. But this time his free hand did not seek my throat. It was engaged in a frantic search amongst the papers and odds-and-ends littering the desk top - the key? Yes, to lock the door to this room, keeping the others at bay until he could dispose of me, set fire to the room - and how quickly the flames would spread over these wooden panels! - and then make his exit through the tower.

Now, as never before, I struggled against him. I don't know from what hidden reserves I summoned up the strength to pull and twist and jerk - until suddenly I had one hand free. Charles, in the excitement of discovering the key amidst the scattered objects, must have slackened his hold on me. Before he knew it, my hand had settled on the heavy inkstand. He was still behind me and had I been able to swing round I would have struck him with it. As it was, the only target presenting itself to my hampered aim was the window - but outside was the night, dark and compact, and the noise of horse hooves kicking viciously on the gravel, and voices, loud and urgent, and the heavy pounding of fists on the hall door . . .

I threw the inkstand at the window with all the force I could muster. Almost in the same instant I was rewarded by the sound of shattered glass and the inkstand thudding on the ground outside.

'Too late, Katherine. I'm not done for yet. Not by a long shot.' He released me, allowing me to turn round and to view the key gloatingly displayed in one hand; inviting me also, in a cat-and-mouse fashion, to make a futile bid at snatching for it. He pulled his hand away, laughed, and started for the door.

'No, Charles . . . it's you who are too late!' Perhaps

because I willed it so much, I was the first to hear the racing footsteps outside in the hall. Their sound gave me the desperate courage to fling myself at him before he could reach the door. He stepped to one side, parrying like a fencer. I was caught off balance. Surprisingly, Charles Northwood caught me. His arm went round my waist, steadying me, drawing my body close to his in a loathsome embrace.

We were standing thus, partly facing the door when it suddenly burst open - but by that time Charles had taken a pistol from out of his waistband, the same pistol, I think, which Mrs Forrest had so eagerly handed over to him in the ballroom. The muzzle was pressed against my temple.

'Stand back, Carne!'

Redmond Carne's headlong entrance was brought to an abrupt halt. He stood just inside the open door, his clenched fist about the handle, completely immobilized by the shock of this confrontation. The dark hallway behind him seemed to be full of people; I glimpsed an open-mouthed Dr Howard, Margaret Rebstock and her brother, both faces gleaming palely from the shadows, stunned by what they saw, and beside them stood a ghastly sobre Jem Forrest. Time appeared to hang suspended. Nobody dared make a move. For just a little while the only sounds were the crackling logs in the fire and the quiet plip-plip of the rain water dripping from Redmond Carne's oilskins to the floor. He was the first to break that awful silence.

'Release her, Charles . . .'

'Damn you if I will. She's my trump card now.'

The gun barrel was deadly cold against my forehead.

'I warn you, Charles. If you harm her . . . if you've harmed her or my daughter . . .'

'Hear that, Katherine? The ruffian admits to fathering that brat upstairs.'

258

At those words Margaret Rebstock stepped back behind her brother and seemed to glide away into the shadows. Dr Howard moved too, forward, attempting to join Redmond Carne inside the study.

'Stay back, Howard! You, Carne . . . if you have any regard for this dainty baggage you'll do as I say. Now close the door . . . Do you hear me, damn you! Close that confounded door and stand over there!'

He had no choice but to obey. A myriad of half-held expressions scurried across Redmond's tense features - defiance, anger, helplessness. He closed the door and then walked carefully over to the chart table, never once removing his eyes from Charles. I was helpless too, pitying him as I watched him move about like some great and powerful creature trapped in a cage, lithe and cautious; eager, yet unable to spring into battle.

'That's better.' Still with the pistol against my temple Charles dragged me over to the door. He put the key in the lock and turned it. 'Much better.'

I was then led over to the fireplace.

'Do what you will with me, Charles, but for God's sake let the girl go!'

'Shut up, Carne! You're far too noble by half. Why, you put a fellow like me to shame.' The mocking laughter sounded harsh and callous in my ear. 'Did you hear that, Katherine? I think the fellow is in love with you, by God! I really do. And you, Redmond old salt . . . I rather suspect that our plucky little governess here is quite taken with your manliness likewise. You're both so bloody noble and self-sacrificing that I think it only proper you should die in each other's arms! Wouldn't that be nice?'

Above his words came the sound of his boot kicking against the fire-grate. He was trying to dislodge one of the blazing logs. 'You were perfectly right to spurn Eliza after she'd shown her true colours, Redmond. This one is much more your type . . . though for the life of me I don't know what she sees in you. Ah, there we have it!'

With the corner of my eye I glimpsed a little shower of sparks as one of the logs rolled out on to the carpet. But my gaze was actually riveted on Redmond's face: like a hawk he had been watching the pistol in my captor's hand throughout all this. It was no longer levelled at my head but pointing directly at Redmond Carne. I knew instinctively that he was about to leap forward, to gamble his life against a single shot - to risk it for me!

'No, Redmond . . .!' I cried in the same moment as he lunged towards us. At the same time I jerked my elbow against Charle's forearm.

There was a deafening report, a flash, the acrid smell of gunsmoke - and before my eyes Redmond Carne spun round in a short half-circle, the instant slam of pain jack-knifing his body. He fell heavily against the chart table and then slumped to the floor.

I broke away from Charles Northwood and rushed over, throwing myself on my knees beside Redmond. A jagged, gaping hole showed in the raincoat just above the knee. I tried to staunch the blood welling up from a deep wound in his thigh. Dark and crimson the blood mingled with the blobs of rain water and defied my endeavours.

'You beast . . .!' My panic and helplessness took the form of scorn-filled venom hurled at our tormentor.

He was carefully re-loading the pistol, looking down on us tauntingly. He had already thrown a pile of papers on to the smouldering log, causing them to feed the little spurts of flame now fanning out across the carpet. It would only take a minute or two for them to reach the wooden panels lining the walls.

I tried to pull Redmond away from a long finger of flame creeping steadily towards where he lay. Charles Northwood stepped around the flames and opened the panel-door leading into the tower. He stood there for a moment, a mocking smile on his saturnine face, surveying his terrible handiwork, merciless and unmoved by my frantic efforts to haul the injured man from the path of fire. By now the flames were licking about the legs of the desk, climbing, swept on by the sharp breeze entering through the shattered window. Redmond was still dazed and half-paralysed by pain. Was there no escape?

'Please, Charles . . . for pity's sake help him!'

There was neither help nor pity in his face. His shrug contained all the callous insouciance of a reckless gambler. 'It's been a luckless throw of the dice for all of us, hasn't it, m'dear? Remember, I lose the chance of a fortune with this little bonfire . . .'

He was partially hidden by the billowing clouds of smoke, his dark attire already merging with the wavering shadows just behind him. The heat was intense and the first flames had already struck the panelled wood. Redmond Carne was now in a sitting position. I had my hands under his armpits - but could I make it to the locked door before the fire engulfed us?

'For God's sake, Charles, help me with him!'

'What's a few more dead bodies, Katherine, one way or the other? Ever since I put a pistol to my brother John's head I've had to . . .' His words broke off in a harsh, choking sob. He swayed in the narrow doorway, one hand reaching out for support, not finding it, pawing aimlessly at an uneven column of smoke. He came towards us with faltering steps, stumbling into the red glare. Under the translucent glow of the fire his face was ashen, the eyes fixed and staring wildly at nothing. Then he fell, face down, at Redmond Carne's feet.

From just behind me came the groan of tortured, splintered timber as the door was smashed in. Suddenly, as if from nowhere, Dr Howard and Sir Arthur were beside me, helping me to lift Redmond Carne to his feet. They were not a moment too soon. At the opposite end of the study the racing flames were climbing steadily to the ceiling. Long, vivid tongues of fire were licking their way across the oaken beams, prising them loose from the stonework.

Just as we reached the door the first beam came crashing down, a twirling cascade of flame that lit up every detail with stark and unforgettable horror. We saw the knife handle protruding from between Charles Northwood's shoulder blades, the dark stuff of his jacket darker still with a growing stain. And we saw Margaret Rebstock standing in the little doorway leading from the tower. The flames were already encircling her, lighting up the dark hatred in her eyes as she looked down on the corpse of Charles Northwood. She had avenged the death of the man she had loved.

Then a second beam broke loose from the ceiling, plunging and roaring down like some gigantic torch to engulf both figures.

In less than a minute Captain Northwood's study, and everything within its blazing walls, was no more . . .

Chapter Fourteen

'Ready, Miss Ainsley?'

'Yes, in just a moment,' I replied, fastening the final clasp on my portmanteau. 'Please come in.'

Mrs Cooper entered first; her husband hovered outside on the landing with a kind of absent-minded diffidence until his wife beckoned to him. 'William dear, be so kind as to take down Miss Ainsley's bags . . .' She turned to me and asked, 'Must you, Katherine? Is there no way in which we can prevail on you? Even for another week?'

'Thank you. I am already too much in your debt.'

'Debt? Nonsense!'

'A great pleasure having you, Miss Ainsley. We have so few visitors, and we will miss you,' the Reverend Mr Cooper added warmly; then his tone drifted back again into what I can only describe (and in no unkind sense) as his pulpit-voice. 'Naturally one would have wished that the circumstances which occasioned your sojourn had not been attended by so much grievous tragedy.'

'Dr Howard thinks you should still rest some more . . . just a few more days perhaps?' Mrs Cooper tried to coax me with a motherly smile.

'You are both far too kind, but really . . .'

'We understand.' The clergyman nodded with grave sympathy. His wife, too, was understanding, the kindly smile fading just a little from her plump face and the eyebrows slanting upwards with gentle solicitude. They had more than an inkling of those personal considerations which made it imperative that I should leave.

Mr Cooper took the two heavy valises. His wife helped me with the smaller things. She linked her arm through mine after she had closed the bedroom door behind us. Together we followed Mr Cooper down the short flight of stairs, the imminence of departure making silent people of us all.

I shall not easily forget the immense kindnesses lavished on me by this couple during the two weeks in which I stayed at Marrambridge Rectory - ever since that night when they'd hurried down in answer to our loud pounding on the hall door, there to find the three of us, Mrs Forrest, Adelaide and myself, all on the verge of hysteria, our clothes soaked through by the rain, our faces streaked and grimy from tears and the blackish smoke of Polmarran's inferno.

How readily the Coopers had thrown open their door to us! Their home proved to be a sanctuary. It offered so much more than shelter and food on a night that still carried the echo of all the dark forces which had so recently terrified us. In the following days it had offered surcease and a gradual return to reality. The nightmare diminished, and the qualities of Christian fortitude and quiet affection exhibited by the Coopers acted as an antidote to the harrowing memories of our last hours at Polmarran.

It was Sir Arthur Rebstock, who, despite his own grief, had taken us to Marrambridge on that eventful night. Tragedy had somehow imbued him with a degree of 'capability' which I had not credited him with possessing. He had taken charge, finding amidst the blazing ruins of his ancestral home latent qualities of self-reliance and leadership: he despatched Dr Howard and Jem Forrest to Rebstock Grange with the wounded Redmond Carne; he brought us to the Rectory; with the Reverend Mr Cooper and those

Marrambridge citizens whom he roused from their beds Sir Arthur then rode off in search of George Northwood.

Towards dawn they found him. He was lying prostrate on the wet sand of Polmarran Cove, his frail body racked by long exposure to the elements, his mind empty of all reason and memory. They carried him back to Rebstock Grange. He never regained his strength, but before he died there were a few brief, lucid hours in which sanity and recollection returned. Under the patient, compassionate enquiries of both doctor and clergyman the jig-saw pieces of his shattered mind were collected and arranged into a coherent pattern.

It became apparent that Charles had convinced him that he, George, was responsible for Eliza's death. That conviction arose from the fact that, years before, George had wandered, quite by accident, into that secluded glade wherein the pool was situated - that same place which had been for me an idyllic haven at first, and then the scene of such indescribable fear. At the pool he happened on Eliza - an Eliza who was naked, bathing, wanton. She tried to entice him, her blandishments turning to scorn and mockery in the face of his timidity. They struggled. George struck her and she fell, her head striking against a rock. In panic and guilt he fled. Hurrying back to the house he met his brother Charles and immediately confessed what had happened. He begged his brother's help. Charles sent the distraught youth to his room, but not before he had counselled George that under no circumstances was he to tell anyone else what had occurred. Then Charles rode to the glade. When he returned it was with the news that their sister-in-law was dead, that George had indeed killed her, but that the body was now safely concealed and buried in the woods. It was to be their secret, the will of God, a just retribution for Eliza's wickedness, an atonement for John Northwood's suicide and their own father's profiting from slave-running - in short, it was to be any one of a dozen reasons which might appease George's conscience and bind him to Charles in a pact of silence!

Somehow - by some process of self-delusion, of willing it to be so - George Northwood had, over the intervening years, come to accept the fact that Eliza had just 'gone away'. From such an acceptance it must have then become a comparatively easy step to efface her completely from his memory. Eliza had never existed! Unless of course some untoward and unexpected event jolted some dark recess of the mind - such as a storm, for instance, its jagged lightning ripping through the curtains of the past, illuminating with stark clarity a snatch of memory, like the night when his sister-in-law had crept into his room to 'comfort' him. Or the inexorable pull of that secluded glade, the desire to test the substance of a vaguely remembered nightmare, and the sheer coincidence of going there on the same afternoon as I was desporting myself at the water's edge in circumstances almost identical to those in which he had discovered Eliza so many years before.

What a shock that must have been to him! I must have seemed the very reincarnation of Eliza. Stunned, disorientated by the personification of his guilt-ridden past, George had hurried back to the house. Back to a fortuitous meeting with his brother. And Charles, though still half-drunk and querulous after the fracas in *The Crown Inn* earlier that same day, had sufficient wit to take command of the situation: George was to go immediately to his room, to say nothing of 'Eliza's' return, to leave everything to Charles. There and then the scheme must have begun to take shape in his mind: creeping furtively towards the pool he'd sketched out a blueprint of terror which should have rid him of all who stood between him and his father's

266

wealth. I shuddered to recall how close Charles had come to realizing his plans!

Now, Polmarran House was nothing but a burnt-out shell; the evil-looking windows of the tower stared blindly and meaninglessly from their blackened sockets. And the last of the Northwoods was dead. Looking back on it all, I found a deep compassion within my heart for George Northwood - futile now, but no less real for all its futility. Poor George! He had trodden dark paths which none of us had ever known or suspected, hounded on by a hideous mixture of guilt and innocence, of fear and vengeance and a grotesque righteousness. And now his heavy sorrows were ended; he had atoned for all his misdeeds, real or imagined, and was at last free in the only way possible for him. And in some strange way his death had also freed Redmond and Adelaide from the past.

With a deep sense of loss I realized that their freedom also meant the end of my involvement with them.

During the past two weeks I had seen very little of Redmond Carne. His leg wound was slow to heal and still quite painful. It kept him indoors much more than he was normally accustomed to, first at Rebstock Grange, and then at the house in Marrambridge which he had taken. For my part I rarely ventured outside the Rectory. To most of the townspeople I had become the 'Polmarran woman', a creature to be gaped at with a curious compound of sympathy, awe, and no doubt, suspicion. In their minds I would always be an outsider, the agency through which all the dark deeds had reached their inevitable climax.

On the day following my arrival at the Rectory I had gone out to Rebstock Grange to see Redmond Carne. I had been concerned and anxious. And also embarrassed at the prospect, lest he should make some mention of the manner in which I had taken leave of him on the previous night: I had taken his face in my hands and kissed him just before Dr Howard's coach had borne him away. En route to Rebstock Grange that day, and seated beside the Reverend Mr Cooper, I had tried to convince myself that the impulse had been dictated by nothing more than relief at our narrow escape from the blazing house, or gratitude, or the release of so much tension after our ordeal. But my heart gave the lie to such conjecture.

My meeting with Redmond Carne had been brief, almost matter-of-fact. I think we were both suffering from some kind of delayed shock, too drained of emotion to enter into any conversation of a personal nature. Thankfully, there had been no reference to my impulsive kiss. Yet, in spite of his illness, Redmond Carne had shown a great determination to explain certain matters to me.

'I want you to know about my daughter . . .'

'Really, there is no need. I'm sure I understand.'

'Please, Katherine, hear me out,' he said, pale-faced and sombre in the cold light of the wintry day. Around his eyes the weather-lines had held more than a hint of entreaty. 'I want you to know why I could never step forward and claim Adelaide as my own. For the Cap'n's sake, you see. All these years I believed that the Cap'n cherished her as his own grand-child . . . John's child. John was ever his favourite, and I believed that he wanted something of John's to hold on to . . .'

'And unknown to you the Captain had in his possession all this time a paper signed by Eliza, naming you as the father of her child.'

Redmond nodded his head slowly, pondering the significance of the past seven years, the short span of Adelaide's years, in which these two men had kept silent out of loyalty and respect for each other.

'Captain Northwood must have loved you as dearly as any of his own sons.'

As if I hadn't spoken Redmond continued: 'After all the sadness and tragedy he'd known in family matters, how could I deprive my Cap'n of the child? For, mark you, I too have a paper signed by Eliza before witnesses. But how could I lay such a paper before the Cap'n believing as I did? Besides, what had I to offer my own daughter . . . no wife and mother for her, and precious little in the way of worldly possessions? Nothing but the burden of a tainted parentage for such tiny little shoulders.'

'That was no fault of yours, Redmond.'

He had shaken his head slowly. There was no bitterness in the ghost of a smile that touched his lips. 'True, Eliza used me. Oh, she was young and wilful and bored at the time of our first meeting and probably didn't intend to be deliberately cruel. But she used my infatuation as a spoiled child uses a toy and then discards it. I had ceased loving the memory of our short time together even before our daughter was born.' He had turned to me then, his expression gentle, urgent, uncertain all at once. 'But I have always loved my daughter and watched over her as best I could. And now, after all she has been through, I am resolved to love her openly . . . to protect her . . .'

'Forgive me for ever having doubted you, Redmond . . . for all my earlier suspicions.'

'It is you who must forgive me. I provided you with plenty of cause for suspicion and doubts. But it couldn't be helped, Katherine.'

And then, just as he had seemed about to reach out to take my hand in his - or had I foolishly misread the movement of his arm across the counterpane? - there came a brisk tap-tap on the door and we were joined by both Dr Howard and the Reverend Mr Cooper.

'Time to leave the patient to his rest, Miss Ainsley. Reverend Cooper has to leave now.'

After that, my few meetings with Redmond Carne

269

had always been in the full glare of spectators. At the Northwood burials first, then before the investigating magistrates when (in company with Sir Arthur Rebstock, Dr Howard and the Forrests) we made, and signed, our respective statements concerning the events at Polmarran. Finally, we had one brief meeting when he called at the Rectory to collect Adelaide and the Forrests and install them in the house which he had rented at the far side of the town for himself and his daughter. Yes, how proudly and openly he proclaimed the fact of fatherhood - like a man suddenly released from an intolerable vow of silence! And how Adelaide had responded! She was overjoyed to discover a 'real' Papa and scarcely wondered at the fact being concealed from her for so long. Nothing in the adult world seemed to surprise her for very long. I was so happy for both of them.

It was a happiness tinged with just a little of my own sadness; for the knowledge that Adelaide and Redmond now had each other made it just that bit less difficult to come to my own decision. It seemed an appropriate juncture at which to effect a discreet withdrawal from their lives. Especially since the arrival yesterday in Marrambridge of the late Captain Northwood's attorney and the subsequent report that both Redmond and his daughter were handsomely provided for in the late Captain's will. Now that the magistrates had concluded their investigations I was free to go. Any lingering, or further contact with my erstwhile pupil and her new-found father, was open to too great a misconstruction. Physically I might resemble the mysterious Eliza, that wilful fortune-hunter who had brought so much misery to so many lives. I was determined that the wagging tongues of Marrambridge should have no cause to hint at additional similarities. I wanted the likeness to begin and end in the matter of looks.

It was time to leave.

In response to my wishes the Coopers had reluctantly agreed to facilitate my early morning departure. No one else was to know. With a degree of consideration and circumspection bordering on secrecy they had arranged a carriage to take me to join up with the Exeter Mail some miles from Marrambridge. I hated the thought of leaving without saying goodbye to Adelaide. And Redmond. But it was better this way . . .

'You *will* write?'

Mrs Cooper's words broke the long silence and dispelled my thoughts.

'I promise.'

'Well then, if we cannot persuade you from your decision it remains only to wish you God-speed and a safe journey, my dear. William, be so kind as to continue with the luggage.'

I followed the clergyman through the door.

Already the first tints of dawn had seeped into the sky. Last night's rain had ceased and the wind was only a sad and muted sighing through the churchyard. Outside the little wicket gate the shifting, impatient hooves struck sharp and clear on the stony road. The coachman stood beside the open door, hat in hand. At the sound of our approach he looked up and then came forward to help the Reverend Mr Cooper with the heavy bags. He walked with a limp, a tall, broad-shouldered man . . .

Redmond!

I stood still, genuinely surprised and more than a little confused. He met my questioning look with the words: 'If you're so set on leaving then I'll drive you to wherever it is. Same as I did the first day I met you. Maybe this time I'll have more luck talking some sense into your head.'

The dark weather-lines of his face held a near-angry frown. Through the cold dawn light I saw that hard look in his eyes and could think of no way to soften it.

'How did you know I was leaving?'

'In Marrambridge every speck of news or gossip is quickly blown about. For once I'm glad of it.' He stood before me, blocking the path, making no attempt to relieve the clergyman of my bags.

Undecided at first, then with a glance at his wife, followed by a shrug, the Reverend Mr Cooper drifted down the path towards the waiting carriage. Mrs Cooper found something of absorbing interest behind the west wall of the church. Redmond Carne and I were alone.

'Why, Katherine? Why like this?'

'I think it best.'

'Without seeing Adelaide? Without as much as a goodbye to me?'

I had no answer.

Redmond too was silent, no longer frowning, but hesitant and uncertain, his hands spread out in that gesture of helplessness which I had come to know so well.

'I couldn't ask you to come into this rented place with us. It wouldn't be seemly, Katherine . . . not in a place like Marrambridge. They'd speak ill of you. But couldn't you stay on here for a while? With the parson and his wife? Look, I intend to take Adelaide from this place soon, to make a fresh start somewhere else.'

'I am glad. I think that's a wise decision, Redmond.'

'Come with us, please!' He reached out and took my hand in his. 'I told you once before, Katherine . . . I can set a course as good as any man, but I need someone to help me steer it. I need you, Kathrine. I need you.'

Now it was I who felt momentarily uncertain. I started to turn my face away . . .

'No. Look at me,' he said in words that were little more than a whisper. His hand took my chin, bringing my face around to meet the final truth in his eyes. 'I love you, Katherine.'

I raised my hand to brush away the untidy forelock from his forehead; instead, I swept away the slight frown of entreaty with my next words: 'I wanted you to say that, Redmond. I've been wanting it for days. I love you too.'

He took me in his arms then, held me close. Slowly, and with extraordinary gentleness, he kissed me.

From some faraway, unreal place I heard Mrs Cooper calling, 'William dear, be so kind as to return Miss Ainsley's bags to the house.'

In the incongruous surrounding of that country churchyard Redmond and I stood, clasped in each other's arms. Time was suspended, forgotten for this brief, ecstatic spell. In the distance we could both see the dark line of hills concealing whatever remained of Polmarran. I knew that I would never again feel any fear. Redmond's arms were warm and strong and protective about me . . .